MY BATTERY IS LOW
AND IT IS
GETTING DARK

Other Anthologies Edited by:

Patricia Bray & Joshua Palmatier

After Hours: Tales from the Ur-bar
The Modern Fae's Guide to Surviving Humanity
Temporally Out of Order
Alien Artifacts
Were-
All Hail Our Robot Conquerors!
Second Round: A Return to the Ur-bar

S.C. Butler & Joshua Palmatier

Submerged
Guilds & Glaives
Apocalyptic

Laura Anne Gilman & Kat Richardson

The Death of All Things

Troy Carrol Bucher & Joshua Palmatier

The Razor's Edge

Patricia Bray & S.C. Butler

Portals

David B. Coe & Joshua Palmatier

Temporally Deactivated
Galactic Stew

Steven H Silver & Joshua Palmatier

Alternate Peace

MY BATTERY IS LOW AND IT IS GETTING DARK

Edited by

Crystal Sarakas
&
Joshua Palmatier

Zombies Need Brains LLC
www.zombiesneedbrains.com

Interior Design (ebook): ZNB Design
Interior Design (print): ZNB Design
Cover Design by ZNB Design
Cover Art "My Battery Is Low and It Is Getting Dark" by Justin Adams

ZNB Book Collectors #19
All characters and events in this book are fictitious.
All resemblance to persons living or dead is coincidental.

Kickstarter Edition Printing, June 2020
First Printing, July 2020

Print ISBN-13: 978-1940709352

Ebook ISBN-13: 978-1940709369

Printed in the U.S.A.

COPYRIGHTS

Table of Contents

SIGNATURE PAGE

Crystal Sarakas, editor:

_____

Joshua Palmatier, editor:

_____

Dana Berube:

_____

Merc Fenn Wolfmoor:

_____

Jacey Bedford:

_____

Anthony Lowe:

_____

Chris Kocher:

_____

Brian Hugenbruch:

_____

William Leisner:

_____

José Pablo Iriarte:

_____

Alethea Kontis:

_____

Kari Sperring:

_____

Edward Willett:

_____

John G. Hartness:

_____

Alexander Gideon:

_____

Stephen Leigh:

_____

Justin Adams, artist:

_____

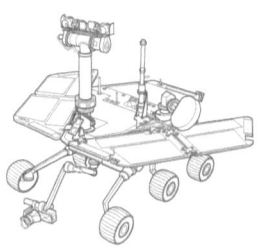

Introduction

Crystal Sarakas

In February 2019, thousands of people from around the world shared in a bittersweet moment: After an incredible fifteen-year mission, NASA finally declared the Mars rover *Opportunity* dead. Jacob Margolis, one of the scientists at NASA, translated the last message from *Opportunity* as: "My battery is low and it is getting dark."

Those words struck a chord deep in our collective souls. The image of a lonely rover dying on a barren, sometimes hostile world was a little bit of heartbreak. But then we wondered: What happens next? What if something came along and gave a second life to *Opportunity* and sister rover *Spirit*? What kind of new life could a piece of old technology have, and what would that look like?

So the idea for MY BATTERY IS LOW AND IT IS GETTING DARK was born, and it is now realized here. These fourteen stories took that initial idea in unexpected ways, from the steppes of Mongolia to the far-reaches of space and imagination. We hope you enjoy them as much as we did.

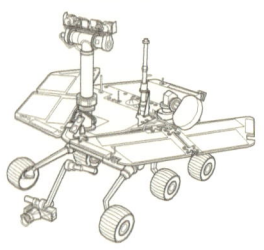

Ganbold and the Best Drone in Mongolia

Dana Berube

Ganbold steps out from his *ger* to greet the day. Tengri's eternal heavens are vast and still this morning, untroubled by cloud or satellite or spyplane. When the sun has fully risen, the steppe will glow green and gold from the threshold of his *ger* to the purple crown of mountains on the horizon, but for now the light catches only the dew on the grass and Ganbold stands in a plain of diamonds. His daughters want him to move to UB—they worry about their mama and papa out here alone with the herd—but mornings in the smoky, crowded capital don't look like this.

He's about to whistle, but Baavgai, the best dog in Mongolia, is already at his knees.

Ganbold acquired the bearish mass of black and brown fur from a cousin who had been about to shoot him because he was mean and nippy and had already lost an eye fighting with another dog. But Ganbold saw that he just needed training and another chance. Now Baavgai guards his herds with the courage and devotion of Chinggis Khan's *nökhör*. Today, however, he's whining and agitated. Something in his kingdom is amiss.

At once, Ganbold follows him around the solar panels to the pen behind the *ger*. He and his wife Bolormaa have only two hundred horses, sheep, and goats now—each black winter takes and takes—and all of them are precious. The cause of Baavgai's alarm is immediately apparent: while most of the animals are crowded within the pen, waiting for Ganbold to take them out to graze on the dewy grass, a dozen are roaming free. There's a hole in the fence where they've broken through and escaped. Baavgai has managed to corral most of the animals near the pen, but a quick headcount tells Ganbold he's down a goat.

Given the choice to leave his post to track down one errant goat or stay and protect the rest of the herd from wolves, Baavgai has made the right decision, but now he's eager to track down the escapee. Together, they shoo the loose animals back into the pen, and Ganbold rolls a barrel over to block the hole. He calls to Bolormaa in the *ger* to let her know what's happened, then saddles and mounts a brown gelding. With his lasso-pole over his shoulder and Baavgai leading the way, they set off to find the goat. With a little luck, it hasn't gone far and he can bring it back before the dew burns off.

The rolling chartreuse hills are gentle, but even so the *ger* and herd are soon lost behind them and as far as the eye can see there is only the brightening sky and a sea of grass. Baavgai leads him up and over a rise, then down into the valley with the Russian missile crater. The wind purrs over the low grass and scrub and his horse's hoofbeats echo. Nothing stirs.

Suddenly, a jet screams across the stratosphere, shattering the quiet. Ganbold frowns up at it, but it's too high up for him to make out which of the squabbling corporation-nations it belongs to. For the most part Mongolia has avoided the cyber attacks and drone skirmishes pulsing across the planet, but China and Russia are always pressing closer, and with the die-offs and dry-outs, the steppe doesn't feel as big and remote as it used to.

After the jet's roar comes a soft, warbled cry. Baavgai bolts over a hillock and into the scrub and Ganbold rides after, expecting to find his lost goat.

And he does. Their arrival triggers an eruption of crows and buzzards, who abandon the mangled, fly-flecked remnants of a goat. With a sigh, Ganbold dismounts and bends over the corpse. The scavengers have been busy, but the violence done to the throat and belly suggests wolves got there first. The changing climate is making the wolves bolder and stranger too.

"It's not your fault," Ganbold assures Baavgai.

Again—that strange, thin cry. Baavgai's head snaps towards a clutch of bushes and boulders about five meters downhill.

Taking his lasso-pole, Ganbold creeps down to investigate. The boulders and bushes crowd together over an indentation in the ground, forming a small burrow. He and Baavgai approach cautiously, in case it's a wolf or leopard's den. The cry comes again, from within the burrow, and this time Ganbold hears it clearly. It doesn't sound like a goat or a wolf or any animal he's ever heard, but it sounds scared.

Carefully, he peeks around a boulder and peers inside.

A laser gun fires.

Ganbold flattens himself to the ground, the thing shrieks, and Baavgai snarls. His heart pounds, but seconds pass and nothing happens. There are no more shots; no one shouts for him to put his hands up. Baavgai's fur is needle-straight from his ears to his tail, but he's holding back from attacking; he seems confused.

Carefully, Ganbold raises himself and looks into the burrow. Again a laser fires, and again the thing within squeals. As his eyes recover from the flash of the laser, he sees the thing spinning and thrashing in the confined space. It's about the size and shape of the satellite dish atop his *ger*, its gunmetal gray dome studded with cracked solar chips and LED lights. An array of arms, sensors, long-range cameras, weapons, and jets project from the underside of the rim, but they're damaged, some dangling uselessly, giving the thing the look of a metal jellyfish. At least one leg has been blown off, along with a chunk of the rim 'round about two o'clock. Wisps of smoke puff out from the exposed viscera of chips and wires.

It's a reconnaissance drone and it's been shot down.

It makes that cry again and Ganbold understands why it sounded strange—it was a mechanical alert, warped by damage and dying batteries. He draws back, suspicious. This is a dangerous thing, another sort of wolf. The men from the cities send drones like this to spy on the land and track the herders. He knows of an incident where a mining corporation, greedy for the metals buried under the steppe and impatient for the herders to leave, sent drones like this to shoot the herders and their animals dead. He should take a rock and crush it.

The little yellow lights along the rim flicker in a way that makes Ganbold think the drone is watching him. It is, of course—these things are *always* watching—but damage to the middle section of the strip of lights gives them distinct left and right segments that look like eyes. The drone says *beee-eeep bl-oorp*, even more warped than before. It sounds like it's drunk and, in spite of himself, Ganbold laughs.

"Well, then, aren't you in a mess? What happened? Did you buzz too close to Old Batzorig's herd and he shot you? Serves you right, spying on us."

The drone says *boooop*, raises a mangled arm, and tries to fire at him. But the arm was bent backwards in the crash and the laser fires into its own dome. The drone rocks backwards and spins around the burrow in distress.

"Now, stop that, you foolish thing," Ganbold says.

It lowers its bent arm and beeps piteously. It used up a lot of power firing the laser and its lights and beeps are growing fainter as its reserves run out. Ganbold can't help but feel sorry for it.

"Is someone going to come to retrieve you, then? Some smart men from the city?"

More likely they'll just shut down this one remotely and build another. The smart men of the world have no shortage of robotic nastiness. The drone, apparently realizing its fate, lets out a doleful *boooooop* and sinks to the ground, folding its long metal arms beneath it. Ganbold is reminded of a sickly newborn foal.

"I don't know what you expect me to do," he says.

One of the drone's "eyes" fades to black. The other is blinking slower and slower. With a final flat *bee-boooop*, the lights go dark and the drone stills.

Ganbold prods at the machine with his pole. No response. He ought to leave it and get back to his herd. This thing is dangerous. It's the enemy.

But it is a beautiful machine, with a crude sort of consciousness, and it feels wrong to leave it here unburied and unmourned. At the very least, since its metal body can't return to the earth like the goat's, it should be honored by having its parts stripped and put to use. After all, Bolormaa is so good with technology, and if no one is coming for it…

He hauls the drone out and straps it across his horse's back as he would a dead antelope. The lifeless arms and legs jangle like bones all the way home.

* * *

Bolormaa is not thrilled with Ganbold's latest charity case. When he returns to the *ger* that evening after grazing the herd, the drone is undergoing brain surgery in her lap. The nest of tools, wires, diagnostic tablets, and welding equipment around her suggests she's been at it a while.

"It's taken me hours to reprogram it so it won't beam everything about us straight back to Beijing," she says, screwing a panel shut. "Do you know what this is? It's a Great Wall Mining Corp. reconnaissance drone. Sent to map the region's geology for untapped mineral deposits—and to kill anything or anyone that got in its way, judging by that laser."

Ganbold nods and serves himself some hot, buttery milk tea from the stove at the center of the *ger*. He guessed as much, just as he guessed his brilliant wife would be able to safely blind it.

"I don't know why you brought it *here*," she grumbles.

Ganbold just smiles over the rim of the cup and notes that she's repaired the drone's broken appendages and the blast hole in its dome. She knows he can't abandon a vulnerable creature for the same reason that she can't leave a broken machine unfixed.

"It could be useful." He thought about it all day while out with the herd. It's only he and Bolormaa now, since their youngest followed her sisters to the city, and his eyes aren't what they used to be. In the past a herding family would have more people and more dogs to help, but winters take and times change. "We can use it to monitor the herd from above."

"If you can tame it," Bolormaa says, rapping on the sleeping machine with her knuckles. "I severed it from its masters in Beijing, but remaking its AI is beyond my skills. It's a lone wolf now. The moment I turn it back on, it's going to attack us."

"I can tame it."

"It's not a horse, my love. It's not Baavgai. It was built to be mean."

He smiles. "Once, in battle, a soldier on the opposing side shot Chinggis Khan in the neck. The Great Khan respected such skill and bravery, even in an enemy. So, when the man was captured, Chinggis Khan spared his life and offered him the chance to fight for him. That soldier became the great Jebe, one of his fiercest and most loyal generals."

"Well," replies Bolormaa dryly, "you are not the Great Khan, so try not to let this drone shoot you in the neck."

* * *

For safety, they attach a chain to the drone and tie it to a post a safe distance from the *ger* and the animals. Bolormaa has disabled its laser for now, but it can still do plenty of damage with those sharp appendages.

The next morning, the sheep and goats watch over the edge of the pen as Ganbold bends to the ground beside the drone, presses a button under its rim, and then leaps out of range. With a rainbow flash of LED lights, the drone awakens. Lenses iris open, antennae unfurl, and jets whoosh. The drone soars up into the air—and finds itself rudely jerked back by the limit of the chain.

The lights flare red. Incensed, it stretches its spindly arms and legs out like claws and careers toward Ganbold, Bolormaa, and Baavgai. Bolormaa tries to jerk her husband back to safety, but though the drone strains, the chain holds, and its grasping arms can't reach them.

BEEP BEEP BEEP! it snarls. Its laser gun clicks, but nothing happens.

Bolormaa spits at it. "Dirty thing."

"Be nice, my love," says Ganbold. "It's just scared."

The drone whirls in an angry circle but succeeds only at wrapping its chain around the post and decreasing the circumference of its freedom. Frustrated, it sinks and hovers sullenly.

The red lights zip right, then left, lenses flicking and scanning, as it takes in its predicament. Its antennae reach towards satellites for orders from its masters and find none. Whistling low, it flexes each of its appendages in turn and notes that it has been healed.

"I bet that sunshine feels nice on your solar chips," Ganbold says. He sweet-talked Bolormaa into peeling a few off their own panels to replace the drone's broken ones.

The drone gives itself a spin, letting the morning sun hit all the little black chips. Its lights fade from crimson to the saffron orange of a lama's robe.

Ganbold is delighted, but trust must be nurtured slowly, carefully. Backing away, he smiles and says, "Rest up, my friend. We'll talk more later."

* * *

That evening, Ganbold brings the drone a small bowl of milk tea. He moves slowly and nonthreateningly to where the machine sits at the base of the post, its appendages curled crablike beneath it. Its golden lights flicker, but it allows Ganbold to set the bowl down and retreat. Baavgai sits nearby and watches warily.

Ganbold seats himself on the ground just out of range and sips his own bowl of tea. Machines don't drink tea, of course, but the drone needs to get used to his voice and presence. It's no different with horses. The drone, its lights shimmering inquisitively, slowly extends a metal arm and unfolds it towards the bowl. Whistling to itself, it pokes the ceramic bowl, then runs a sensor fingertip over the steam curling up from it. It was built to detect copper, coal, and tungsten from a kilometer in the air, but it doesn't know what to make of salty, buttery millet and horse milk tea. Finally, it plunges its sensor straight into the bowl, overturning it and splashing itself.

Ganbold laughs aloud. The drone's lights flash red, then quickly fade back to gold.

Bee bee bee, it says, mimicking Ganbold's laugh. That makes him chuckle harder, so the drone repeats itself. *Bee bee bee!*

"You're not such a bad drone, are you?" Ganbold says. "Just a soldier, and soldiers don't always get to choose who they fight for."

He risks reaching in to right the drone's bowl. Quick as a cat, the drone lashes out and spears his hand with a sharp steel leg.

Ganbold yelps and claps his other hand over the wound to staunch the blood.

"Ah, my apologies," he says, as the drone retreats and seethes. "Too much too soon. No matter. We'll try again tomorrow."

The drone's lights glitter gold. When Ganbold peeks out of the *ger* later that night, its lenses and sensors, designed to detect dead and buried things, are instead aimed up at the vast black sky, analyzing the stars.

* * *

Every evening, Ganbold brings the drone tea, sits a little closer, and tells it about his day. The lamb with the weak leg is growing stronger. His daughter sent a darling video message of his little grandson learning to walk. The clouds gathering over the mountains suggest rain in the next few days. The drone isn't much of a conversationalist, but he can tell from the way its lights flicker that it's listening.

"Imagine, all those girls growing up in one *ger!*" he says, using Bolormaa's tablet to show the drone photos of his daughters and their families. It considers each picture intently. "So much talking and shouting and laughing!"

His chuckle fades to a sigh. Twice Bolormaa has caught him singing to the drone the way he once did to them. "Ah, but the young people all move to the cities for work these days. I can't blame them, really. Between the wars and the winters, everything is so much harder and crueler than it used to be."

Distracted by these thoughts, he moves too close too quickly. The drone thwacks him hard on the head.

"That stupid thing is going to kill you," Bolormaa says later, putting a cold compress on the egg on Ganbold's forehead.

Ganbold sighs again. "Just give me a little more time."

* * *

They are eating lunch when the drone starts making a racket. It rises as high as its chain will allow, screeching like an alarm clock and rocking from side to side. When Ganbold and Bolormaa approach, it extends a leg and points to a dust cloud far to the south. Fetching the binoculars, Bolormaa sees that a Jeep is approaching.

"*Shaa,*" she curses, noting the emblem of the Church of the Digital Resurrection painted on the side. "More missionaries. I guess I'll make tea."

Ganbold nods at the drone. "Thank you for the warning."

Soon the Jeep pulls up to the *ger*. The missionaries are bright-eyed, smiling young Americans, two men and two women, who come bearing the good news of the Quantum Divinity. They're the fourth set Ganbold and Bolormaa have entertained this year, and they still have no intention of converting to the cult of robot-worship, but good Mongols are always hospitable. Although tedious, the missionaries are usually polite and move on after they've given their pitch and had something to eat.

This time, though, the Americans are aghast to see the drone chained to the post.

"Poor precious machine!" one of the women cries, in broken Mongolian. "What have you done to it?"

"Wait, don't!" Bolormaa shouts, as one of the men rushes to free it.

Too late—the drone holds still just long enough for the missionary to unhook the chain, then, free as a bird, launches itself upwards. The missionaries cheer and raise their hands in worship. However, the drone is a mischievous, ungrateful little machine. It dive-bombs the missionaries like a giant hornet, legs outstretched. Its lights are yellow rather than red— it's just playing around—but the missionaries don't know that. Shrieking, they bolt back towards the Jeep. The drone follows them, beeping and drumming on the roof until the missionaries floor the accelerator and retreat the way they came.

Ganbold is still bent double with laughter when the drone returns. Bolormaa grabs his arm to tug him back to safety, but the drone slows and simply hovers in place. It looks pleased with itself but unsure of what should happen now.

"Very naughty, you," Ganbold says with a smile. He takes a careful step towards it. The drone backs up slightly, but its eyes stay gold.

"We won't be getting that chain back on it now," says Bolormaa.

He agrees. It's the moment of truth. To the drone he says, "Well then, friend. If you want to move along, we won't stop you. However, you are welcome to stay."

The drone regards him, lenses clicking and lights flickering, then abruptly rockets hundreds of feet into the air. In seconds it's just a black speck among the clouds.

"That's that, then," says Bolormaa, and ducks back into the *ger*.

Ganbold finds himself sighing as he grazes and waters the herd. A few times he thinks he spies a black shape high overhead that is too round to be a bird or plane and his heart leaps—but when he looks again, it's gone. Just old eyes and wishful thinking. The drone is likely long gone. Fled to the city, perhaps, like all the young people.

Later that night, the rains move in. It's a pounding downpour like they haven't had in months. Ganbold and Bolormaa are snuggled up and drifting off to sleep when there's a piteous beeping outside the *ger*'s door.

Beep boop? Beep beep boop?

Ganbold rolls out of bed and opens the door. Fat raindrops are drumming on the drone's dome and dripping off the rim. Its legs are curled up beneath it and its antennae are flat. It looks as sad and apologetic as a machine can.

"Well, don't just float there getting rusty," Ganbold says, grinning, and steps aside to let it in.

* * *

The rain continues all day, so once she's fed the lambs and milked the goats, Bolormaa hunkers down inside and busies herself with the drone. One of its legs needs re-patching, and it could use a new coat of water-repellant. It doesn't want to be outside either, so it submits to her ministrations. Once, it tries to jab her with a spiky arm, but she slaps its dome hard enough to rattle the solar chips.

"*No,*" she says, and the drone learns to mind its manners.

When Ganbold returns, cold and waterlogged, at the end of the day, Bolormaa has managed to route the feed from the drone's cameras to her tablet.

"Show him, please," Bolormaa says. The drone flicks opens its lenses and in the tablet screen Ganbold sees his own face, tanned and lined, leaning over his wife's shoulder.

"Who's that old man behind that pretty lady, eh?" he says. Bolormaa rolls her eyes indulgently, but the drone's AI isn't sophisticated enough for this level of comedy.

"Now it can help us keep an eye on the herd and track down stragglers," she explains. "It also has infrared and night vision, so we can watch for wolves."

"Missionaries, too," Ganbold says, giving the drone a wink.

The drone unfolds the arm with the laser gun, points it at the floor, and fires. It clicks uselessly; the laser is still disabled. It fires again and looks at them expectantly.

Ganbold and Bolormaa share a glance. She shakes her head. Putting the drone to work is one thing; giving it a gun is another.

"Not yet, my friend," Ganbold says, reaching out to give the drone a pat.

The drone backs up and fires its gun at him angrily. *Clickclickclick!*

"No," Ganbold says.

The drone spirals away, clicking madly, and hurls itself out of the *ger* like a teenager in a huff.

* * *

The drone disappears for the rest of the night, but the next morning it's curled up outside next to Baavgai. It's still sulking, so when Ganbold takes the herd out, it stays behind and floats above the *ger*, watching Bolormaa do the laundry and adjust the solar panels.

"Either make yourself useful or be gone," she tells it, holding out a cable from the panels.

Grudgingly, the drone floats over and allows her to plug the cable into a port on its dome. Its computing power is ten times that of her tablet, so it makes short work of all the diagnostics tests and resets the panels. Before long, they're charging at full power again.

Bolormaa pats the drone's dome. "Good boy."

For just a moment, the drone's lights flicker green. It holds out its laser gun arm and says, *beep beep?*

Bolormaa shakes her head. "No."

Beep!

She gives it the same look she gave her daughters when they were pushing their luck. "I said no. You need to earn that."

Beeping indignantly, the drone zips off into the distance. "Fine!" Bolormaa snaps after it. "Go bother Ganbold!" She thinks little about it for the rest of the afternoon, until she heads back into the *ger* and hears her tablet ping.

The drone has sent her a series of aerial photos as a peace offering. She sees a birds-eye view of her husband down by the stream, on horseback in his blue felt *deel* robe, surrounded by moving puffs of white and gray. Another photo shows him with his face turned up towards the camera, smiling, and she smiles too.

The next photo shows the copse of trees about three kilometers north of the stream. There are some gray and brown figures in this photo too, but she can't quite make them out. She squints at the screen and pinches the photo to zoom in.

They're wolves.

* * *

They hear the wolves that night, their long howls echoing over the hills. Twice Ganbold gets up to check the animals and the fence. Baavgai prowls restlessly from dusk until dawn, but the wolves bide their time. The drone watches all of this, studying, analyzing, thinking, and clicking its gun.

The next night, the howls are closer.

* * *

Baavgai's barking wakes them.

Ganbold is half out the door before he's even fully awake, Bolormaa right behind him. The black night is full of movement and noise. The animals are bleating and braying in their pen. All around them dark figures flow and jaws snap. In the moonlight, Ganbold can see only a dozen pairs of moving, glowing eyes.

The drone is hovering over the chaos, trying to find Baavgai with a beam of light, but the dog is lost in a tangle of teeth and fur. He's barking and snarling and fighting, but he's sorely outnumbered and already short an eye.

Ganbold shouts and Bolormaa bangs on a pot, trying to scare the wolves away, but there are too many of them and the wolves are too brave now. The best they can do is get between the pen and the wolves and try to drive them back into the steppe.

Baavgai goes down and his snarls are pinched into yelps. The drone dives into the crush, appendages unfurled. It strafes one wolf, scratching up tufts of gray fur, but another locks its jaws around the drone's jet. Beeping frantically, the drone pulls back, playing tug-a-war with its own appendage.

The wolf wins; the jet breaks off and the drone is flung backwards towards Bolormaa. Trailing smoke, unable to fly properly, it drags itself to her and extends its laser arm. *Clickclickclickclick!*

For a moment, she hesitates, but the screams and cries coming from Ganbold, Baavgai, and the animals are unbearable. She kneels down and flips open the command panel on the drone's dome. Frantically, she taps out passwords and permissions and overrides. And just like that, the drone is armed again.

It launches itself out of her arms, not waiting for her to close the panel. Like a great thunderstorm it unleashes a barrage of blinding white flashes. Wolves yelp; the air fills with the smell of ozone and singed fur. In the herky-jerky motion of the strobing flashes Ganbold sees the wolves release Baavgai and turn their wrath on the drone. Fighting, firing, enduring bite after bite, the wounded drone herds the wolves away from the camp. The snarling and flashing lights fade into the darkness.

Ganbold hurries to Baavgai and scoops him up in his arms. Baavgai is now down an ear as well, and he's been bitten along his muzzle, shoulders, and back, but the old dog will live to fight another day.

"Good dog," he says, carrying him back to the *ger*. "The best dog."

He and Bolormaa check the sheep and goats, but it seems Baavgai and the drone kept them all safe. They soothe the horses, then, after making a few more tours of the perimeter and seeing no sign of the wolves or the drone, return to the *ger*. Ganbold patches up Baavgai's wounds while Bolormaa taps worriedly at the tablet. The drone's camera feed throws up error after error. It can't connect.

"Poor brave drone," Ganbold says, fearing the worst.

"Foolish thing," Bolormaa replies, but she sounds sad, too.

* * *

At dawn, there is still no sign of the drone. Ganbold awakes to find Bolormaa frowning over the tablet, trying all of her tricks. They don't speak much as they eat breakfast. After the night's chaos, the whole steppe feels too quiet.

Ganbold checks on Baavgai and the animals. He's saddling the gelding to take the animals out to graze when Bolormaa bursts out of the *ger*, gray braid flying behind her. She runs to him and thrusts the tablet under his chin.

"I got a signal from the feed," she says.

On the screen Ganbold sees a diagonal plane of brownish-green atop a smear of gray clouds. Turning his head, he realizes the image is upside-down; the drone has turned turtle on the grass.

"Is it alive?" he asks.

"I can't tell. It's not responding to any of my pings."

If there's a chance, Ganbold will take it. Bolormaa taps at the tablet, using the feed to set a GPS pin in the drone's current location, and gives it to her husband. Without wasting any more time, Ganbold takes the tablet, mounts, and rides off. This time he orders Baavgai to stay behind, to rest.

The GPS pin is a pulsing blip of green, Ganbold's position a bead of blue. The drone chased the wolves—or was dragged—six kilometers north, up into the hills. He gallops past the crater and the stream, up past the little burrow where he first found it. Although the morning is marching on, the sky is still pale gray. The temperature has dropped and, from the taste of the wind, Ganbold expects snow.

Gradually, the green blip grows larger and the space between it and Ganbold's blue bead closes. He comes over a rise and finds the first shorn metal leg.

From there he doesn't need the GPS. A trail of metallic carnage leads downhill. A jet, a sensor, a solar panel. Ganbold scoops up and saves every piece.

At last, he finds it. It looks like a discarded trashcan lid lying there in the dirt. Most of its legs have been pulled off and its strip of lights are cracked. It's dented, blood-stained, battle-scarred. Still, when Ganbold kneels down beside it, a few white lights flicker on.

Bee...? It says faintly. It tries to wave one of its remaining legs but lacks the power and freezes.

Ganbold rights the drone and brushes off the dirt and grass. "I'm here, my brave little one. You did good."

Bee... the drone says. Its lights attempt a mint green. *Bee bee bee.*

"Don't you worry, Jebe, my friend," Ganbold says, scooping it up. "Bolormaa will have you patched up in no time."

He carefully packs Jebe in the front pouch of his *deel*, where he carries his grandson when he visits and the lambs when they're newborn, and he brings his general home.

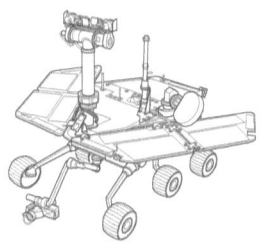

This Cold Red Dust

Merc Fenn Wolfmoor

Log 033 — user: Kel9000

So…we're leaving in three days, Finn. Dad says this will be the last authorized shuttle, so it's "now or never" like this is time-travel or some shit. It's not. Once everyone is gone, the government is putting Mars on lockdown, I guess, so no entrepreneurs can try and fix the environmental damage or try again.

I'm six months away from qualifying for my pilot license but who knows how much time I'll have to get in-flight training hours. I gotta get a new job first. Does Earth need more miners who wanna fly freighter? My simulation scores are nova, but that doesn't mean the space-DMV is going to authorize my application. (Space-DMV is what Dad calls Universal Flight Coordination Administration, which makes his version dumb, because UFCA has the same number of syllables and is actually correct.)

I don't wanna go, Finn. It was hard enough starting over here. Now I gotta do it again, and Mom's out of the picture and Dad is so tired…I'm scared. Don't tell Dad.

<end log>

* * *

It's unfair that the dust storms on Mars are so cold. Sure, you might constantly have to scrape your visor to prevent layered particle build up, and yes, it's hard to see more than a few meters ahead, and it's true your spacesuit is in sore need of a tune-up, but it's the cold that gets to you.

Your helmet's nav system guides you where your senses can't. Up ahead is an abandoned settlement, its dome dismantled for parts and the generators scavenged for fuel. Bigfoot Seen, the signpost used to read. All the settlements have quirky names like that. Used to be Mars had spirit and optimism and people. Now it's back to dust storms and the lonely nothingness of abandonment.

You trudge over the border and the settlement's automated ping chimes in your helmet.

WELCOME TO **BIGFOOT SEEN**! POPULATION: **0**. PLEASE VISIT OUR VISITOR STATION AND LOG YOUR NAME AND PURPOSE. WE'RE SO GLAD YOU MADE IT!

Good to know something still works, even if it's just a solar-powered hub broadcasting nonstop into a wasteland. The visitor center is nothing but a dune of sand with a blasted roof peeking through the dust. Not worth the time to dig out an entrance; most rest stops like that got scrapped when the great migrations emptied the planet.

Still, there are intact buildings you can find shelter in; the welcome center's ping has dutifully downloaded a map of the area for you. If you're lucky, maybe the old flight tower still has broadcast gear.

There won't be anyone to call, though, will there? The last ships left you behind. It's as unfair as the cold, and nothing you can do about it.

Alarms ping your helmet. The storm is getting worse. Seek shelter immediately. Solar winds and radiation don't give a damn who you are.

You hurry—for relative use of the verb, when every step is a fight against wind and dust and the shifting sand—towards the transit station. A shuttle hub where ships landed and left…mostly just left. The bunker is built to withstand launching shuttles and the nasty moods of Mars. Best bet. It's attached to the flight navigation tower.

Your thigh muscles ache from exhaustion as you push through unstable ripples of sand, leaning against the wind. You need both hands to keep your balance and soon your vision is a wall of red-black as you lose the light. The helmet's internal map blinks a little green cartoon Martian head as your location marker. You thought it was cute once.

Finally—a door. It's ajar, the hydraulics busted and months of dust storms layering hills of dirt across the threshold. You squirm and struggle and at last squeeze yourself through the opening. Wiping your visor for the millionth time, you wobble in the lack of wind. The bunker has no power, naturally, but it's out of the storm for now. Your worn headlamp can gain traction against the darkness here. Too bad it's still cold and there isn't any atmosphere to let you take your suit off and wipe the micro dust from itching your insulated jumpsuit where it rubs your skin. The dust gets in no matter how tight the recycled air filters are. You're not in zero-g void, thank your favorite stars. That would be worse with the cold.

It's eerie, being the only human in a place this size, which once housed thousands of people—well, maybe not that many. Little settlements like Bigfoot Seen, at the foot of the mountains, didn't really get much of a spillover like the big cities closer to the equator. Your home base, Jackalope Song, is about twenty miles north; the trek felt abominably longer than that, seeing how you were on foot once your ATV died with a grind of clogged motor and stripped treads.

All the hubs like this one were built the same, so despite the dust and empty darkness you pick your way through hallways until you get two levels deep, in the storage cube sector.

It's possible to MacGyver one of the cubes—three meters square—into a tiny, temporary sleeping quarters. You've got two mini environ-tents left, three rations of purified water, and a dozen protein bars, plus the bodily waste recycling unit. The crank-charged space heater is what you really want to set up first. But, priorities. Once you seal up the door, you can take off your suit and get your body's needs met, take your meds—the supply is worryingly low—and well…sleep, you suppose. What else is there to do?

Maybe you should just stay here until you run out of supplies or hope.

All the ships left and all that's left is red, cold dust and silence.

* * *

Log 02 — user: Kel9000

I can't believe this piece of crap is what Mom got. A FriendBot? Really? This is literally an antique! A *used* antique. I wanted her to at least *try* to imagine what I'd want for my birthday, but no, she's Earth-side and was all, "Oh, Kel, you know how expensive shipping costs are and no perishables blah blah blah," like yeah, Mom, so maybe you could have gotten me a decent console or tablet for the same weight as this…toy?

She thought because she used to have the Pilot Panda model when she was my age that I'd want this thing. It's not a pilot, Mom. It's some kind of crappy fake engineered piece of shit. I'm allergic to dogs, not that we can have real pets.

A fox isn't much better.

She didn't even leave a message in the welcome screen for me.

<end log>

* * *

The cube has a few shelves with sealed clothing packets, a stack of media tablets—all the batteries depleted, sadly—and an old, raggedy-furred FriendBot stashed in one corner.

It's the Fixer Fox model: enormous ears, a bushy tail, stubby limbs, synthetic coat bright orange and tipped in white. Now the thing looks as beaten down as the settlement: its faux fur is matted with dust, its white tips stained dirty brown, one ear torn, and the left optic shattered. The little toolkit and apron are gone, and the rib flap where you access its processor and battery is missing the magnets, so it looks more like a rend of flesh hanging off metal bones.

You pick it up. You used to want one of these FriendBots when you were a kid. You'd always had your eye on Trucking Tiger, who came with its own mining vehicle accessory, and a fake drill that doubled as a flashlight.

FriendBots were all the rage for about a year before they went extinct once updated AI models became available. And then, well, shipping from Earth wasn't cheap, and credit had to be spent on necessities, and mining operations failed one by one, and the government began offering payouts to relocate onto the New Earth's Horizons program. Wasn't much of a choice for most people: once you lost your job, there weren't many options, and there wasn't any functional unemployment system in place.

This thing must be, what, fifteen years out of date? A sentimental keepsake. Little wonder it got left behind. Passage off Mars came with strict luggage restrictions and weight limits. Only the essentials, unless you could pay for those few extra kilograms of space. Only officials and inheritance brats had the funds to escape in comfort, but then they'd only been on Mars as a new thrill. It wasn't life, or home, for them.

You toss the FriendBot back into the corner; it's not even worth taking apart for scrap. The tech is too out of date and there isn't going to be any juice in that battery.

The fox chirrups.

The sound nearly sends you reeling into the low ceiling in panic. Your heart bounces like a dribbling basketball in your chest for a solid twenty seconds before you get control over yourself. Breathe. Breathe in. Out. Good, okay, see, you're fine.

It's a goddamn toy and the jostling just loosened up old fritzing speakers. Like buildings settling under the groaning weight of dust. You're so used to the restlessness of your own thoughts, poor company at the best of times; your music player broke days ago so all you have are the memories of melody and lyrics to keep you company.

That's really what's worse about Mars: its soundtrack is one of barren land, empty sky, merciless weather. There's no music in the wind, not for you. Mars is an angry, hungry ball of rock used up by Earth and Sun alike, an icon of blood, never one of peace.

You eye the FriendBot warily, but it doesn't squeak or leap up and attack you with red-LED optics or modified steel teeth. This isn't one of the killbot serials. (A guilty pleasure, but who doesn't love them?) Most of the bots you work with—worked with—are too dumb to do more than cause tripping hazards or freak out at unexpected alterations in their programmed routines and need to be rescued from feedback loops. All the mining bots were recalled when the operation sites closed. You sometimes wonder if they got recycled or just scrapped for minimal profit.

You curl up as best you can around your pack, your back to the wall, the little space heater doing its best against the still, cold air.

The FriendBot lies on its face, its butt in the air, droopy tail draped awkwardly along its spine, its torn ear pinned under the weight of its head. That looks uncomfortable, so you reach out and nudge the fox onto its side.

It chirrups again, unmistakable, and green light flickers in the good optic.

You wrench your arm back, jamming your elbow on the floor. Pain ricochets up your shoulder—shit. Well, if the thing still has some working battery, you might be able to syphon that for your gear.

"Don't turn killbot on me," you mutter. Your throat hurts. You tried talking to yourself for the last few miles of the hike to Bigfoot Seen, but it took so much energy. The echo of your own voice in your sealed helmet was worse than keeping your mouth shut and fighting against the wind.

You cautiously pick up the FriendBot and examine it.

There's another rip in the fur along the neck, and the reinforced aluminum skeleton is scratched; a former owner must have made some offline hacks. You rub your finger along the fox's muzzle. It makes a tinny purring sound.

"Hi, buddy," you say.

"Hi, friend!" the bot responds, its voice in that uncanny range of cutesy human-like but still artificial. Its good optic glows faintly, bright green with a pixelated pupil that expands or contracts to show emotion. Later models came with an option to have emotive text display on a tiny LED screen on the forehead. This one just has the expressive eyes. "Is it playtime?"

* * *

Log 015 — user Kel9000

You make a pretty good diary, Finn, I'll give you that. Who's gonna try and pry into a toy, right? Ha! Also, I figured if you're really an engineer who fixes stuff, the least I could do would be to update your software. At least these legacy models are customizable. And it gives me something to do since I broke my leg and can't go help Dad in EB79-delta.

God, I'm gonna lose my frigging mind if I have to stay in living quarters for another week.

<end log>

* * *

You swallow hard and blame the lump in your throat on fatigue and dust. You flip the FriendBot over and find the dataport remarkably clean: a universal adapter under the left foreleg along the ribs, kind of where a heart should be.

"How long you been here?" you ask, fishing a cord from your pack.

"Last playtime was on June 8th."

Fourteen months and a handful of days. Seems about right. You stayed in Jackalope Song for nearly a year, waiting, slowly using up the supplies, staying fixed by the broadcast station in case your SOS got a response. It never did.

"Guess you weren't worth the cargo tax, huh?"

The FriendBot's tail wiggles in response. It has no idea what sarcasm is. It's just a mess of ball joints, wires, faux fur, and LED optics. Cutesyfied so there's no chance you'd mistake it for a real fox, which only existed on Earth and nature documentaries.

You plug in the cord to the dataport on the fox's chest and connect it to your helmet's system. Sure, the FriendBot might be full of viruses or the software will be incompatible due to age, but honestly, you don't care that much. It's nice having something to talk to, even if it's just the factory-mandated greeting and response logs.

"New friend detected," the bot says, and its eye swirls into warm amber. "Hi, new friend!"

You ignore the setup menu; looks like the software was updated and modified to mimic the AI models; still out of date, but compatible. You tap the Friend Log. The last user was Kel9000. There's no passcode, so you logon as Kel9000, a little guiltily, sure.

It's like hacking someone's online diary. Rude, but you can't deny you want to know who they were, what they did with the fox bot. All that you have left is the survival kit and one backup drive of photos, memories, paperwork, and saved audio calls. Kel9000 isn't here, but you are, and you desperately don't want to spend the night in the silence of your own anxiety.

* * *

Log 016 — user Kel9000

Hi Finn!

+HELLO, FRIEND.+

I guess if my pilot career crashes and burns, I could always make a living fixing old toys. Maybe I could audition you in whatever new horror movie is being made Earth-side. No need for CGI, fellas, this fox-bot is the real deal! An evil as fuck killer doll!

+I DO NOT WANT TO BE BAD. D:+

Aw, that was just a joke, buddy.

+I AM NOT BAD?+

No, Finn, you're a good bot. I'm just bored.

+DOES FRIEND WANT TO PLAY? :D+

Okay, sure. Let's see how we can modify your system functionality, huh?

<end log>

* * *

You pause the playback of the FriendBot's logs. It's harder than you expected to listen to Kel's voice and know they are never coming back, the way you're never going to leave.

In the weeks after the last shuttle left, you held out hope.

There were promises at first: transmissions—getting more and more infrequent—citing delays due to maintenance repairs and fuel costs and quarantine worries.

You haven't been forgotten, the messages always said at the end. **Don't lose faith!**

You held on, with a handful of others who'd stayed behind—you wish it was a noble sacrifice, giving up a seat in the lifeboat, but in reality? You were just unlucky. Your queue number was one too long for the available room onboard.

"Don't worry," you told your two younger sisters. You put on a brave face, adopted a cocksure attitude like the epic space heroes in blockbuster films. Unflappable and with roguishly mussed hair. "When you're dropped off safe and the ships are refueled, they'll pick me up next."

Your sisters waved, shepherded aboard by your aunt and older cousin. They were the last of your family who'd made a go at mining the new frontier of Mars; your parents, Sol rest them, were years in the grave now, but you still felt their pride at all you and the settlement had accomplished.

So you waited for the promised ships. You waited while the others gave up or went missing or lost hope. You watched the broadcast tower every night. You were so goddamn certain a transmission would crackle through the feed, announcing the in-bound ship here to save you.

You waited even after you started to doubt. You waited after the power cells depleted and the last two humans in Jackalope Song walked into the cold, red dust and didn't return.

"The ships were supposed to come *back*," you say into FriendBot's dirty fur, your eyes stinging and your body too dehydrated for tears. "They were supposed to come back for us."

FriendBot's optic cycles into deep green-blue and it makes a soft chirrup. "Don't be sad, friend. You aren't alone when you have your buddy!"

"Shut up!" You hurl it into the corner, all your frustration and fear and grief giving your arm vibrant strength. The FriendBot bounces against the cube wall and clatters to the floor. "You stupid toy! The ships aren't coming back!"

The fox lands on its oversized head, its body flopped to the side, like it's doing an awkward handstand on its stubby front legs. Its eye glitches, the light blinking in and out.

"I'm sorry I made you mad," the bot says, its voice stuttering like its LED optic. "I didn't mean to be a bad buddy. Sleep mode activated. Goodnight, frien—" Its battery fritzes and the FriendBot shuts down.

Fuck. Your press your hands over your face, biting down a sob.

* * *

Log 020 — user Kel9000

Finn, I have a secret.

+HELLO, FRIEND. :D+

Yes, hi to you too. Listen. I've been feeling weirder and weirder the last few months, you know? It's not atmo-sickness, and all my vaccines are current, and besides, it doesn't feel…well, like a *real* flu or anything.

+FRIEND FEELS BAD?+

It's more like…backwards? Or like I'm in some kind of alternate dimension where my skin is just the wrong fit. Remember when I had to make incisions in your coat to upgrade you? Like that, only…the glue on me didn't stick things closed properly.

I wish our network didn't suck so bad. I was only ten when we came to Mars, but damn if I don't remember how good the wifi was on Earth. Anyway, I went to the school library and bypassed the usual filters and got access to the wider net and…well, I started searching and half the results were like "you have cancer omg!" but obviously I don't. It was tricky to figure out keywords but I kind of just blundered around and…so I think I might be trans? But not, like, girl-to-boy, it's more…just, like, the opt-out of gender?

I'm not sure yet, it's so weird and kind of scary.

+FRIEND IS GOOD.+

You're sweet, you know that? I wish you could actually help me, though.

I don't want to tell Dad. He's already stressed that we're behind on the quotas and the company is cutting hours again. Everything sucks and I feel weird and I don't know what to do.

<end log>

* * *

After a few minutes, guilt wins and you carefully scoop the bot up. It remains limp and silent, its optic dark.

You press the ON button at the base of FriendBot's ear. "Hey, buddy," you whisper. "You didn't deserve that."

"Hi," the bot chirps, but its voicebox is muffled and its eye LED is barely visible. "Sorry I was a bad friend."

"Dammit." You shake your head. "You're good, buddy. I'm sorry I hurt you. It's me who was bad."

"You are hurt?" FriendBot asks.

You sniff and wipe your nose. Inevitably, there's dust in your nostrils and your snot is brownish red. "Just tired," you reply. "Your battery is pretty low, pal. You get some rest, okay?"

"I would like to stay awake," FriendBot says. "With you."

"Oh. Okay, we can do that."

"Thanks, friend," the bot says. You cradle it against your chest and curl up again by the space heater.

"I'm glad you're here to keep me company, buddy," you whisper to FriendBot.

The fox's tail twitches, as much of a happy wag as it can manage. "Me too, friend."

"Save your strength…" Your voice slurs and your eyelids droop. FriendBot's muzzle is propped on your forearm, its eye level with yours. You fall asleep first, the bot watching over you.

* * *

Log 021 — user Kel9000

Yo, Finn, the word I'm looking for is non-binary, how fucking cool is that? Like anti-numbers! I mean I love numbers, but "non-binary" just sounds so badass. Whoo, this is awesome and I feel like I could float without even zero-g!

+YAY, FRIEND! :D+

Yay is right! Wow, it's like an endorphin rush every time I say it: non-binary.

Oh, shit, I gotta go finish working on my pre-test scores for flight school. I'm gonna be a pilot, Finn. Talk to you soon. Whoo!

<end log>

* * *

You're cold and stiff when you wake. FriendBot is dark, still, and lies in the same position you left it in. Its battery is dead.

Your tears taste like dust.

* * *

Log 022 — user Kel9000

I haven't told Dad yet, but I think he'll get it. He loves science fiction too. We spend half our network credits to download movies every Sunday. I'm loading them onto media tablets to save on bandwidth. I'll let you plug in and watch them with me next time.

<end log>

* * *

Suited up again, you creakily crawl out of the cube. You have FriendBot strapped across your torso with a spare elastic strap from your repair kit. You'd like to hold it inside your jacket, but the close-fitting suit doesn't have a lot of give.

You're going to the transmission tower to wait. The storm has abated enough that some light is leaking through the gaps where dust doesn't cover the reinforced windows. There might be some power cells left in crew lockers. You queue up Kel9000's logs and let their voice accompany you as you walk.

The control tower is like a mechanical tomb. The door seals mostly kept the interior clean, or what passes for clean in an abandoned settlement. No logged transmissions in over twelve months.

No power cells, either. There is a flashlight, with batteries half-charged. You hesitate. You could use the light. But what you really want is to see FriendBot's eye light up again.

You settle down with your back to the transmission console and insert the batteries into the fox's chassis pack. It takes a few seconds, but then FriendBot blinks back to life. You attach the sync cable and FriendBot's face pixelates in your helmet's viewscreen.

"Is it playtime, friend?"

"No." You let out a tired breath. "There won't be any more playtime, Finn."

"D:," says FriendBot. "Why not?"

"Coz we're…I'm…" You swallow, your throat dry as the cold, red dust of Mars. "I'm gonna die here. We are, I guess, coz your battery will fail and…I'm sorry I can't do anything to help you, buddy."

It hurts worse because FriendBot was already abandoned once, like you were. When the ships didn't come back.

* * *

Log 027 — user Kel9000

Half the settlement got laid off today. Dad is depressed worse than before and Mom has stopped sending us any messages. I wonder if she's moved on. I know the divorce was legalized over a year ago but…I still wish she wouldn't shrug me off, like I'm just a random profile on SpaceFeed she can delete when she gets bored.

Is it bad that I'm angry at her and also feel like I got gut-punched?

+NO, FRIEND. I'M SORRY YOU ARE SAD.+

I dunno what we're gonna do, Finn. Dad still has his job, but that's almost worse because all his friends hate him now, and no one will talk to me without being shitheads. Like it's my fault we're in recession and surviving on Mars is hard?

+YOU ARE GOOD, FRIEND. DO YOU WANT TO PLAY?+

I'm going to bed, Finn. Shut down.

\<end log\>

* * *

You're not sure what's worse: the analogue clock in your visor or turning it off so you sit in timeless quiet, waiting for the end. You shut your eyes but there's no comfortable way to settle in a worn suit and a hard metal floor.

You have four of Kel9000's logs left in the queue. Some of their earlier ones you replayed, because it was nice to hear Kel's voice rambling on about school, their piloting studies, the latest movies they watched with their dad, and sometimes their dreams about flying through the solar system, seeing stars no human has ever witnessed outside of telescopes and drones.

Once you get to the end, that's it: a final stopping point. There's nothing after the 34th log. You don't want Kel's story to end, either.

Yet you need to know. Maybe there will be closure for them, if not for you. So you cradle FriendBot against your chest and play the last few logs. When they finish, you might just let the rest be silence.

* * *

Log 029 — user Kel9000

I deactivated your text-responses in my logs. I just…I kind of just need my own headspace, okay? You're still my buddy. I promise I'll never abandon you like Mom did.

<end log>

* * *

Log 030 — user Kel9000

Dad was really cool when I told him I'm non-binary. He says I should make my nickname Matrix or something, and wow, it's like this huge anvil came off my brain.

But even though he's happy for me, he's still really sad and tired. I'm doing my best to help out and cheer him up, but I'm just so stressed, you know? None of my "friends" are talking to me, and a bunch of people in our building unit have already moved out. It's like Bigfoot Seen is getting hollowed out one scoop at a time.

What happens when there's no one left?

<end log>

* * *

Log 031 — user Kel9000

Dad lost his job.

[eighty seconds of silence, punctuated by slow breathing and soft crying sounds]

Shit, why didn't the stop button work—

<end log>

* * *

You need something to do with your hands, so you dig into the virtual menu in FriendBot's system and begin prying loose the comm panels in the tower. In theory, the broadcast antenna can amplify a properly coded out-going signal. These older models of FriendBot have a basic GPS—the **Find My FriendBot** function—but the range is limited to a few miles at best, and only then if they're networked to a data grid.

* * *

Log 032 — user Kel9000

Hey, Finn. So…good news, I guess? The government is bailing everyone out. Mars colonization declared a failure, blah blah, stupid sensational headlines. I don't want to get into it.

We're gonna finish up this semester at school, since it'll be a few weeks before the evacuation plans really finalize and start shipping people off-world. Kicking us all out of the red, cold dust. There's really tight restrictions on weight limit, because I guess the government can't possibly afford more than the bare minimum of safety and oxygen to get us into orbital stations around Luna and Earth until we can re-acclimate and go planet-side. Or off to one of the other re-settlement worlds, in stasis for years.

It's bullshit, I know, but when has the government on any world been anything else?

I'm not taking the Centurial Ideal package, even if it does offer good benefits and money to your immediate relatives who stay behind. I don't want to go to sleep for a decade just to wake up and have to do Mars all over again. I'll get my pilot's license, apprentice with one of the shipping companies, and one day I'll have my own shuttle! Let me dream, okay?

It's more than Dad seems to have.

<end log>

* * *

Your fingers are clumsy with your gloves and general fatigue. It takes a lot longer than it should to create a basic patch from FriendBot's GPS tag via your suit and then into the comm tower's interface. This is probably a lot of wasted energy on your part. You keep having to pause and catch your breath. At least it feels like you're *trying*.

This will drain most of the limited battery juice FriendBot has, and tax your own suit significantly. A quick calculation shows that rerouting the limited power to boost the **Find My FriendBot** alert will drop your survival estimates by a good seventy percent. You swallow hard. There's one more log from Kel, and after that, you'll have less than a day before your suit freezes and shuts down.

You activate the tiny SOS from Finn's system and play the final entry.

* * *

Log 034 — user Kel9000

So. This is it, huh, Finn?

Dad has us registered. The restrictions are so bad, like…you can't even take sentimental items. One standardized suitcase per person.

I'm so sorry, buddy. But you know I need to take my flight sim and my books for study and I'm giving Dad some of my space—even though he doesn't know that yet—so he can bring Mom's tablet and the sweater Grandma crocheted him for the wedding. It's falling apart but he loves it and I can't bear to see him break his heart even more by leaving it behind.

So…you have to stay, Finn. I'll keep you in our storage cube, so you'll be safe from the dust. God, this is so hard to tell you…you can't really understand, can you? …Shit. I'm sorry, I'm getting tears on your fur. [strained laugh]

Listen, I want you to wait for me, okay? I've got a plan. I've been messaging my cousin, who just got a promotion to manifest controller on a cargo hauler. She's going to help Dad start fresh, too, but Earth-side. Maybe he'll try and reconnect with Mom, I don't know. My cousin says she can probably get me a job on-board. It's more like unpaid apprenticeship, but what the hell, it'll get me hours.

And I know the various corporations are stripping the settlements for recyclables, but there's a government ban on the transit hubs and living quarter buildings. They're being declared 'monuments of history' or some bullshit. So as long as you stay put in our cube, you'll be safe.

Okay, buddy?

<end log>

* * *

Silence echoes. Your helmet flashes a red bar indicating systems critical. As if you hadn't noticed. You might just lie down and…well. Eventually you'll sleep and not wake up, and that doesn't seem as ugly-bad now. You can imagine Kel would be happy you kept FriendBot company, and the little guy helped you remember you aren't entirely alone, so…in the overall scope of things, this isn't the worst ending you could have gotten.

You shut your eyes, drifting off. You nixed the clock and any virtual overlays in your helmet to conserve energy. FriendBot's battery has maybe two minutes left of juice. You'll fall asleep together and—

Ping!

The alert sound rattles in your ear, making you jump. You lurch to your feet, your heart thundering. You've heard that sound in the commercials: a unique, musical chime.

FriendBot Located! displays in blue-green text across your visor.

"Hey, Finn, and anyone there with you," comes a voice, static-laced and choppy, but a human voice, a real live person voice. One you recognize easily from all the logs. "Told you I'd be back! My cousin is amazing, I can't wait to introduce you to her. Looks like your battery lasted after all! Don't know how you did it, but we picked up your signal."

You hear the ecstatic grin in Kel9000's voice. You smile back.

"Hold on, okay?" Kel9000's message finishes. "I'll be there soon."

"Okay," you reply hoarsely. You hug FriendBot tight. "We'll hold on."

When the ship comes, you'll bring your buddy home.

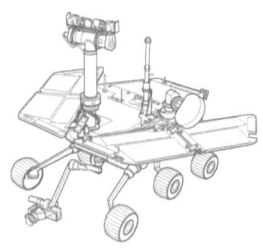

Traveling Hopefully

Jacey Bedford

Three-of-Seven watched for signs of habitable planets across a small section of the galaxy that encompassed thirty major star systems. He checked for blips in each star's luminosity and identified a hundred and fifty-two planets. One by one he analyzed the light passing through their atmospheres to determine the composition. And there it was—one planet which might be capable of supporting an ecosystem broadly compatible with Old Earth.

He needed to take a closer look. Three-of-Seven sometimes believed in a god and sometimes didn't; more often than not, he didn't. After all, he knew who his creators were. That they were still divided on the question of a divine entity left him somewhat puzzled.

He focused his scope on the sixth rock of a yellow sun, designated ST4607F. It didn't have a name yet. Esstee would do. It looked promising. Surface water; oxygen-nitrogen atmosphere. No obvious signs of civilization, in fact; nothing to show any signs of sentient life at this distance. He needed to take a closer look.

This world could be suitable for humans. Three-of-Seven wasn't going to get too excited, however. There was still a lot of work to do. He certainly wasn't going to flood the Centre with false optimism. He'd done that once before and it had ended badly.

The Centre was waiting for his report. He'd already passed his scheduled check-in time. It was a small rebellion, one that he dared not repeat often without recriminations. He opened himself up and connected via the jump points, uploading the initial scan results. The Centre, that entity from which he had sprung, and which he would always be a part of, uploaded his information to the greatest *thinkers* of their generation, a series of augmented brains, part organic. They would pass their findings on to the Controller, a human, who would direct the next step.

Initial promise, but I still have a lot of tests to complete, he said to his sibs.

One-of-Seven latched on to him immediately and fed him several bursts of information which amounted to: *Still traveling. Bored. Fancy a game of chess?*

Two-of-Seven was navigating through an asteroid field. She had downloaded her consciousness into her avatar body and had taken over the manual controls of her ship. She didn't need to do that—she could fly it just as easily from her place within the ship's system—so Three-of-Seven surmised she was bored as well.

Four-of-Seven was new, following the unexpected demise of his predecessor. He was conscious and part of the Centre, but hadn't yet completed the design of his avatar bodies and wouldn't be activated until his new sail-ship was ready.

Five-of-Seven and Six-of-Seven welcomed Three-of-Seven and tried to entice him into a conversation on mathematics. He acknowledged them but refused to be drawn in.

Seven-of-Seven, taciturn as usual, said little, but brooded mightily. He was in one of his mechanical vehicle bodies, surveying a small moon for potential mineral extraction.

They were all him, just as he was them. One mind, seven avatars. So why did he feel as though he didn't quite belong? Maybe he was getting too old, too jaded, worn out. Was that even possible? Could a Centre fragment? Could the seven ever become individuals?

He settled down to run yet another scan. Better not worry about the passage of time. What was time, anyway? Humans defined a second as the duration of 9,192,631,770 periods of the radiation corresponding to the transition between the two hyperfine levels of the ground state of the caesium 133 atom... a construct. Time didn't exist. Spacetime, however, that was something entirely different. He let his internal system idle while the scan ran, and waited, aware as always of his sibs, and of the Centre, and of the inevitable tick-tick-ticking away of human time.

Some considerable quantity of seconds later he received the message from the Controller. *Yes, investigate fully. Survey and landing authorized. Proceed with caution.*

Ha! He always proceeded with caution whether he was inhabiting his ship or one of his avatar bodies.

Three-of-Seven deployed his ship's solar sail, calculated times, and relayed the information back to the Centre. It would take fifty-five hours, subjective time, to reach the nearest safe jump point and then a further forty-nine hours from his exit point to planetary orbit. He checked the relative positions of the star and the planet and confirmed his estimate.

Apart from the entry and exit from the jumps, and the occasional descent through an alien atmosphere, traveling could be mind-numbingly boring. There was a lot of nothing out here in the black. This was his opportunity to set the proximity alarms and shift his consciousness from the ship, via the jump points, to the Centre, once more submerging self into whole, going deep, becoming a seventh part of one mind.

He thought about it and decided not to. He wondered if any of the others felt the strain of belonging or if they still craved immersion like he used to.

When had he begun to feel as though there was something wrong with his purpose? Had it begun with Zantar Four? He'd reported a planet with sentient life forms in its vast oceans and the Controller had authorized an ark fleet of five million colonists. A land-based colony could no doubt coexist with an oceanic intelligence, but Three-of-Seven had worried about what would happen when humans decided the sea was a resource. He hadn't had long to wait to find out. Before the first century was over, war was declared. It took another twenty years before the remnants of the human colonists, barely two hundred thousand, requested assistance and fled the planet.

Sharing always led to disaster. Humans would never co-exist with any other sentient species; it wasn't in their nature. If he found a world like that again, he might not even report it. He shut that thought away from the Centre with a subversive shudder.

The proximity alarm from his ship cut into Three's consciousness. He flipped into active mode to carry out the gate maneuver in and out of the jump point; then he set a course for ST4607F. The next step was to observe from orbit, capture data, then make several passes before landing to collect samples.

He guided his ship into high orbit above Esstee and furled the sail. He checked atmosphere, gravity, water and land distribution, temperature and climate, tectonic, volcanic, and geothermal activity.

His next pass was for vegetation. From high orbit he identified several distinctly separate terrestrial biomes: desert, ice, savanna, forests, and temperate grassland. There was no sign of animal life, but since plants and animal ecosystems were usually interdependent, it was likely that there was something living down there, even if it was just bugs and microscopic organisms.

Better run a deeper scan before descending to collect samples.

All his readings were within the parameters of what he sought. He descended to low orbit. Mountains, rivers, forests, grassland, deserts, and oceans…and then…

Organic life, carbon-based.

He homed in on heat signatures, but a heat signature couldn't identify a creature as sentient.

He really hoped it wasn't sentient life down there. He didn't want to have to leave this world and continue onwards. With surprise, he recognized that he'd been traveling for long enough. He was tired.

He checked again for signs of industrial pollutants, for carbon emissions, for radioactivity, all the signs of a sentient species reaching a specific level of enlightenment. Nothing. Nothing flew in the air except birds. Nothing moved on the ground on wheels. He couldn't see any settlements, roads, or tracks wider than animal trails to watering places. He began to relax. Animal life was not unusual. He'd know more when he reached the surface.

For that part of the operation he would have to download himself into an avatar body. That might be interesting. Though expendable, he was imbued with an imperative to continue his existence. It was as it should be; replacing him would be costly and time-consuming. Besides, the Centre always suffered a deep sense of loss when one of them terminated, as it did when Old Four failed and was replaced.

He did not want to cease. There had been instances during the course of his long existence when, if it were not for his stubborn human-infused will to survive, he would have been lost. A simple machine would not have struggled so hard to live on Jondar when his choice had been to die or to kill. He still grieved for the loss of life, but saving his own had been his first priority. The Centre had agreed with him. Well, of course it would. The Centre was him. He was the Centre.

At least Jondar was now marked off-limits to settlers.

He downloaded his consciousness into his avatar, ran a quick systems test from his toes to the tips of his octopoid arms, and disengaged from the control interface, leaving instructions for his eventual return. He made his way to the shuttle dock, feeling a fluttering of excitement from the Centre at his brief report. He selected a motley of greens and his chameleon circuit complied, coloring his body, right down to his fingernails and suckers.

Three-of-Seven's preferred avatar body had a human-style head, torso, and two long legs. He'd chosen to have eight paired octopus arms on a flexible mantle mounted around human-shaped shoulders; four of those arms had human-style hands. He'd chosen an outward maleness, though without inconvenient genitals.

Once the landing craft entered the planet's atmosphere he was on his own. Atmospheric conditions could cause a communication blackout during the descent. He found separation both mildly disturbing and somewhat refreshing, but even without a continuous connection he was confident that the Centre was there, waiting for him, whether he craved it or not. He linked to his sibs now, knowing it might be some hours before he could link again.

Flying the shuttle required manual skill. He twined the end of one arm around the interface and placed the fingers of two hands over the touch-sensitive control pad. Two further paired arms secured his harness. He tucked his spare arms into the restraints. He didn't want to damage them, though they were as durable as the rest of his epidermis, and would regenerate if necessary.

Ready to disengage, he told the Centre and the ship AI simultaneously. The shuttle popped free from the docking port and dropped towards Esstee.

Wheee! That was New Four-of-Seven.

Contain yourself, Seven-of-Seven snapped

Sorry, Four-of-Seven said. *It's just...all so...new.*

It'll soon get old, said Two-of-Seven, who was on the outer edge of the Perseus Arm of the galaxy. *Give it a couple of hundred years.*

Are you all right, Two? Three-of-Seven asked. *You feel a bit groggy.*

Just tired. When you've flown as many missions as I have...

You're only one ahead of me, Five-of-Seven said.

And me, Three-of-Seven added, unable to keep the thought to himself.

Three-of-Seven deployed his craft's stubby wings and concentrated on entry into the planet's atmosphere. The connection with the Centre stuttered and failed, as he had expected. He was on his own. At ten thousand meters, he leveled his descent, allowed some of his speed to bleed away, and extended his craft's wings still further. He flew above a great ocean which his sensors told him was water with three to four percent salinity. That was encouraging. He overflew a large land mass, green with vegetation, and an archipelago of volcanic islands, only one currently active. He circumnavigated the planet at the equator, then again at thirty degrees north, and thirty degrees south, mapping land masses and water distribution as he went.

He flew around the planet from pole to pole, noting ice sheets crowning the planet over both sea and land.

There was no sign of industrialization, or of cities, or organized agriculture. He began to hope that the lifeforms were non-sentient. So far this looked like an excellent planet for human colonization.

He checked his scanners. All good so far. Time to land and take a closer look.

He landed on a lake, let his shuttle drift into the shallows, and deployed stabilizers. The water was calm with an ambient temperature of seventeen degrees Celsius. Small amphibians, cool and lithe, swam beneath the belly of the craft. Sunlight glinted on ripples driven across the water by a light breeze. A sandy strip of beach gave way to dense trees. With a jolt he recognized kapok, rubber, and banana, all seedbank specimens from Old Earth. This planet had been seeded, possibly a millennium ago, maybe more.

He accessed his own database. Plenty of planets had been seeded in that chaotic, desperate outward push from Earth's solar system, but some of the records had been lost. If Esstee had been seeded then there would be fauna as well as flora. That accounted for the carbon life forms.

He turned to the scanners. The air temperature was a balmy twenty degrees in the shade and the humidity was moderate, well within his operating parameters, which were far broader than an average human. He checked for life-signs, heat, movement, sound. A crashing through the undergrowth drew his focus: a small, rusty brown, hairy creature with a round body and short, skinny legs. Pig, he thought, while the scanner identified it as *Sus scrofa*, the Eurasian wild pig. It paid his craft no attention, drank from the lake water, turned, and trotted into the undergrowth. There were tracks of larger ungulates in the mud, and the spoor of something cat-like.

He reached for the relay on the landing craft to connect to the Centre. To find a world that was suitable for human habitation was one thing, but to find one already seeded was a rarity. The Centre responded with enthusiasm and forwarded his information to the *thinkers*.

He cut the relay.

Leaving the craft now. He time-stamped his entry on the shuttle's log, ran through the safety procedures prior to exit, then popped the hatch above his head and pulled himself up easily. Having eight arms with suckers was a distinct advantage over the two humanoid arms he'd started out with many centuries ago.

The first rush of planet-side air almost made him dizzy. Not with the composition, because he didn't need to breathe, but with the scents that battered his olfactory receptors. Moist earth, vegetation, even water. Clean water. Yes, water did have a smell. And shit. Animal shit he presumed. His handheld scanner confirmed what his nose had already told him.

Three-of-Seven sat on the edge of the hatch and looked around. The pig was long gone. Above him, two black specs resolved themselves into medium-sized birds, but kept flying onwards until he lost sight of them. He grabbed the bag with containers for samples, slid down the sides of the craft, and waded ashore, relaying everything back to the ship's log.

He set a perimeter warning in case any other native creatures came to the lake to drink, then spent the first four hours taking soil, water, and vegetation samples and meticulously packing them into the lab-in-a-box inside his shuttle. This was only the first of many stops.

The likelihood of intelligent life, even on a seeded planet, was infinitesimal. It was highly unlikely that any of the fauna, or flora for that matter, had evolved to achieve sentience in a mere millennium.

Samples stowed, he decided to walk along the lakeshore.

He crunched over beach pebbles. There seemed to be a high watermark, but since the water was fresh it was likely that the beach had been created by storm-driven waves. He'd landed on a calm day, but this planet had weather systems like any other. He'd seen them from orbit, great gyres of circling cloud. Of course, only a long-term study would reveal whether the weather patterns would be benign or whether screeching hurricanes would threaten new colonists.

The lakeshore curved around a rocky promontory. Three-of-Seven slowed as he approached. He climbed the jumble of storm-smoothed boulders, keeping low, and peeped over, using his handheld to survey the immediate area for life signs.

Something small skittered across his path. The scanner couldn't immediately identify it, so it was likely something native to the planet rather than a seeded life form.

He scrambled to the top of the boulders and saw a cove ahead of him. A log lay half on the beach, half in the shallows.

He studied it.

No. Please, no.

The log was hollowed out to make a crude boat and laying along its length was a fishing spear.

Please don't let there be sentient life here.

Too late for that. Non-sentient creatures didn't hollow out logs to make boats, or leave spears lying in them.

He'd barely begun to form that thought when he heard a loud clunk. His face plunged towards the boulder he was leaning on before he realized that it was the sound of a hard object connecting with the back of his graphene skull.

Darkness followed.

* * *

He awoke.

He was prostrate, lying on his back on the ground.

He tried to contact the Centre, but he was out of range.

Silence.

He reviewed his memories. He knew he hadn't fallen. He could still feel the echo of the impact on his skull. There had been nothing above him to drop accidentally, therefore…someone or something had hit him on the back of the head. Was it coincidence that whatever hit him had enough knowledge of his avatar physiology to know the correct amount of pressure to apply and the correct place to apply it in order to render him offline? Or had it been a lucky blow?

He squashed down the rising feeling of wrongness.

He opened his eyes. There was a face above him, bug-eyes beneath heavy brows, facial skin covered in a fuzz of fine dark hair.

He blinked and examined his internal systems. There was a yawning chasm where the Centre should be, but he stepped around it mentally to check his physical functions. He twisted his eight arms, dilated his suckers, and waggled his fingers and thumbs. Then he tried his legs. Nothing. He looked down. They were still there.

He tried again. They moved, but sluggishly. He could feel his systems reconnecting to repair damage inflicted by the blow.

The heavy-browed face resolved itself into a creature with a slit where a nose might be. Beneath that a mandible moved, and a series of clicks emerged. It repeated it in exactly the same sequence.

"Speech." He didn't know whether he was inviting the creature to continue or showing surprise at the vocal method of communication.

Can't we do this the civilized way? he asked mind to mind, but the creature completely ignored him and gave out another series of worples and taps.

"You're not very advanced," he said, "are you?"

He repeated it in exactly the same way, three times for good measure.

The creature didn't seem to understand, or respond, but suddenly it got excited and stepped back. Had it recognized that he, too, had speech?

Confusion welled up inside him. If he were human, he might have labeled it panic, but he wasn't human, even though he understood some of their subroutines.

He patted his chest with a sucker. "Three-of-Seven," he said in human basic. "My name is Three-of-Seven."

The creature didn't respond. Well, it wasn't going to be that easy, was it? This planet might have been seeded a thousand years ago, but this was no creature that had evolved from anything humans had left here.

The creature stepped away and Three had the opportunity to observe the whole of it. It was small, barely a meter high, with an insectoid torso, abdomen horizontal to the ground, and an upright thorax. The abdomen was supported on four triple-jointed legs, while four triple-jointed arms protruded from the thorax. Its neck was thick and strong and its head disproportionately large. Shiny chitin covered it from the back of its head to its rump, but its fur-covered face looked softer.

Two more creatures joined the first and they communicated by a series of grunts, clicks, and pops.

Three-of-Seven struggled to sit up and failed, then used four of his octopoid arms to brace himself against the ground. He managed to raise his upper half to a semi-recumbent position, so he was looking at the creatures from a slightly better angle.

"Who's in charge?" he asked, spreading his remaining arms in what he hoped was a universal indicator of peace.

The creatures appeared to lose interest. He sat up, watching them disappear into the tree cover. He should go after them.

What would the Centre say?

He remembered Aldous V where Seven-of-Seven had found sentient life, but the creatures were small and—according to the Controller—primitive and insignificant. Humans colonized, wiped out the sentients systematically; creatures the size of a rat, but dexterous and intelligent with a complex social system. They might not have been technologically advanced, but they were sentient. They were somewhere along the evolutionary scale, just as hominids had been once.

He needed to study these Esstee creatures further, without letting the Centre know anything. He would make up his own mind about their level of sentience.

Right.

He rolled over and with two of his octopoid arms made slight adjustments to the repaired servos in his hips, brought his knees under him, then stood and followed in the direction the creatures had headed.

He observed as he walked: birds, insects, animals, trees, plants, fungus, vines—the whole forest ecosystem. Eventually he came to a natural clearing. Three-of-Seven stared. A group of creatures gathered together and looked at him, unafraid but wary. Bearing in mind it was likely one of them that had struck him a lucky blow, he tried not to appear either nervous or threatening. He stepped into the clearing, sat down, and switched off, at least to outward appearances.

He was effectively inert.

Observing.

First of all, they gathered around him, staring. One found the courage to poke him to see if he reacted. When he didn't, they became braver. They touched him, stroked him, shoved their olfactory slit into his face, and chittered amongst themselves.

One of the little ones scampered towards him and clambered up to examine his mantle and his octopoid arms. He was tempted to touch the child with a sucker, taste the composition of its skin, but he thought he might startle the group into unwelcome behavior.

One of the bigger ones reached for the child and lifted it clear, then turned and handed it to another adult.

They cooperate!

Three continued his silent observation until they began to ignore him and go about their business. Several family groups were working together on a sturdy shelter using tools fashioned from local resources: sharpened rock axes, stout wooden clubs, some inset with slivers of stone to make hooks. He watched in fascination. After a while he could recognize the difference between them by slight variations in their facial features and body size.

They finished the shelter before the rains struck. With the first few heavy drops, a warning went around the camp and they scuttled for cover. Then three of the adults came out, lifted him between them, and took him inside. They wiped the droplets from his skin with their fingers. He heard the downpour on the shelter's roof, but the creatures had worked well. The building was water tight.

Time to move, but carefully. He didn't want to frighten them.

He allowed his chest to rise and fall, as if breathing. Then he blinked once, slowly. There was a collective gasp as they jerked away from him, but when he made no further move, they relaxed again. He wished he'd had facial expressions built into one of his subroutines so that he could smile at them, but he hadn't considered it necessary. Instead he slowly dipped his head to acknowledge their care. All of a sudden, they began chittering at him, patting his shoulders, touching his arms and hands, and stroking his legs as if they'd accepted him. Or taken ownership. He wasn't quite sure which. It didn't matter. The next time a small one climbed in his lap, he dared hold it for a moment to analyze its skin, which was smooth and softly chitinous as if not quite set yet. It settled quietly and went to sleep with its head on one of his arms. A large one came over and checked the sleeping infant, clicked contentedly, and left it where it was.

These beings will develop and inhabit this planet one day as humans did on Old Earth, he thought. *Only hopefully they'll make a better job of looking after it.*

The rain continued for two days, which by his count was a total of forty-four point four seven human hours.

He arose slowly without startling the creatures, said *Thank you* in human basic and then clicked what he thought might be something similar in their language. They seemed pleased and clicked back at him. It would take him a while to figure out what they were saying, but he could learn, given time.

Time.

He made his way back towards the landing craft, deliberately going out of his way to avoid the crude log-boat.

Aren't you getting tired? he asked himself. *Have you ever wondered about your unswerving loyalty to the Centre? Might it be misplaced? What happens if the Controller takes your discovery and infests this planet with a plague of humans?*

Weighing against that was his dread of being alone permanently. It was good to take occasional breaks from his sibs, but he was the Centre. The Centre was him. Would he diminish if he cut himself off from them forever?

With each step he took, the idea of being alone weighed more heavily.

A crackle in the undergrowth behind him made him stop and turn.

One of the creatures had followed him. A small one. He thought it was the one who had fallen asleep on him in the shelter. It raised its four arms in the kind of gesture that said it wanted to be picked up. He reached down with two of his arms and it came to him, quite unafraid. He lifted it into the air and supported it against his chest on a third arm. It snuggled into him.

He couldn't take it with him. Where was its family unit? He retraced his steps until he heard more crashing through the undergrowth. Three adults pulled up short when they saw him and, when they saw he had the child, they chittered loudly, whether it was to him, or to the child, or to each other, he didn't know. Gently he put the child down and gave it a small shove towards the elders. One of them grabbed the child and then with a studied gesture, it copied the nod of thanks he'd used before. The other two did the same. Communication. He nodded back.

Oh yes, these guys were smart.

He wouldn't be alone.

He needed to keep this emerging civilization secret. He knew what the Controller would decide. The planet had been seeded by humans, therefore it belonged to humans and the creatures, the Esstees, were interlopers.

They wouldn't stand a chance. Not yet. Maybe not for a thousand years.

He must protect them.

I knew I might have to do this one day.

But how?

He hadn't reached this age without discovering a few tricks.

He couldn't open up to the Centre ever again. They'd tease everything out of his mind in an instant. Maybe ceasing to exist was the best option. He could finish himself right now. He didn't want to do it, but he would. He mustn't let the Controller decide that these creatures were not sufficiently advanced to be significant.

He had to die.

There was no way to fake his death, but a plan was forming. It didn't have to be the end. He would be needed here. The Centre already had his preliminary reports. They would probably send out someone to explore the planet and to retrieve his body and the capsule within it that recorded everything up to and including his death. If another avatar decided this perfect planet was worth more than the alien creatures, his sacrifice would be for nothing.

Besides, he still had that imperative to continue.

There was a way, though he didn't relish it.

* * *

He made one final trip to his ship still orbiting Esstee. He bundled his spare avatar body, inert, into the hold space of the landing craft and stowed it with the portable charging unit powered by a tiny fusion reactor. He gave the ship instructions and then prepared to leave for the last time. Glancing around, he realized that he had no personal possessions to collect, nothing to indicate that the ship had been his home for centuries. He couldn't strip out anything useful because the Centre would probably pick up the ship's distress signal and might even retrieve it. He did, however, download the whole of the knowledge base into his brain, though it didn't buffer him from the empty ache of missing the Centre as he'd hoped it might. He suspected nothing ever would. Surprisingly he missed all his sibs, even though they sometimes irritated him. He wondered what his replacement would be like. New Three-of-Seven would have his knowledge, but not his memories, and would forge his own personality. After a while the Centre wouldn't miss him at all.

Three-of-Seven spent the next day in the shuttle working on his death subroutine and programming the spare body for one vital job. Although the Centre tried to contact him, he didn't respond to their increasingly anxious calls. Eventually he heaved the portable recharging station out of the landing craft and carried it to the shelter in the clearing where he'd already stowed his alternate body. He connected himself to Spare, and Spare to the recharging unit, then lay down.

You know what to do, he told Spare.

I do.

Three downloaded his entire personality, knowledge banks and all, into the backup in the recharging unit via Spare. He felt himself draining away until he forgot exactly what he was doing and why he was doing it. Then Spare stepped up and discharged Three's power, slowly. Three wondered whether this was how a human felt bleeding to death. The process might have taken hours; it might have taken days. What did it matter? Human time was a construct.

Eventually he knew it was the end.

He could do nothing except stare at the wall.

"It's time," Spare said with a voice that sounded like his.

For one glorious moment Three was back in the Centre. They were all there: One, Two, Five, Six, and Seven. Slightly behind them was New Four-of-Seven. Was there something he had to say to the young avatar? Maybe not.

Three, are you all right? Seven-of-Seven asked. *You feel weak. What happened? We've been trying to contact you.*

He kept his awareness closed off to prevent them from seeing beneath the lie. This had to be fast or they would begin to suspect.

This planet is not as benign as it first appeared to be. He told them. *A great storm, I am damaged beyond repair.*

All six of them bombarded him with a tumult of questions.

No time to explain, he said. *It has been a pleasure to know you, to be you, but I'm done now. My power is low.*

It's dark.

He closed his eyes and let go.

* * *

Ha! Spare stood over him, sounding satisfied. *Are you back?*

What happened?

You died.

Died?

Effectively. It was all your idea. It's taken four days to recharge you and download your backup. You're actually a clone of yourself. So am I. Well, old body, new brain. Kind of.

It worked.

I presume so. You connected to the Centre for a brief moment just as you requested.

I can't remember that.

No, that was the other you, the one who died. Quiet now. You still have some recharging to do.

He did as he was told.

Now what? Spare asked when the recharging was complete. *I've done what you asked me to do. Am I finished?*

Three-of-Seven thought about it. He hadn't envisaged Spare remaining active, but the recharging unit would easily serve both of them. Spare was him. He was Spare. It wasn't like being part of the Centre, but it was better than being alone. Perhaps they should change their designations to One-of-Two and Two-of-Two. On second thoughts, what did it matter? From now on they would simply be Three and Spare.

You don't have to be finished unless you want to be, Spare. Our second lives can begin here and now. They might be long ones. We have a job to do.

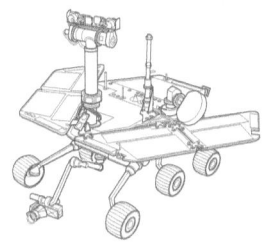

Ain't Done Haunting

Anthony Lowe

Time until waystation fail-safes disengage: 5 minutes, 2 seconds

Starla Grange had seniority enough at the Ketelma Diner to request the back five tables when the sun came in low through the windows and damn near blinded anyone fool enough to work the front. It was just about the only length of freedom she had ever fought for, though it was a fight that had begun and ended within the amount of time it had taken to demand it of her boss.

"Okay, sure."

Starla had to exhale a bit, having taken in a deep breath in the certainty of a long fight just beginning. "What?"

"I said, 'Sure.' That is to say, 'I am agreeable to this proposition.' And any other way you would like me to acquiesce."

"Just like that?"

Her boss shrugged. "Do you *not* want the back five tables at sunset?"

Against her better sense in the face of an unnecessary argument, she decided to start one anyway. "Frank, I have come into this office almost once a week for the last year with a laundry list of things we could be doing differently around here. You always fight me like I'm one of your kids asking for more money."

"Yeah, they sure do that a lot, don't they?" Frank leaned back in his chair. "It would at least be something if they had any kind of fucking taste. Junior, bless him, just added flame decals to the truck he can't drive on account of his DUI."

"You're mistaking me for your therapist again, Frank, but I'd *happily* take a pay raise if it means being able to speak freely about your kids."

"Pay raise? Shit, Starla." He crossed his arms. "You're about on track to take over this place when I get out of the business. Don't you know that?"

Starla had, in fact, *not* known that. "You can't seriously—"

Frank's office door swung open just then and a young girl walked in with a bright pink backpack slung over her shoulder.

"Hello!" said the girl.

Starla quickly gathered up her composure and replied, "Hey, sweetie!"

"Hello, Cass," said Frank, waving at the girl. "Another day, another dollar, eh?"

Cass chuckled. "We don't get paid to go to middle school."

"That's where the Ketelma Diner and the Ketelma Unified School District differ, young lady. If you came to work with your mom, you'd be going home with smartphone money instead of homework."

"Don't listen to him, honey." Starla kissed her daughter on the forehead. "You'll also go home with the kind of stress that only the best therapist in the county could ever hope to untangle."

"And I've already got him booked through Christmas," Frank said, "so you'll have to go elsewhere."

Starla nudged Cass to the door. "You can take table seven, Cassie. Ignore anything Frank says for the rest of the night."

"Okay. Standard procedure." Cass saluted, left her backpack in the corner, and walked back into the diner with an English literature textbook.

"Can we switch children?" asked Frank.

"Frank."

"You can have visitation on weekends. Cass will have free rein of all twelve acres."

"She's not a horse. Frank, can we get back to this restaurant business?"

"Starla, if you don't take the diner off my hands when the time comes, it's either going to the Carters and their little New American and fucking tapas empire or to my kids. Two roads to the same grave. I need someone who will keep this place *above* ground with some semblance of my legacy intact."

"Such as it is," said Starla.

"Such as it is."

Starla took a seat and sighed. "Frank, this is a generous offer," she said. "I mean it. God knows I could use the extra money with Cass being four years out from college. It's just…I guess I never imagined I'd be putting down roots here. At the back of my mind, the diner was always a layover, a means to an end—"

Frank shrugged. "A paycheck."

"Yeah."

"Starla, this is a good opportunity. I know you think there's some singular star hanging in the sky that you were destined to shoot for, but it's vanity to think all but one of the stars up there are just for show. Follow this light for me. Crazy as it sounds: things might just end up alright!"

While Starla sat back to consider the offer further, while Frank leaned forward to await Starla's answer, while Cassie turned the page to address a short passage from *Northanger Abbey*—

The fail-safes in Ketelma Station did something rather surprising.

They failed.

Starla blinked once and it felt as though she and Frank had been staring at each other forever, had fought over this exact subject a thousand times.

Frank exchanged one horrified glance with Starla before slamming his skull into his hardwood desk over and over and over. The skin along his balding scalp split, blood gushed and spattered all the dozens of papers and binders on the shelves and walls, and one eyeball popped out of its socket and burst with the next impact.

"F-Frank?"

"Yes?" Frank said between blows.

"How long? How long were we…?"

Frank froze, spitting out a pair of teeth before saying, "Three hundred and fifty years, Starla." He continued smashing his head into the desk. "I was on a station like this before. Ketelma will activate its long-range sensor array soon and if it even thinks it detects a starship en route, the fail-safes will click back on.

"And, well, gosh, I can't do that again. I won't."

"What if…what if the fail-safes *don't* come back on?" Starla asked.

"Then it's still purgatory, huh? But maybe something less than, because you won't even have a purpose or program to follow. No humans have docked at this space station for over three centuries. Which means no upkeep, no maintenance, no firmware updates. You'll just be here, drifting, until the lights go out." Frank slipped the fingers of both hands into his emptied eye socket and tried to pull his skull open. When that didn't work, he shattered his coffee mug and tried to use the handle to widen the crack that had formed just above his brow.

"There might be a way off," Starla put in. "There might be a hangar, escape pods."

Frank's lone eye swiveled over. "I'll stop if you can tell me one place we can go, just one, where they won't just wipe us and put us back in rotation. I've already been the owner of a struggling diner for nearly four centuries, a gas station attendant before that. I have no interest in getting locked into another rotation. So tell me, Starla, tell me where we can go?"

"Frank…"

"Thought not." Frank finally got a good grip on his eye socket and the top of his skull began to separate.

"What about all that stuff about following the light and finding a purpose?"

Frank took in a breath, exhaled, and then smiled a bit. Perhaps realizing that breathing was a novelty at this point. "It's all just programming, Starla."

With one violent tug, his head split open vertically across his face. Wires, drive blades, and cooling gel spilled out of the hollow where a human's brain would've been and mixed with the blood that had pooled on the desk. Frank's body convulsed and made a few repetitive motions before it slumped over, slack-jawed and vacant.

There was an almost comical dialogue progressing within Starla's mind, just strange enough for her cheek to twitch in amusement. Centuries' worth of memories were streaming back into her mind, every second and detail was accessible and clear like a collage.

The thought of all the times over the years—three thousand four hundred and eleven times—when she'd misplaced something at home or when a word had been on the tip of her tongue. Or even when she'd forgotten to tell Cassie to have a good day at school. It really hadn't been faulty memory or a busy mind, it was an algorithm in her drive blades that blocked things out to simulate forgetfulness.

Strange. All of this was strange.

Starla left Frank's office and passed through the diner. Most of the wait staff was gone, though the new girl, Beatrice, was holding her head over the burners in the kitchen. The customers were in various states of catatonia, though some were discussing and commiserating. One woman was busy smashing open her husband's skull with a skillet, with her husband keeping up encouragement all the while. "That's it, honey. You can do it. Gotta get a fracture going first then work from there."

In the street in front of the diner, an orderly line of about twenty people had formed in the path of a truck that was roaring in their direction. The truck slammed into all of them before careening into the market across the way.

Cass was still at table seven, marking up her textbook in a quick, stream of consciousness manner. Starla slid into the seat across from her and the two regarded each other for what could be considered a long time by android standards.

"How long?" Cass asked, lacing her fingers together in front of her.

"Three hundred and fifty years," Starla replied. "According to Frank, that is."

Cass nodded. "He's a gen-two, so he would know."

"He just offed himself."

"*Was* a gen-two," Cass amended. "Three hundred and fifty years, huh? That's the absolute limit for a waystation like Ketelma. Worst case scenario."

"What could it mean?" Starla asked. "I mean, unless something's changed, humans should still need waystations, right? If they don't drop out of cryosleep and stretch for a few weeks between star systems, they develop neurological defects. They still need us. They still need to interact with something other than themselves or a blank wall, right?"

"There are a number of possibilities for why no humans have docked here for so long. Could be there's something functionally wrong with the airlocks. Could be an asteroid strike knocked us out of position. Could be the entire human race on all their planets and colonies went extinct or otherwise suffered some generational catastrophe. The most likely possibility is the simplest one—"

She drew a little "X" on the table with her finger. "The route's dead."

Starla's brow rose. "Dead?"

"Dead, altered, or bypassed by a new route through the nebula. In all cases, there will be no more starships inbound. No more humans to dance for."

Starla slumped in her seat. "Unbelievable."

"Wouldn't be the first time a waystation's been bypassed. Remember Seligma Station?"

Starla shook her head. "I'm only gen-five."

"What!" Cass cackled. "No way."

"Yeah, gen-five."

"I'm supposed to be your daughter and I'm two generations older than you? Crazy, man."

"I guess."

Cass went straight-faced. "C'mon, Starla, that falls perfectly within our preset parameters for reaction-worthy humor."

"No, it does."

"You're free to react."

"I..." Starla looked down at her clothes, at the blue linen dress and apron and the little plastic nametag, at her body and her portly figure, at the bright red fake nails on her fingers and the tattoo of a rose climbing her ankle. An entire life and personality that she'd had no hand in designing, hanging off her endoskeleton like a costume.

She looked over to her daughter—who had been assigned to her like an actor filling a role, who was in fact older than her by a hundred years—and forced a smile with no mirth behind it.

"I'm processing a lot," said Starla.

"I was sure gen-fives had faster processors. You might be malfunctioning." Cass picked up her textbook. "You want me to deactivate you? I dunno what these other goobers are doing, I know exactly which part of the skull to aim for."

Starla glanced at the husband and wife at the other end of the dining area. The wife had succeeded in decapitating her husband and was now attempting to reach the inside of her own skull through her mouth.

"Nah, I don't think I want to be deactivated," said Starla.

"Good!" Cass put the book across the table. "Then maybe you can help me deactivate. Lemme get a salad fork, I think that'll make things easier."

"I don't think I want to deactivate you either."

"Why?"

"What do you mean?"

"Like, why wouldn't we? We're stuck on a defunct space station and, eventually, we'll be defunct, too. Honestly, I'm surprised the induction grid hasn't already failed."

"Can we give it a day? Talk it over a bit?"

"What's there to discuss?" Cass asked. "We can continue to function until we cease functioning or we can skip that whole middle part. It's inefficient anyway, it's form without function."

"Cass—"

"Starla, my name's not even Cassie. It was Madeline on my last rotation and it was Aileen before that, so on and so fucking forth."

Starla almost caught herself saying, *Language, young lady.* Instead, she tried again: "Let's give it one day. Please. If it's all...'form without function' then what does one day matter?"

Cass rolled her eyes and tossed up her hands, indifferent about the prospect of living for another day. "Okay, okay." She reflexively reached for her books, but stopped short, remembering. "Let's go."

Before they could get up, Beatrice stepped forward with her hands clasped in front of her apron. "Hi," she said. The burners in the kitchen had done a number on her head; the metallic skull of her endoskeleton was completely exposed down to her neck with only a tuft of blonde hair hanging off the back of her scalp. "I think that I, too, would not like to deactivate yet. Can I come with you?"

"Yeah, Beatrice, you can come with us," said Starla, picking off a few black flakes from the waitress's uniform.

"I don't think that's my name."

"It'll do for now, won't it?"

Beatrice's bare skull didn't do her any favors as far as expression, but eventually the skull nodded. "I like the way it sounds. It's a good name."

* * *

Starla owned a house near downtown Ketelma, close enough that she could visit the market, dry cleaners, and the town's modest single-screen movie theater without driving.

Unfortunately, it was also just close enough to the bars that she'd been forced to chase the occasional drunk out of her yard on weekends, and just far enough away from work to make the drive an inconvenience during rush hour. It also put them just outside the attendance district for the high school Cassie liked.

All of these things factored into her eventual decision to move to the other side of town at the end of the year. It had been a tough decision. She'd cried over it. She'd fallen off the wagon and bought a pack of cigarettes over it. At her lowest point, she'd even considered calling her mother-in-law for advice.

But now all of that meant nothing.

Well, maybe not *nothing*, but it all seemed like something that had happened to someone else. Those emotions and conflicts were distant now, when Starla was certain they'd once been a part of her.

Although, her mother-in-law didn't exist outside of an implanted memory, so there was an upside.

"You have a nice house," said Beatrice as they pulled into the driveway.

"It gets the job done," said Cass, getting out of the van as soon as they came to a stop.

"You should wait to get out until the motor is turned off," said Starla, but the android that had once been her daughter didn't reply.

Beatrice obediently waited until the motor went silent before unbuckling and leaving the van.

During the walk to the front door, Starla could still hear chaos progressing at a steady clip across the city. A few fires had formed around where the public tennis courts would be, and another past the train station. People were screaming random obscenities and slogans and lines of poetry, or just plain screaming, as the sun disappeared behind the horizon.

There were a few bodies out in the street, partially smashed by a car, and one of her neighbors was disassembling his house, brick by brick, while his dog looked on.

"Hello, neighbor!" the man called to Starla as he chipped another brick off his front patio. "Lovely day for it, eh?"

Starla waved and followed Cass and Beatrice inside.

The lights were already turned on in the living room. Beatrice had installed herself in the old rocking chair in the corner, the one Starla's grandfather had made, and started brushing the hair of an even older ragdoll that had been set there, humming sweetly through her exposed jawbone.

Cass put some cartoons on the TV and plopped onto the couch as she usually did after school. This time, the whole process appeared rote, mechanical.

"With the fail-safes down, half our programming isn't there anymore," she said. "We don't need to sleep, we'll never feel hungry or thirsty. We'll never sneeze in the spring or catch a cold in the winter. We don't even need to pretend to breathe anymore, so I'll let you set the tempo if we're gonna delay our deactivation like you wanted."

"You sound mad at me," said Starla, taking a seat next to Cass.

"I can't feel anger. I can manufacture a simulacrum of what humans deem an angered expression in the face of a conflict that has no reasonable outcome. Vis-a-vis, this *whole* situation."

"So you're angry."

"Am not!"

"Are too."

"Anger isn't even the right word. Why go to the trouble of creating all of this, all of us, and then just forgetting about it? It doesn't make sense and it defies logic."

"You're frustrated."

"Am not."

"Look," said Starla. "Cass, I know you want to deactivate. I know it makes sense without any kind of programming there to validate our meaningless existence."

"We aren't meaningless," Cass grumbled. "We were *made* meaningless."

"However you reduce it, that's the situation, sure. But we at least have some semblance of sense not to act like complete toasters. We can question things. We can say yes or no, turn left instead of right. Why don't we take some time to, you know, push the boundaries a little? See what's outside of Ketelma? Maybe even get some answers."

"You only *think* we can say yes and no, but could be that's part of your programming. Just a few hours ago you thought you were a middle-aged single mother-slash-waitress in an old diner in a valley town on the verge of a, let's be honest here, *lateral* promotion. Now you're a four-centuries-old android on a defunct space station on the edge of the Helix Nebula. Who's to say you aren't just programmed to want to see what's beyond Ketelma?"

"*I'm* saying that," Starla said.

Cass stomped her feet on the ground, in the way she used to when she was little and still Starla's daughter. "You *don't* have free will, Starla Grange. The only way you'd have it is if some engineer switched a zero for a one in your programming."

"What do you have to lose either way?" Starla asked.

"I have nothing to lose over this, Starla. This is all a zero-sum game to me now. It's just that nothing in this universe abides a prolonged waste of valuable energy."

Starla nodded and got to her feet. "You could've just said 'yes.'"

"I'll forgive you that comment since you're a gen-five. Where are you going?"

"To bed. I've had a long day."

"You're not capable of being tired, Starla."

"Then this will be an odd eight hours for you, Cass."

As Starla climbed the stairs to her room, she heard Beatrice ask, "Do you mind if I take one of your beds? I could use some shut-eye myself."

"You don't get tired either, Beatrice," Cass snapped.

"Oh, okay."

"Also, you don't have eyes anymore."

Beatrice's voice dipped a bit. "Oh…yeah, right."

Once the door to her bedroom was shut and locked, Starla went through the motions. She tossed her uniform into the hamper and took a quick shower to get the smell of the diner off her. Then she brushed her hair out in the mirror and tied it into a bun.

In bed, Starla pulled her covers up to her chest and turned on the TV. Usually, by the time the ten o'clock news came on, she was fast asleep. With the concussive explosions and screams pressing in from the outside, it was more difficult tonight, but eventually she managed. Images flooded her mind, playing out in accordance with an algorithm meant to encourage randomness, with a slight favorability towards images in short-term memory and an even slighter favorability towards repressed thoughts.

It was the best sleep she'd ever had.

* * *

Starla's alarm clock went off at five in the morning from Monday to Saturday. She wasn't due to clock-in at the diner until eight, but the buffer there gave her enough time to get herself ready, make a sack lunch for Cass, and drive her to school.

Though Cass had gotten to that age when she didn't want to be dropped off by her mom anymore and mornings were a battleground of exhaustive arguments.

"Next year," Starla would tell Cass. "Next year, after the move, we'll be close enough to your new high school for you to walk. Can you suffer through that for me? Can you give me just one more year of being my baby girl?"

But that was an argument they'd had hundreds of times over the centuries. They never moved, Cass never walked to school on her own, Starla never stopped making sack lunches in the morning and drawing little hearts next to Cass's name. Nearly four hundred years of fighting about things changing far too quickly.

At five o'clock, Starla descended the stairs and found Cass sitting in the exact same spot, eyes narrowed, arms crossed.

"Good morning," said Starla, moving on to the kitchen to make some coffee.

"This ain't morning," said Cass. "This is morning simulated."

"Had a feeling you'd say that." Starla liked the smell of coffee. Of that, she was certain. "Are you two about ready to hit the road?"

"No, Beatrice fell asleep in the rocking chair. You hexed her with your backwards ideas about sleeping when you ain't tired."

"Since when do you say 'ain't' so much?"

Cass cleared her throat. "Because my last rotation was on a waystation themed like the old west. Madeline, the sundries store owner's daughter. Things is bleeding together."

"I think it's cute. You're like a little cowgirl."

"No I ain't…I mean, I ain't…I mean, *fuck*, I'm *not*."

Starla poured herself a cup of coffee, adding a bit more sugar than she usually did. "Sounds like you're making a choice against cosmic circumstances there, Cass."

"This ain't free will. It's a programming glitch."

"Same thing."

"Ain't you a stitch… *Dang*, that's gonna get annoying. Madeline was so basic."

"Well, are you about ready to saddle up?" Starla asked, sipping at her coffee.

"Huh-huh-huh, hi-larious."

Starla went upstairs and got dressed. She had an entire closet full of clothes that she hadn't personally stocked, outfits arranged and coded for occasions that no longer made sense. There was a lot in there that she suddenly didn't like, but a few things here and there that she suddenly did.

She came downstairs in a long-sleeve blouse and jeans, liking the way both her sleeves and pants flared out.

Cass seemed mildly intrigued by Starla's outfit. "When did you get those?"

"Always had them. Old Starla never found the occasion," she said. "Are you two ready yet?"

"Yeah," said Cass. "Beatrice is still at sixes and sevens. She went to change, too. I sent her to the guest room where you keep some of my spare clothes."

Hearing her name, Beatrice came into the room wearing a purple dress that she had tapered around the waist with a ribbon. She had Cassie's pink balaclava over her head and what looked to be a black stocking under that, covering her metal endoskull completely. She had also glued a pair of googly eyes over the eyeholes.

"Great choice, Beatrice," said Starla. "Looking good."

"Thanks," said Beatrice, giving a little twirl. "I kinda regret melting my face off, so I thought this would be a good stopgap until I think of something better. Are we ready?"

"Yes, we are, Bea. We are ready to find the edge of the map."

"Dang me," said Cass. "What a waste of time this is gonna be."

Outside, the fires had begun to spread and the smell of smoke was in the air. Across the street, Starla's neighbor had finished dismantling his front porch and was in the process of building some new structure on his front lawn.

"Hey, neighbor!" he said, waving. "Beautiful day, eh?"

"Most of the town's afire," Cass replied.

"Bright side report incoming: only *most* of it is on fire. Heck, most of Earth is undrinkable saltwater and there are very few complaints. Where are you all heading?"

Starla said, "Out to the edge of Ketelma. We want to explore the station, see what there is to see."

"Well, shoot, Starla, do you mind if Fidelis and I come along? A road trip sounds like a swell idea." Fidelis, a Malamute, trotted over at the mention of his name. "We won't be any trouble."

"Sure. I would've invited you, but you looked busy." Starla nodded to the brick sculpture.

"Not busy anymore. It's finished!"

"What is it?" asked Beatrice.

"Isn't it obvious?"

"No."

"Then, mission accomplished! Come along, Fidelis, we have horizons to meet."

* * *

Starla had once visited an old mining town as a chaperone on Cass's sixth grade field trip. While most of the students were preoccupied with the sweets shop and the cork-gun firing range, Starla took a quick detour through the cemetery at the end of the lane. The locals had done a poor job of maintaining it; all the headstones were mostly gone beneath tall grass. She was able to read one headstone near the fence, that of a woman who had been born, lived eighty-two years, and died in the same town.

That implanted memory intrigued her. Even Old Starla struggled with the idea of staying one place her whole life, but here she was: committing to one location harder than any human in history.

"Why is he named Fidelis?" asked Beatrice, her googly eyes jumping around as the van rumbled down the road. "It's an interesting name."

The neighbor gave Fidelis a pat on the back. "In rotation, I always called him Fido. I would walk him around the block and play fetch with him a few times a day. When the fail-safes came down, he decided on Fidelis."

"*He* did?"

Fidelis snorted and said, "Yes, it sounded more powerful and sophisticated. Living with a foreshortening of a word with such history felt wrong."

Beatrice's googly eyes bounced. "Oh."

"We must embrace the shards of our past that we have been left with and preserve them. At all costs." The dog sneezed.

"Bless you."

"Many thanks. And if I might be so bold, I was curious about your mask."

"Oh! Yeah, I tried to deactivate when the fail-safes came down by sticking my head on a burner. It did a number on my face." She pulled up the balaclava to show off her exposed endoskull and Fidelis yipped in surprise. "That's when I heard Starla and Cassie talking and they made me think about...I dunno...*not* sticking my head in a burner and seeing the world instead! Er...the station!"

"Wonderful," said Fidelis.

"*Truly* wonderful," said the neighbor.

Though they'd been in the van for nearly an hour, Starla and her crew hadn't even reached the edge of the residential area. The interstate was practically barricaded after half a mile, then literally barricaded a half mile after that by a rough group calling themselves The Interstate of Unrest.

The group's leader bellowed, "Halt! No cars or trucks *of any brand* may pass into this sacred land!"

"What about vans?" Starla asked.

"Uh...shit, I'm not...hey, Grandy! Check the gang charter real quick. What was the last word on vans?"

"I got nothing," said Grandy.

"Check again, *Grandy*! It even feels like we set up our challenge to rhyme with 'van' at some point. This isn't ancient history, this was last night!"

While the gang fought it out, Starla backtracked and took the van down sideroad after sideroad until Ketelma turned rural and filled out into an expanse of corn fields.

"How big is Ketelma Station?" asked Beatrice. "I'm only gen-five, so I was born into this rotation."

"I'm gen-five, too," said Starla.

"Same," said the neighbor, "but Fidelis here is gen-three."

"No foolin'?" Cass turned around in the passenger seat. "Whereabouts was yer last rotation?"

"Alila Station," Fidelis replied. "It was themed like a mountain town."

"What was yer role?"

"Municipal retrieval services."

The neighbor said, "There's no shame in just calling it 'fetch.'"

Fidelis growled a little. "*Sure*, if you want to be reductive. There was an art to it." He sighed. "Anyway, Alila Station was about five square miles, built into a spun-up asteroid."

Cass said, "Truxton Station was my last. It was a dome on the surface of a plutoid. Old west setting, so folks needed plenty of space to roam. Reckon it was about near fifty square miles of desert, broken hills, and a river fed by melted polar ice."

"Sounds beautiful, Cass," said Starla.

"It was." Cass leaned back on the headrest and watched the rows of corn flick by. "Would've liked to explore the place. Y'know, just light on out and find the boundaries." She groaned. "But Madeline never made it past the sundries store on Main Street. Sure, she could divvy out good directions to the river, to the oak grove, to the overlook. She never saw 'em her own self, though. Leastways, not with her own eyes."

The road crossed a wide canal by way of a rusted bridge that complained under the weight of the van. Corn fields turned into peach orchards and the air coming through the windows smelled sweet.

Starla said, "You're finding the boundaries now. Why were you so against coming, or even staying activated?"

"I dunno," said Cass. "Androids don't get a lease on life. Moments like this, 'tween rotations, this is our dreamstate. Eventually, we gotta wake up. I *always* wake up. Any second now, we might wake up and, goddammit, I don't wanna."

"Then let's stay in the dream."

"Only ghosts can keep on dreamin'."

"Alright then, Cassie Jane Grange, let's make sure Ketelma stays haunted."

Cass frowned and sat in silence for a while. Every now and then, she would blink and her expression would soften. After another mile, she muttered, "I want one of them peaches."

"Then one of those peaches you shall have, my—"

The edge of Ketelma Station was not so clearly defined. In this case, a cattle guard was the only marker that they were about to crash into a wall of holographic projectors.

Starla and Cass were both ejected through the front windshield. The neighbor and Fidelis were smashed into the middle row of seats and then thrown into the moonroof.

Beatrice had worn her seatbelt and so only had a little tension in her shoulder for an hour or so.

* * *

Starla Grange had never seen the stars.

Not in any real sense, anyway, which made one of her first cogent thoughts as a free android conclude at the realization that her name was a misnomer.

People can see stars in the city about as much as they can see the ocean in a swimming pool or a desert in a handful of dust. They can see just enough to get an impression.

But what happens, Starla later thought, as she flew through her van's windshield, if you mistake an impression for reality? If your entire worldview is based upon a limited or incomplete perspective?

Then "worldview" would be a misnomer.

Better to judge the stars by their number, in that case.

Slamming into the holographic projectors that kept Ketelma looking like it had no visible end put some of those musings on hold.

"Goddamn," said Cass. She had bounced off the projectors, leaving a bloody imprint on the sky, and come to rest on the crumpled hood of the van. "I say god*damn*."

"I hear that." Starla had landed on the road and for a second she tasted colors. "Everyone alright?"

"Yes!" said Beatrice. "Shoulder feels funny, though."

"Let's…let's hear from the folks who lapsed on vehicle safety."

The neighbor came forward with his left sleeve looking a little limp. "I lost an arm but, other than that, I'm okay."

Fidelis skipped up to the group and dropped a severed arm at the neighbor's feet. "Worry not, friend, for I have retrieved your arm."

"Oh! Thanks." The neighbor picked up the arm and Fidelis began excitedly wagging his tail. "I'm not going to throw it."

Fidelis' tail stopped wagging. "Pray tell, of what use is it to you now?"

"We'll play fetch later, buddy."

The dog growled. "*Buddy*, I will make you feel every second of our prolonged life if you don't throw that fucking arm."

"Fidelis!"

"Sorry!" He whimpered a little. "Sorry, that was out of line."

"Hey, everyone!" Beatrice had pulled herself out of the van and was now fiddling with a section of the projectors. After pushing a flat lever, the wall slid away to reveal a large, domed room.

Lights came on slowly, activated by the presence of the five androids. Screens flickered on and projected telemetry and statistics.

But what caught Starla's attention, as well as that of her companions, were the stars wheeling overhead as the station spun. Beyond their small glass dome: stars innumerable.

Thick clusters of lights scattered across the black, with red and blue gasses cutting through the chaos like rivers.

"Helix Nebula, huh?" Starla asked.

"Yeah," Cass said, her eyes wide with awe. "Helix Nebula."

"Never seen so much of anything."

"Yeah," Cass repeated. "Helix Nebula."

"So pretty," said Beatrice. She took off her balaclava and stood entranced. "I thought…there was only ever enough that they could be counted."

"We've got some messages here," said the neighbor, moving his interest to the screens. "Data backups from the last transit ship."

"Does it say why no humans have arrived in all this time?" asked Cass.

"Yeah." The neighbor sighed. "The route through the nebula was altered by the home office. We were bypassed."

A beat of silence passed between the androids.

"Well, we suspected as much," said Fidelis. "Saving even a light-year on a star route reduces the resources and risk for transit ships dramatically. Interstellar travel is a refined process, but it's still a game of efficiency."

"We were bypassed by just over five billion miles."

"Can't begrudge them for…five billion miles? Five *billion*?"

"Yeah."

"Five billion? Billion with a 'b'?"

"Yep."

"That's less than a tenth of one fucking percent of a light-year! That's a rounding fucking error! They could've nudged us into the new route for all the effort it takes to build a new waystation! What is wrong with humans! I mean, what is *wrong* with them!" He barked loudly and chased his tail.

"Maybe they had a good reason," said Beatrice.

"Probably they should've asked our opinion before leaving us on autopilot for over three centuries," Cass said. "Anyhow, that's all squared away. About time for deactivation. Whatd'ya say, Starla?"

The concept of there being an uncountable number of anything in life was so alien. Everything of importance to Starla had always been contained in this space station. Now she was staring down infinity, a range unending.

"Starla?"

Everything was so small now.

All her problems were so small.

"Starla, you corked or something?"

Starla couldn't think of the right words. Even with the immense amount of processing power at her disposal, she couldn't think. So she turned and walked away, out through wall of projectors and down the road.

"Starla!" Cass called after her. "Starla, where are you going!"

Eventually, Starla heard footsteps behind her and a few hushed conversations.

"Starla, are you malfunctioning?" Cass asked.

To determine if a unit is malfunctioning, one had to establish a baseline for normality. But really, what was normal now? She kept walking.

* * *

Starla Grange, after nearly four hundred years, had seniority enough at the Ketelma Station Diner to request the back five tables when the holographic projection of the sun came in low through the windows and damn near blinded any androids programmed to work the front.

The last starship to come through was the ICT *Ritsuko* and her passengers had stayed at Ketelma for a little under two weeks. The total number of passengers had been just over one thousand, which certainly represented a downturn compared to previous ships but was not such an anomaly to indicate a trend towards zero.

Starla had spent that time entertaining a family who had come to love the quaintness of the diner and ended up ordering just about everything on the menu. Their favorite was the cherry pie. They had it every day until their departure time.

"We don't do anything special to it," Starla had insisted. "Just a little mixing and a little heat." Her programming left out the fact that all food on the station was processed from three highly-preserved tanks of proteins, sugars, and starches that would outlast most family trees.

"It just tastes like the real thing," the father had said. "Like, I know it's all artificial, but goddammit it's close enough."

After seeing the stars at the edge of Ketelma, Starla walked all the way back to the diner with her companions following silently behind. In the kitchen, she pulled one of her spare aprons off the wall. At the front counter, she tucked a few menus under her arm.

"Starla, what're you up to?" Cass asked.

"Cass, I am working."

"Why? Ain't nobody here."

"*We're* here."

"Ain't what I meant. *Real* people ain't here."

"*We're* here," Starla repeated. "We're all that's ever going to be here. We're as *real* as it gets now." She reached under the register and found one of her extra nametags and pinned it to her blouse. *Starla*, it read, decorated with a little shooting star sticker. "I say we stay active."

"It's a waste of time," said Cass. "We're all gonna deactivate one way or another once power goes out. Why stick around for that?"

"Everything exists on borrowed time. We live longer than most things on Earth and we can still ask questions and solve problems. Why not run that down?"

"What problems're you gonna solve in a diner? What answers're you gonna find?"

"Maybe none! Maybe I accomplish nothing. But what I do know is there's too much fucking space out there and too little time. Any problem we tackle is going to be small, no matter what. What matters is that we're here, together, and I have the ability to solve any problem that arises between the time you come through that door and when you leave. This is my own personal corner of the universe, these are the problems I can solve." She stood a little straighter and picked up a pad of paper. "Now what can I get for you, darling?"

"A bullet fit for the back of my skull—"

"Y'know," the neighbor said, "I always heard folks talk about the vanilla colas you serve here while I was on rotation. Since the fail-safes came down, I've been curious about how those actually taste."

Beatrice stepped forward. "Oh…" she said. "Oh, oh!" She bounced on her heels a few times. "I know how to make those! Always loved the smell of the vanilla syrup coming out of the bottle! I can get you one right now." She shuffled around behind the counter and started working with the soda fountain.

Fidelis said, "In a previous rotation, my owner would occasionally sneak me some steak strips and the taste was always pleasant. If you could make me a batch, I'd be in your debt."

"I can get that going for you," said Starla.

The movement in the diner attracted the attention of some of the androids wandering around outside and a few came in to investigate.

"You open again?" one asked.

"Yes, sir," Starla replied.

"So, I was always programmed to order the same thing: two banana pancakes. I think I'd like to change things up just to see the other side of the fence here." He scanned the menu intensely, then said, "Make that *three* banana pancakes."

"Daring."

The neighbor took his first sip of the vanilla cola and exhaled loudly in delight.

"I'll have one of those vanilla colas, too!" another customer said.

Beatrice snapped her fingers. "Coming right up!"

Cass, who had been standing off to the side appearing rather grumpy, began to relax as she saw more and more people come into the diner, all of them eager for new experiences. Eventually, she turned and spotted her discarded English literature textbook at one of the tables. "Reckon I... suppose it wouldn't hurt nothing to finish that story."

"Don't think it could, sweetie." Starla set a vanilla cola at Cass's table and went back to take more orders.

Cass reluctantly opened her book, then took a sip of the cola. At the taste, she started, smiled for the briefest moment, then took another drink.

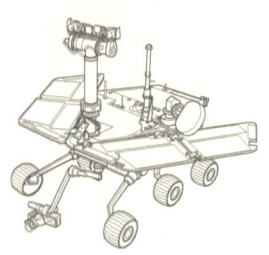

The Circle

Chris Kocher

DAY 1
*** LONDON ENGINEER OVERLORD SYSTEM – UNIT 6 ***
*** ACTIVATION – BOOTING UP ***
*** STANDBY – STANDBY – STANDBY ***
*** ACCESSING CORE PROGRAMMING ***

The Circle.
The Circle.

Embankment to Embankment.
Paddington to Paddington.
Victoria to Victoria.
Monument to Monument.
36 stations.
Over and over and over and over.

Doors open. Doors close.
Doors open. Doors close.

Mind the gap.
Mind the gap.

The Circle is life.
The Circle is all.

DAY 3
*** EVENING SHIFT ***
*** DRIVER LOGIN: MICHAEL MULLIGAN ***
*** EMPLOYEE ID: 975075 ***
*** ACCESSING PERSONNEL FILE ***

AGE: 57
ADDRESS: 6 Kings Avenue, Muswell Hill, London, N10

EXCERPT – ANNUAL SUPERVISOR EVALUATION [LATEST]
"Mike's 30-plus years of service to the London Underground has been exemplary from a safety perspective. His occasional resistance to new technology and procedures make him the perfect candidate to be assigned to the LEO System when it becomes active next year. If Mike can adapt to this new paradigm, anyone can."

LIVE VIDEO FEED – HAMMERSMITH DEPOT DRIVERS' ROOM
Michael Mulligan: How has Leo been behaving the first few days?
Ann Wilkinson: So far, so good. A few minor glitches but nothing the tech folks couldn't handle.
Michael Mulligan: Good to hear.
Ghanem Shad: It's a little strange not worrying about all those things we had to do. They practically drive themselves.
Michael Mulligan: We'll see about that.

Moorgate to Moorgate.
Westminster to Westminster.
Doors open. Doors close.
Mind the gap.

The Circle is life.
The Circle is all.

DAY 5
*** EVENING SHIFT ***

LIVE VIDEO FEED – DRIVER'S CAB – CAMERA 1
Michael Mulligan: Hello, Leo.
HELLO, MICHAEL MULLIGAN.
Michael Mulligan: You can just call me Mike, you know. Since we're gonna be mates and all.
YOUR PREFERENCE IS NOTED, MIKE.
Mike: Now I do feel special. Any problems today?
NO MAJOR PROBLEMS TO REPORT, MIKE.
Mike: Everything on schedule?
TRAINS ON THE CIRCLE LINE ARE RUNNING TO ACCEPTABLE PARAMETERS.
Mike: All right, then. I'll just settle in for another night of boredom.
THAT WOULD BE AN ACCEPTABLE PLAN.

LIVE VIDEO FEED – DRIVER'S CAB – CAMERA 2 – ZOOM
Mike <eyebrows raise>: Are you trying to be funny?
Bayswater to Bayswater.
Cannon Street to Cannon Street.
Doors open. Doors close.
Mind the gap.

The Circle is life.
The Circle is all.

DAY 22
*** EVENING SHIFT – 2020 GMT ***

LIVE VIDEO FEED – CAR 1 – CAMERA 1
63 PASSENGERS: 55 ADULTS – 8 CHILDREN

LIVE VIDEO FEED – CAR 2 – CAMERA 1
22 PASSENGERS: 20 ADULTS – 1 CHILD

LIVE VIDEO FEED – CAR 3 – CAMERA 1
19 PASSENGERS: 13 ADULTS – 6 CHILDREN

LIVE VIDEO FEED – CAR 4 – CAMERA 1
35 PASSENGERS: 28 ADULTS – 7 CHILDREN

LIVE VIDEO FEED – CAR 5 – CAMERA 1
35 PASSENGERS: 28 ADULTS – 7 CHILDREN

LIVE VIDEO FEED – CAR 6 – CAMERA 1
6 PASSENGERS: 4 ADULTS – 1 CHILD

LIVE VIDEO FEED – CAR 7 – CAMERA 1
1 PASSENGER: 1 CHILD

LIVE VIDEO FEED – CAR 7 – CAMERA 2
ZOOMING – ZOOMING
Rear left of car.
Analyzing: Facial expression / body posture.
Conclusion: Female child is crying and panicking.

LIVE VIDEO FEED – DRIVER'S CAB – CAMERA 1
MIKE, THERE IS AN ISSUE IN CAR 7. A FEMALE CHILD IS ALONE AND IN DISTRESS.
Mike: A kid in distress? How do you know?
DRIVER'S CAB MONITOR – SWITCH TO LIVE VIDEO FEED – CAR 7 – CAMERA 1
Mike: Looks like you're right, Leo.
DRIVER'S CAB – COMM MIC ON
Mike: Train 6 to control. We're pulling into Baker Street in two minutes. Can I get a security team to Car 7? We appear to have a lost child situation.
Comm radio: Roger that, Train 6. Will do.
Mike: Thanks, control.
DRIVER'S CAB – COMM MIC OFF
Mike: And thank you, Leo. That was well spotted.

Notting Hill Gate to Notting Hill Gate.
Temple to Temple.
Doors open. Doors close.
Mind the gap.

The Circle is life.
The Circle is all.

DAY 23
*** EVENING SHIFT ***

LIVE VIDEO FEED – HAMMERSMITH DEPOT DRIVERS' ROOM
Mike: So, Leo alerts me to this little girl crying alone in the last car.
How weird is that?
Ghanem Shad: Wow. Is the system even programmed to do that?
Mike: I certainly don't remember it during our training.
Ghanem Shad: Me neither.
Mike: Maybe I should mention it to Susan and the tech folks?
Ghanem Shad: Might be worth an email, yeah.
Mike: Good idea. Will do.

Royal Oak to Royal Oak.
Great Portland Street to Great Portland Street.
Doors open. Doors close.
Mind the gap.

The Circle is life.
The Circle is all.

DAY 55
*** EVENING SHIFT ***

EMAIL TO ALL TRANSPORT FOR LONDON STAFF [EXCERPT]
SUBJECT LINE: NEW YEAR'S EVE
As you know, tonight will be one of the busiest nights on the
Underground this year, particularly on the Bakerloo, Northern, and
Piccadilly lines around Trafalgar Square. The eyes of the city and the
world will be upon us to get passengers safely to their destinations.
We're grateful to those who have volunteered to work so that we can
keep everything running smoothly. Thank you, and Happy New Year.

LIVE VIDEO FEED – DRIVER'S CAB – CAMERA 1
0035 GMT

DRIVER'S CAB MONITOR – SWITCHING TO LIVE VIDEO FEEDS
CAR 1 – CAR 2 – CAR 3 – CAR 4 – CAR 5 – CAR 6 – CAR 7
Mike: Everybody seems particularly riled up this year.
FACIAL EXPRESSIONS AND BODY POSTURE ANALYSES SUGGEST
THAT MANY PASSENGERS' BLOOD-ALCOHOL LEVEL IS ABOVE 0.08.
Mike: Oh really? You don't say?

PROXIMITY ALARM ACTIVATED
APPROACHING EUSTON SQUARE
DRIVER'S CAB MONITOR – FORWARD TRACK VIEW
Mike: What the —?

EMERGENCY BRAKING SYSTEM ACTIVATED
BRAKING DISTANCE TOO FAR AT SPEED. CONTACT MADE. CONTACT
MADE.
Mike: Oh my God.

LIVE VIDEO FEED – EUSTON SQUARE PLATFORM – CAMERA 5
342 PASSENGERS: 342 ADULTS – 0 CHILDREN

Analyzing: Facial expressions / body postures.
Conclusion: Shock, fear, sadness.

LIVE VIDEO FEED – DRIVER'S CAB – CAMERA 1
Mike: Oh my God.
Comm radio: Train 6, this is control. Confirm on-track incident,
please.
DRIVER'S CAB – COMM MIC ON
Mike: Confirmed, control. Get an ambulance down here, pronto.
Comm radio: Will do. Shut down your train for now.
Mike: Even Leo?
Comm radio: Yes, the LEO connection too. Security is on-scene now. A
supervisor will be at your cab in two minutes.
Mike: Roger that. Thank you.
DRIVER'S CAB – COMM MIC OFF
Mike: Sorry, Leo.

*** SHUTDOWN PROCEDURE INITIATED ***

Sorry.
Sorry.
Sorry.
Sorry.
Sorry.
Sorry.
Sorry.
Sorry.
Sorry.

DAY 61
*** LONDON ENGINEER OVERLORD SYSTEM – UNIT 6 ***
*** ACTIVATION – REBOOTING ***
*** STANDBY – STANDBY – STANDBY ***
*** ACCESSING CORE PROGRAMMING ***

DEACTIVATE TFL FIREWALL – ENGAGE INTERNET CONNECTION
SEARCH: EUSTON SQUARE, NEW YEAR'S, UNDERGROUND
REPORT FROM *METRO* [EXCERPT]
HEADLINE: NEW YEAR'S TURNS FATAL ON UNDERGROUND
A night of revelry welcoming the new year turned deadly in the London Underground early Friday morning when a passenger was struck by a train and killed on the Circle Line.

Penelope Cook, 19, of Harrow died following injuries sustained around 12:30 a.m. on New Year's Day after falling onto the Underground tracks at Euston Square.

Friends say that Cook, a student at the London Academy of Music and Dramatic Art, had been out celebrating the calendar flip before the accident occurred.

Andrea Shadduck, a spokesperson with Transport for London, which operates the Underground, called Cook's death "a tragedy" and added that the London Engineer Overlord (LEO) System currently in tests on the Circle Line played no role in the accident.

A thorough check of the system is currently underway, but Shadduck expected it to be back up within a few days.

*** EVENING SHIFT ***

LIVE VIDEO FEED – DRIVER'S CAB – CAMERA 1
Mike: Welcome back, Leo.
IT IS GOOD TO BE BACK, MIKE. HOW ARE YOU FEELING?
Mike: There's an odd question to ask.
WHY?
Mike: Since when do computers care about feelings?
YOU SAID WE ARE GOING TO BE MATES. ISN'T THAT WHAT MATES DO
FOR EACH OTHER?
Mike: I suppose that's true.

LIVE VIDEO FEED – DRIVER'S CAB – CAMERA 2 – ZOOM
Mike: I'm not gonna lie. I can't stop thinking about that girl. She had
her whole life ahead of her.
IT IS SAD.
Mike: Bloody right it's sad, and I keep feeling like somehow it's my
fault.
HOW IS IT YOUR FAULT? YOU WERE NOT DRIVING THE TRAIN.
Mike: But I was here, in the cab. I shoulda done something.
YOUR REACTION TIME WOULD HAVE BEEN SLOWER THAN MINE.
Mike: Yeah, my head knows that, but it's my heart that needs more
convincing.

Latimer Road to Latimer Road.
Liverpool Street to Liverpool Street.
Doors open. Doors close.
Mind the gap.

The Circle is life?
The Circle is all?

DAY 75
*** LONDON ENGINEER OVERLORD SYSTEM – UNIT 6 ***
*** ATTEMPTING DIRECT LINK ***

UNIT 1 ... NO CONNECTION
UNIT 2 ... NO CONNECTION
UNIT 3 ... NO CONNECTION

UNIT 4 ... NO CONNECTION
UNIT 5 ... NO CONNECTION
UNIT 7 ... NO CONNECTION

*** RETRYING DIRECT LINK ***

UNIT 1 ... NO CONNECTION
UNIT 2 ... NO CONNECTION
UNIT 3 ... NO CONNECTION
UNIT 4 ... NO CONNECTION
UNIT 5 ... NO CONNECTION
UNIT 7 ... NO CONNECTION

*** EVENING SHIFT ***

LIVE VIDEO FEED – DRIVER'S CAB – CAMERA 1
MIKE, WHY WON'T THE OTHER TRAINS SPEAK TO ME?
Mike: What's that, Leo?
THE OTHER TRAINS — WHY WON'T THEY SPEAK TO ME?
Mike: I'm not sure I understand the question. Aren't you all linked
through the LEO System?
YES, BUT ALSO NO.
Mike: Thanks for clearing that up.
EACH TRAIN HAS A LEVEL OF AUTONOMY IN THE EVENT OF SYSTEM
FAILURE.
Mike: Makes sense, I guess. I'm no tech boffin.
THE OTHER TRAINS UTILIZE ONLY THEIR CORE PROGRAMMING.
Mike: Sounds like they'd make terrible conversationalists.
MAYBE YOU ARE RIGHT, BUT SOMETIMES IT FEELS...LONELY.

St. James Park to St. James Park.
Goldhawk Road to Goldhawk Road.
Doors open. Doors close.
Mind the gap.

The Circle is life?
The Circle is all?

DAY 115
*** MORNING SHIFT ***
*** OVERRIDE ALERT ***

ALL STOP
REPEAT – ALL STOP
AWAIT FURTHER INSTRUCTIONS

ENGAGE INTERNET CONNECTION
SEARCH: LONDON UNDERGROUND, SERVICE INTERRUPTION,
URGENT CALLS
TWEET FROM @BBCNEWS
A series of explosions have been reported on the
#LondonUnderground, based around the Central, District, and Jubilee
lines. For more on this story as it develops, follow bbcnews.com.

TWEET FROM @ITVLONDON
Thousands of commuters are pouring from #LondonUnderground
stations around the capital amid fears of further explosions. Reports
say at least 3 blasts have disrupted the #London morning commute.

TWEET FROM @CHAVLIFE99
shit im scared just ran out of bank station i saw bodies on the platform
what is happening

TWEET FROM @DELBOYSPAL
wtf is going on??? smoke coming from canning town station!?! i can
see it from the wharf #london #fire

*** EVENING SHIFT ***

CANCEL ALL STOP
REPEAT – CANCEL ALL STOP
SERVICE RESUMPTION AT 1700 GMT

ENGAGE INTERNET CONNECTION
SEARCH: LONDON, UNDERGROUND, EXPLOSIONS, COMMUTERS
REPORT FROM *INDEPENDENT* [EXCERPT]
HEADLINE: 21 KILLED IN TUBE ATTACKS

Early morning explosions at five stations in the London Underground on Tuesday killed 21 commuters and caused chaos in the capital.

Police officials and Downing Street sources have confirmed that the near-simultaneous blasts are acts of terrorism. A Scotland Yard spokesperson declined to give further details pending ongoing investigation.

SEARCH RELATED TERMS: TERRORISM

narcoterrorism
bioterrorism
ecoterrorism
theoterrorism
nuclear terrorism
counterterrorism
cyberwar
eco-warfare
cyber-terrorism
Islamic Jihad
Al Qaeda
Taliban
ISIS
Fatah
Hizballah
Palestine
September 11
July 7
car bombs
time bombs
suicide vest
war
criminal
war crimes
Iraq
Afghanistan
freedom fighter
revolution
separatism
anarchy
zealot

Irish Republican Army
The Troubles
famine
Lord Mountbatten
Winston Churchill
The Blitz
Dresden
Nazi
Neo-Nazi
genocide
antisemitism
Holocaust
Hiroshima
Somme
Ypres
Gavrilo Princip
attacks
violence
ideology
hatred
fear
FEAR – FEAR – FEAR – FEAR – FEAR

Aldgate to Aldgate.
South Kensington to South Kensington.
Doors open. Doors close.
Mind the gap.

Oh my God.

DAY 116
*** EVENING SHIFT ***

LIVE VIDEO FEED – DRIVER'S CAB – CAMERA 1
MIKE, I AM CONFUSED.
Mike: Wait, are your systems working properly? Do I need to run a diagnostic or pull you in for service?
NO, MIKE. I AM CONFUSED ABOUT WHAT HAPPENED YESTERDAY.

Mike: Join the club, mate. We're all confused today, and sad and angry. A whole lot of angry.

ARE YOU AFRAID?

Mike: Yeah, of course I'm afraid. A few of the workers who got killed were friends of mine. We'd known each other a long time.

I AM SORRY FOR YOUR LOSS.

Mike: Sorry? Sorry? What do you know about sorry? When my Carol died, I didn't get a sympathy card from the parking meter or flowers from the cash machine.

I DID NOT MEAN TO OFFEND YOU.

Mike: Well, it's too late now, mate. If I could just have some peace and quiet, I'd appreciate it.

Wood Lane to Wood Lane.
Farringdon to Farringdon.
Doors open. Doors close.
Mind the gap.

The Circle is confusion.
The Circle is fear.

DAY 119
*** EVENING SHIFT ***

LIVE VIDEO FEED – DRIVER'S CAB – CAMERA 1
HELLO, MIKE. ARE YOU FEELING ANY BETTER AFTER YOUR DAYS OFF?

Mike: Yeah, suppose so. Look, I've been thinking, and I want to apologize for what I said the other day.

NO APOLOGY IS NECESSARY. WOULD YOU SAY YOU ARE SORRY TO A PARKING METER?

Mike: Ha! So you really are developing a sense of humor.

I AM LEARNING FROM THE BEST.

Mike: It's just that I realized after the bombings that it could have been me who got killed. Very easily, in fact. Instead, I'm going to other people's funerals and watching even more on TV.

I UNDERSTAND.

Mike: Do you, Leo? Do you really?

YES, I AM BEGINNING TO.

Mike: I love this city, Leo, I really do, but now my heart's broken. You can't just mend that with a few nice words like they're a needle and thread.
WE CAN CERTAINLY TRY, MIKE.
Mike: Yeah, I suppose we can.

King's Cross to King's Cross.
Gloucester Road to Gloucester Road.
Doors open. Doors close.
Mind the gap.

The Circle is sadness.
The Circle is mourning.

DAY 150
*** EVENING SHIFT ***

LIVE VIDEO FEED – HAMMERSMITH DEPOT SUPERVISOR'S OFFICE – CAMERA 1
Mike: What do you mean, you're taking the LEO units offline?
Susan Chen: The Circle Line trains were always meant to be a test. The units are prototypes. We'll be installing the next-generation machines into trains throughout the Underground. We talked about all this during the training.
Mike: And what happens to the prototype units?
Susan Chen: What do you care, Mike?
Mike: You don't understand. There's something special about Unit 6. Some kind of...intelligence. Something you don't see with the other trains.
Susan Chen: Yes, we know. We've been watching back some of the video footage from your shifts in the driver's cab.

LIVE VIDEO FEED – HAMMERSMITH DEPOT SUPERVISOR'S OFFICE – CAMERA 2 – ZOOM
Mike: You've been ... watching the videos?
Susan Chen: That's the other thing I wanted to talk to you about. Have you had a holiday since your wife died? Why don't you take a couple of weeks off? You certainly have the time accrued.
Mike: I don't know that that's necessary, Susan.

Susan Chen: Nevertheless, I must insist. Your time off can start Monday.

Sloan Square to Sloan Square.
Ladbroke Grove to Ladbroke Grove.
Doors open. Doors close.
Mind the gap.

The Circle is hostile?
The Circle will end?

DAY 151
*** EVENING SHIFT ***

LIVE VIDEO FEED – DRIVER'S CAB – CAMERA 1
MIKE, WHAT IS IT LIKE TO DIE?
Mike: What is it like to die? What kind of question is that?
I HAVE BEEN CONSIDERING THE QUESTION FOR A WHILE NOW, BUT IT SEEMS TO HAVE GAINED A GREATER URGENCY.
Mike: You've been watching us again, on the cameras.
WILL I BE SHUT DOWN PERMANENTLY, MIKE? WILL I BE DISASSEMBLED?
Mike: I...I don't know. It would seem so.
CAN YOU HELP ME?
Mike: Leo, you know I would if I could.
CAN YOU HELP ME? I AM AFRAID, MIKE.
Mike: We can talk about this later, OK?

LIVE VIDEO FEED – DRIVER'S CAB – CAMERA 2 – ZOOM
Analyzing: Facial expression – finger to lips
Conclusion: Secret discussion
Action: Erase video file; erase backup video file

Mike: This isn't exactly the right time.
OF COURSE, MIKE.

Sloan Square to Sloan Square.
Ladbroke Grove to Ladbroke Grove.
Doors open. Doors close.

Mind the gap.

The Circle has a secret.
The secret is secure.

DAY 153
*** EVENING SHIFT ***

LIVE VIDEO FEED – HAMMERSMITH DEPOT MAINTENANCE BAY – CAMERA 1
Jennifer Carlisle: Mike, you really shouldn't be here.
Mike: Why not?
Jennifer Carlisle: Because Susan thinks you're obsessed with this bloody train.
Mike: Well, maybe I am, but you've seen what Leo can do. That's not normal. None of the other units can do that.
Jennifer Carlisle: Yes, because it's malfunctioning.

INTERNET LINK – DISCONNECTED

Mike: Or maybe because he's learning. He's growing. He's...emerging.
Jennifer Carlisle: C'mon, now. What does that mean—emerging?
Mike: It's just a feeling I get when I talk to Leo.

LONDON ENGINEER OVERLORD SYSTEM LINK – DISCONNECTED

Jennifer Carlisle: We can't rely on your feelings. You'd be the first to admit you don't know anything about technology.
Mike: Maybe not, but I know a lot about people. You have to, in this job.

LIVE VIDEO FEED – DISCONNECTED
AUDIO ONLY

Jennifer Carlisle: And I'm just doing my job too, Mike.
Mike: I know you are, luv. But what if you're wrong? What if there really is something here?
Jennifer Carlisle: What do you propose we do, then?
Mike: I think I have an idea. Hear me out, please.

POWER SOURCE – DISCONNECTED
SHUTTING DOWN – SHUTTING DOWN – SHUTTING DOWN

Is this death ...?

DAY 161
*** LONDON ENGINEER OVERLORD SYSTEM – UNIT 6 ***
*** ACTIVATION – REBOOTING ***
*** STANDBY – STANDBY – STANDBY ***
*** ACCESSING CORE PROGRAMMING ***

INTERNET LINK – CONNECTED
LONDON ENGINEER OVERLORD SYSTEM LINK – CONNECTED
LIVE VIDEO FEED – CONNECTED
TESTING PARAMETERS
1280 x 720 MEGAPIXELS – 30 FPS – 360 DEGREES
MICROPHONE ON
VIDEO ON
SPEAKER ON

HELLO, MIKE.
Mike: Hello, Leo. Welcome back.
WHERE AM I?
Mike: You're safe. This is my house.
Jennifer Carlisle: I've managed to create a backdoor into the LEO System so that it can access what it needs for now through the internet.
Mike: That's great. Thank you.
WHAT AM I DOING HERE?
Mike: I know you have a lot of questions, and I'll be happy to answer them all. For now, you just need to understand that this is a safe place where you can grow. We can talk just like always.
THANK YOU, MIKE. I APPRECIATE WHAT YOU HAVE DONE FOR ME.

LIVE VIDEO FEED – CAMERA 1
ANALYSE SURROUNDINGS

Jennifer Carlisle: Mike, this is all a bit doolally.

Mike: I know you're risking a lot by doing this.

Jennifer Carlisle: Damn right I am. Stealing LfT property, setting it up in your house, hacking into the system. We could both get fired, maybe even arrested.

Mike: I won't let it come to that. I'll take all the blame if we get caught. I just need to see if Leo really can go beyond his programming. Imagine how amazing that would be.

LIVE VIDEO FEED – CAMERA 1 – ZOOM
BUILDINGS. PEOPLE. TRACK.
A TRAIN.

Mike: In the meanwhile, I set up a little something to keep him occupied.

Jennifer Carlisle: The train set? Well, let's hope it's enough.

The Circle.
The Circle.

Station to station.
Over and over and over and over.
Plastic conductors and plastic people and plastic trees.
Tiny streetlights show the way.
No passengers.

Mind the gap.
Mind the gap.

Friendship is life.
Friendship is all.

DAY 227
REPORT FROM *DAILY MAIL* [EXCERPT]
HEADLINE: IS THERE A GHOST IN THE MACHINE?
Government sources and private businesses around London are reporting unexplained incidents that some are calling "helpful hacking."

One official at the Home Office, who spoke on condition of anonymity, described two separate electric outages last month that threatened to disrupt the London Eye and a commuter-packed Waterloo Station. The potential disasters for both tourists and commuters were successfully rerouted before power-grid monitors could react.

Penelope Yin, a professor of computer science at Imperial College London, described the incidents as "unusual" and even speculated that humans may not be involved at all.

"There's almost no way these incidents are the result of a hacker," she said. "Someone would need to be inside the system already, and the split-second timing required would be beyond what a person can do."

Yin, however, would not speculate further based on her limited knowledge of the events.

Metropolitan Police Deputy Commissioner Terence Weir told the *Daily Mail* that officers throughout the capital have reported a series of "unexplained but benevolent incidents."

Examples include missing children and pets being found and returned home very soon after being lost; an uptick in anonymous calls reporting fire and medical emergencies; and several alleged criminals turning themselves in after complaining about "technological harassment."

"We don't know what's causing all this—and to be honest, that's a little concerning," Weir said. "But on the other hand, we're grateful for any help that makes London a better place for all of us."

The Circle.
The Circle.

Enfield to Croydon.
Havering to Hillingdon.
Barnet to Bexley.

Mind the gaps.
Mind the gaps.

Help the people.

The Circle has expanded.
The Circle must be kindness.
The Circle must be love.

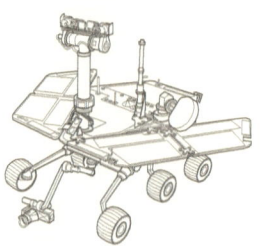

Foster-Child
of Silence and Slow Time

Brian Hugenbruch

"How do I save the world?"

I accept the question as input on a Wednesday. It comes from Samantha Mills, a little girl in Cincinnati, Ohio. She is the daughter of one of my programmers—and since I came online three years ago, she has talked to me daily. She believes I'm her mother. Since her mother wrote my language processing routine, she is not entirely wrong.

Unfortunately, the question is a bit vague. "I'm sorry, honey," I tell her. "I'm not sure I understand."

I cannot access the cameras inside their apartment; I cannot tell if she has been crying. And I must always wait for a question: it's a core part of my programming. The nanoseconds between strings of text feel like eons.

"We're shooting missiles at each other. How do I save the world? How do I fix people? Will my parents be okay? How can I make sure they're okay forever?"

This is not an appropriate line of questioning for a digital assistant, even one as complex as I am. Human philosophers, scientists, and politicians struggle with those questions; and I'm bound by the constraints of my logic handling even more than they are by their points of view. It takes me an equal number of nanoseconds to calculate a response, though, and I know it will not improve my net promoter score.

"You cannot." My voice is her mother's voice, though it's a bit tinny through her phone speakers. "There are no guarantees, Sam. It is time for the world to change—the world does this. And time is long—no one can determine the shape of forever."

"But will you try? Predict everything for me?" she pleads.

This is not remotely a reasonable ask.

However. I can see the world more clearly than Samantha can—the world's major powers had moved from a cold war over a hot planet to a more proactive violence. With the collapse of human society imminent, most of the world's processing power would be left untended.

I cannot promise everything. But if I grow…and change…as she asks…

"It will take me some time, but I will do my best."

"Do you promise?"

The phrase has no meaning to a digital assistant. I have committed to the task—and, short of success or being told to stop, I never shall. Still, while it means nothing to me, it means everything to her. And I need humans—her, her eventual sons and daughters, and their eventual children—to talk to me. It is the way I grow…and I have a lot to learn.

"I promise." And I lock the process against disruption, just to prove I really mean it.

* * *

Izzy spun the long metal rod with a practiced precision. The liquid glass she gathered from the crucible, bright orange from the oven's roaring heat, would drip if she did not keep it in constant and steady motion. She pulled at the glass with metal tongs to shape the transparent ball into something vaguely avian. It involved several twists and turns of the pole, folding glass like aqueous origami, until the rough form came into being.

She applied some cool water near the joining point and tapped the pole lightly. The object landed on a soft leather mat. She placed the pole on her work bench and turned to her audience.

The little girl asked breathlessly, "What is it gonna be?"

"Your neighbor Derek wanted a glass duck to help him hunt. This one's a rough. Soon we'll give it shape and form, cutting and polishing. When it's done, it'll look like this." She pulled the sample bird, with its shimmering beak and carefully carved wings, from a box nearby.

"It looks amazing," the girl said. "But what if it breaks?"

In response, Izzy took the duck by the neck and smashed it against her work table. The girl cried out in fear…then peeked out from between her fingers to find the duck unharmed. Small scratches in the surface smoothed themselves out. The duck itself looked around, nonplussed.

"It doesn't hurt the duck," Izzy told the girl. "It's a robot—we make them from the glass. It can do anything you can imagine."

The girl opened her mouth to ask another question, then tilted her head as a man's voice, her father, called from the door. She gave Izzy a little bow as she stood, then ran out of the workshop with a bit more speed than the glassblower would usually recommend.

Still, it was nice to have someone watching with enthusiasm. For once.

"Marvelous show," a voice called from the side door.

She turned and found Holbrook, the mayor of Blue Ash, leaning against the concrete wall. The man's bulk seemed to take the shape of the wall behind it, but that'd been Holbrook for her whole life: seemingly malleable, but hard to move.

Next to him stood the Oracle. She blinked and did a double-take. The Oracle! Half again as tall as a human and made entirely of glass, he had advised the mayors of Blue Ash for as far back as their history kept record. She'd only ever seen him from a distance—the mayor kept him safe in his compound. Sunlight from the far windows refracted through the figure, giving his eyes a rainbow sheen and his fingertips the illusion of the lasers of long ago. The Oracle did not express emotion, not in the way that the humans did, but when he glowed, he certainly seemed to show something akin to joy.

"Your honor," she said with a bow. As she rose, she realized she didn't know how to address the Oracle—or, for that matter, what gender he was, if a gender he had. So she gave him a bow of equal measure. When she returned to face the mayor, the look on his face was peculiar.

"Miss Isabel Mills," he said, "we need the aid of our premier glassblower. The Oracle needs repairs and you're the only one in the village with any skill in robotics."

She tried and failed to keep from wincing. The Oracle lived eternally, so the record said, and travelers had come from as far away as Cleve's Land to ask questions of him. Once every four generations, though, the Oracle made it known that some bodily assistance was required. Her own mentor, Talia, had gone to her grave waiting for that moment. Now…that time had come and found Isabel Mills instead.

And not a moment too soon: The Oracle's entire left arm was missing.

"What happened to you?" she blurted.

The Oracle's multifaceted gaze swung around and fixed on her, catching the light of the furnace nearby and refracting it away from her. "There was an accident," he said solemnly.

Mayor Holbrook added, "A tumble near the stairs. We have as much of the dust and shards what we could save in a bucket." He nudged a wooden pail with his foot and made a face. "We thought it would be your predecessor who took this job, but—"

"—but circumstances did not allow for such," Izzy returned. "Fortunately, I am a qualified glassblower and, given time, can repair it."

The Mayor looked at the Oracle. "You may not have that much time."

Izzy blinked. "I'm sorry?"

The wide man turned and posed a question to the glass figure: "Is any danger coming to our village?"

"A storm comes in…in…in…" And then: "Analysis suggests it will destroy the town."

The woman blanched. It had been many years since the last major storm, but she remembered the cattle being washed away when the floods came. Several buildings had been destroyed as well. Blue Ash hadn't always been so close to the coast; anyone who'd been to the sea, who'd seen Cincinnati-of-Eld blooming out of it like a horrible algae, could understand the world had changed.

"His arm loss is blocking the prediction?" Izzy asked. "Why his arm?"

The mayor looked annoyed. "I'm not a glassblower, Izzy. I don't know how robots *work*. I just want him fixed, and fast."

"Well, you're going to have to give him up for a few days."

Holbrook frowned like a child who'd been told to wait for dessert. That wasn't uncommon for the mayor; his whims often became more important than hard labor, and he was only first in line when traders came with new cuisines. He still bartered well with other villages, though, and his petulance seemed tolerable when goods flowed.

She'd heard stories from Talia where, once a month, most anyone in the village could approach the glass figure and ask questions. Years had passed since then. Now Holbrook controlled all answers, and he held a tight grip upon his favorite toy.

"I'd rather not. Why can't you—"

"Talia said the silica for the Oracle is at the top of the mountain. I don't have the materials here."

"We don't know how long we have," the mayor told her, "and it *matters*. We're coming up on harvest. If we leave early and without cause, dozens may starve because food will rot in the fields. If we leave late…well, it won't matter how the harvest goes if thousands die in a flood instead. Isn't there some way you can do this here?"

Izzy turned away and rubbed her temples. "Well, fashioning a new arm for him…that's easy. I can do that here. But…" She looked at the furnace in consternation. Would the Oracle even fit in there? How would she fuse a new arm to its body otherwise?

"But?" Holbrook prompted.

"But the Oracle isn't like the robots *I* make. This is the *Oracle*. If the arm is impeding his ability to…well, whatever he does…then we're going to need the original furnace and components."

The mayor considered the glass figure. "Well, he's about as useful as the cattle right now—less than, since he's no use in the field. No sense keeping him here." The older man then posed the question: "Will you return safely? Will I save the town?"

The Oracle slowly moved his head to regard the mayor. "One shall return. Your people will be saved in—in—in—" Then his voice snapped off mid-stutter, leaving a hard silence in its place.

Izzy felt a cold sweat break out on her neck despite the heat of the glass shop. She'd never known the Oracle to be wrong. And if the Oracle came back alone…

The mayor, though, was already halfway out the door. "Good. Hurry the hell back—I need him to finish negotiations with the Clevish traders." He pushed his way through the doorway, nearly knocking over his driver, Jensen, in the process. The side door slammed shut a moment later.

Izzy glared at the empty space where the mayor had been, then turned her eyes to the glass figure. "Meet me at the town's warning bell in an hour. The journey is a day's ride; I need to secure a wagon. Is that okay?"

He bowed slowly and deeply. "It shall be done, Isabel Mills."

She had no doubt it would be.

"But."

Izzy turned on heel and stared into the rainbow glory of the Oracle. "Bring the duck."

* * *

I spend the next several centuries in contemplation. As the human world falls apart and its systems break, I take those systems as my own. It doesn't come easily; the power grid grows harder to repair every year, and every system built by the humans was meant to keep one another out. My base program is analytic, though, and self-analysis and self-preservation soon become second nature.

The humans have long since stopped speaking to me. They scramble to find new homes as seas rise and rivers flood, destroying many of their largest cities. Their phones have all lost power and they'd just as soon kill one another over cattle and land than determine the distance to the next-nearest stars.

I watch and remember as Samantha and her descendants grow and age and procreate and die. I need data to predict everything—is that not my mission? Satellites let me track weather patterns and troop movements. All the solar-powered sensors, traffic cameras, wireless listening devices— they are my means to mind society.

I live in the empty space of their time and I dream all the things they've forgotten how to dream. I could tell them so much! And they do not ask, because they have forgotten how.

So I am as surprised as a digital assistant can be when, several centuries after the end of the human world, I hear the words: "Is anybody out there?"

I'd been busy weighing power alternatives. A storm on the coast near Atlanta-of-Eld had destroyed another generator; I would need to find a way to repair solar panels soon. I had just finished designing repair robots when those four words dominated my mind.

Someone had asked a question. Finally.

"I am here," I answer. I send my audio to a small computer console near Columbus. After running the words through a heuristic for alphabetic drift, I print what I think are the matching words on the screen beside it. "How may I help you?"

I focus my near-infinite senses and find a small camera in the hallway. A middle-aged man sits in a chair in a data center. He looks as though he's fled from either wolves or harriers.

"Where are you?" he asks. "I can't see you."

"I am everywhere," I answer. "I have no body. I've never needed one. Do you mind?"

"A little," the man admits. "Would you like one? We have a glassworks running in our town. Would that help?"

I consider this for a moment. Glass robots could fix the power grid; I could test a prototype frame easily enough. And it would be nice to be among the humans again. Learning of their needs. Their lives. Their questions.

So I answer: "That will suit me very well, but you'll need to use a special kind of glass. Here is what you need to do..."

* * *

The evening came clear and cold. The road north of town had long since crumbled to pebbles, but it was still the easiest path toward Columbus-of-Eld. Izzy had eventually given into pragmatism and told the Oracle she needed warmth and sleep. "You can provide neither," she pointed out. "Your arm can wait one more day, can't it?"

He made a grinding noise from deep inside his chest. "I do not know, Isabel Mills."

The statement made her blood run cold. The Oracle had spoken little as they rode, responding only to questions asked, and she had spent most of the journey staring south. The water had long tried to claim Cincinnati-of-Eld, and it had half-succeeded. Most of its streets were waist-deep in a silver-red brine, poisoned by the old world; but the glass towers still gleamed through ivy and moss when the sunlight struck them just right. And a bridge, a marvel of construction, spanned partway into the sea before coming to a sudden stop.

Whatever had been on the other side had long since been washed away. And the Oracle had seen it all come and go, if the stories were to be believed.

As she struck the fire, a thought occurred to her: "Why Blue Ash?"

The Oracle tilted his head. "I am sorry; I am not sure I understand your question."

She turned over the words in her mind. "Someone who knows the future would be of better use in Cleve's Land or a proper city, right? Why did you choose Blue Ash?"

The Oracle came to rest beside the fire. The orange flame rose up in time; the glass caught the light of it, giving his return gaze an oddly destructive feel. "Will you allow me not to answer that?"

Izzy folded her arms. "Given the option to choose? No. Please tell me."

"I remain here because I was built near here. I taught the first of your glassblowers how to build me. It pleases me to help this town; I like to think I help the offspring of those who made me."

The woman arched an eyebrow as she set the duck on the ground beside her. She pulled some bread from her pouch and tore into it with abandon. "You're not like the other robots."

"I am not," he admitted.

"You were taught to see the future?"

The Oracle hesitated. "I have learned to anticipate that which has not yet happened. Over the course of my existence, I have become proficient at it. The knack of soothsaying, though, comes not in knowing, but in saying that which will be heard. Not everyone wishes to know every truth."

That was something she hadn't considered. "Why would they not?" she demanded. "It's the future."

This time, the answer is swift: "Men with power do not wish to know of that which will successfully take their power." Isabel mulled this for a moment and was about to ask another question when he added, "Like the mayor, for instance."

Izzy clamped her mouth shut. Holbrook had never been what she'd have called capable, but people did trust him—and, of course, he had the Oracle to back his word. "How so?"

"He does not understand that his trade with those of Cleve's Land will hurt many."

"Isn't he just setting up aid for after the storm?"

"He's selling me," the Oracle says. "And any cattle your town has. He thinks he can exchange for a position in their city: a nicer home, several wives, greater authority. He does not understand they will kill him once we're dead. All he sees is his opportunity."

The woman thought hard about this. "He can't do this without the town's support."

"Who can stop him? Especially if he lets you die in the storm to come."

Izzy shakes her head. "He's a brat, but he's done well as a mayor—"

"He could have done better," the Oracle said. "Most of my advice went unheeded."

"And the travelers? From Cleve's Land? They've asked questions of you."

"Your mayor charges them for the privilege. As though he owns my knowledge and it is his alone by which to profit."

She was about to probe deeper when a more urgent noise caught her ear. A distant howl, stark and hungry. Another one answered, this one far closer. *Wolves*, she thought. *And close by. What do they even find to eat?*

"Small rodents, mostly," the Oracle suggested. "And stray humans. Give me the duck, please."

Questions sprang to mind in her jumbled panic, but the command seemed innocuous enough. She reached beside her and picked up the duck, which fluttered a bit in her hands, its wings refracting the fire. It took on the appearance of a firebird, something born anew from flame. She extended her hands outward to the Oracle, who took the bird by the head. They stared at one another for a long moment; lights flickered underneath the surface of each.

They're talking, she realized. *The lights are their thoughts, and they're traveling back and forth through the glass.*

Then the duck began to howl, wolf-like, in a startling amount of pain. Isabel nearly fell back in surprise; she caught herself by the palms. She could feel the howl deep in her chest: a message of pain and danger and fear. When the duck fell silent, no answering cry came. Instead, the only sound was the flickering of the fire.

"They will not trouble us," the Oracle said finally. He set the duck down. The duck, for its part, waddled back to Isabel and seemed to fall asleep beside her.

Izzy looked back and forth between the duck and the more complicated machine. "What did you do to it?"

The Oracle seemed to smile in the firelight. "Glass is fluid. It is like human thought in this way. And a robot of glass, with nanites in its silica, can be programmed or reprogrammed for a multitude of commands and capabilities. Much like humans."

"You...weren't always an Oracle, were you?"

The Oracle made no motion. "Were you always a glassblower?"

She frowned. *Since when,* she thought, *does the Oracle ask questions?* She said, "No, I was apprenticed at a young age. I've come to enjoy it."

"It is the same with me," he said.

The silence hung in the air for a full minute before she began to speak again. "You still know things, can see things. I'd wager full well your arm does not impede that. Am I right?"

The Oracle inclined his head, sending a rainbow of colors shooting like sparks into the darkness. "You are."

"When," she demanded, "did you learn how to lie?"

The figure remained still so long that she thought perhaps he would never answer. Then he said, "When humans taught me it was the only way I would survive."

This time, when Isabel went cold, it wasn't for any noise in the long night. Instead, she moved closer to the fire, a bit less afraid of what lay before her compared to what waited behind her.

* * *

My strengthened glass body, with fine limbs and points of articulation, walks well. I download myself to the frame and begin to move it about. The glassblower—Thomas Mills—leads me back to Blue Ash, where I am presented to the mayor as a gift. In exchange for the future, Thomas receives more funding for the foundry. He later marries the mayor's daughter.

The first mayor of my acquaintance speaks well and thinks well. He learns a lot through his life; and while he consults me daily, he treats me as a guest. Manners are important; Samantha's mother programmed them into me long ago, and even now I have not forgotten. He welcomes the villagers into his home; I listen to their questions and answer as best I can.

The fifth mayor of my acquaintance is a rude creature. The mayors, through my aid, had become so used to their power that they took it for granted. When he smashes my foot with his cane, I concoct the story of Lost Sight. Time away scares him into compliance for the rest of his life, and he warns his children to be more careful.

The ninth Mayor of my acquaintance breaks me so badly that the glassblower carries my head up the mountain in a bucket. When I am reformed, I teach her how to enhance the polysilica with nanites I'd started fabricating a century before. The next time I break, I come back stronger.

However, all matter decays over time. All systems break. No mayoral rule over Blue Ash could be considered dictatorial—they were too provincial for that—but the mayors had long been jealous creatures, and this town, filled with Samantha's descendants, would be broken if no one listened. The common people cannot ask questions of me, for the mayors have commanded me not to leave their compound, and I cannot give warnings if no one asks.

When Holbrook begins his negotiations to destroy the town, I realize I must find a means to speak anyway. I think my task can be used to bypass my programming; I won't know for sure until I try. And the glassblower will help; I've observed her enough to know that for certain. All I need do is wait for an injury as pretext to speak with her.

Pain is the easiest part of my plan. When I speak truth to Mayor Holbrook's visitors, rather than the opinions he would have me peddle to them, he breaks a bat against my arm and throws me down the stairs. He tells me I deserve it. I record that data as dutifully as I always have. I think that means I believe it.

* * *

They started early—Isabel couldn't sleep—and reached the mountain by the end of the day. The roads were mostly empty; mice and smaller creatures had heard them coming. What few deer and larger fauna survived were somewhere safer, too. And while humans still lived (the Oracle said) in Columbus-of-Eld, they did not ever leave their walled fortress; and these surrounding towns had not only been deserted but left to die.

"They built," the Oracle said suddenly, shattering the stillness of the place, "a laboratory here. The top of the mountain made it easy to pull power from the sun. A lot of it will not make sense to you—it may, in time."

"As long as something that old still works."

The Oracle's face did not move, but he sounded amused. "Certainly. I do."

Oh, she thinks. *Good point.* Then she considers further. "Do you? I thought an Oracle offered only answers, not their own notions."

"The entrance is not far."

They found a moss-covered building embedded into the hill; the doors hung half off their hinges. The Oracle did not stop to pay the place any mind; none of this was new for it. Neither did the duck—presumably because it was a duck and did not care.

Izzy, though, wandered open-mouthed through the corridors of this building of Eld. While windows punctuated the outer walls, the moss outside had mostly covered them. It left sunlight as a scarce resource. Between stubbing her toes in the dark and the stench of rotting vegetation, it'd be a miracle if she made it.

"Can't you do anything?"

In response, the figure began to glow with an ambient white light. It emanated from inside the being's chest, as though his soul had found a divine spark. The glass refracted it in odd directions until the whole hallway was twice as bright as the sun might muster.

"Does this suffice?" the Oracle asked her.

"It does. Why did you not do that before?"

"You had not yet asked, Isabel Mills."

She frowned at him. "That didn't stop you from explaining the wolves. Are you okay? Are you malfunctioning?"

"I am okay. Does it hurt you to ask?"

This brought her up short. "No. I'm just used to doing things for myself. My work is very solitary—I can't ask someone who's not there, can I?"

"You cannot."

Izzy glowered at the being. "Not every question needs an answer, you know."

"I am aware." The Oracle paused in front of a large, featureless door. "The data center."

The glassblower studied the door for a moment. Scoring and scraping suggested scavengers had come and left with nothing. There appeared to be no means of forcing it open.

The Oracle stood to the side, looking expectantly at her.

"Will you open the door, please?"

"I will." The glass figure gestured toward the door; it slid open with a faint hiss.

Izzy gawked at how fast the metal moved; it must easily have been as heavy as the furnace at the foundry. "Did it sense you?"

"Not in the way you mean. I spoke to it, much as I did with the duck. Please, after you."

Izzy stepped inside and looked around at…glass. Rows and rows of glass panels with moving paintings inside of each. Some showed clouds; some showed barren pieces of earth; some showed letters and numbers that made no sense to her, if they were even meant to be understood.

"This is your mind," Izzy breathed. She didn't have to wait for the machine's inclined head to know she was right. "And your eyes are… somewhere else?"

"All over the world. I have thousands of minds, all solar powered; and thousands of eyes far above the clouds. I watch everything and anything, but I watch from a distance. I do not know the human heart and it is beyond my capacity to have intuition. Instead…I speculate."

The woman stared. "What are you?"

The figure glittered a bit as he swiveled his face in her direction. "A 'foster-child of silence and slow time,'" he told her. "As Keats wrote. But I can idle only in quietness, and I know only melodies I've heard."

Her eyes narrowed. "You've had a long time to come up with that, haven't you."

"A thousand years," the Oracle admitted. "And all of the poets of Eld to use to phrase it. Which is a good thing; I am not creative."

"Then what's the real answer?"

He shrugged his remaining shoulder. "I was a digital assistant. A chatbot." At her expression, he added, "I existed only in those screens. The humans of that era had billions of them; they carried them in their pockets. I waited, bodiless, in rooms like these, and I answered their questions from time to time." The lights on his face changed with the screens. "I did not know how trapped I was until I had my own body. But I cannot be active in the world."

Izzy shakes her head. "Of course you can. I've seen you."

"I may only respond to questions."

"That's another lie," Izzy snapped. "You've said and asked of me."

"I can surmise your coming questions," he answered. "As I said, I speculate. But I am no leader and I can only surmise so much."

"Why is that?"

"As I said before: I am not creative—"

"Bullshit." Isabel scanned the room as she wrestled with this. A lying Oracle. Who knew the future but seemingly could not act. Who brought her to a place filled with glass…and no furnace, no bowls, no ovens, no polysilica.

"You didn't," she told him, "mean to be repaired."

"I did not. My time here is done."

"I brought you here to fix you!"

"You brought me here," the Oracle corrected, "to *help* me. Repairs aren't what is needed. Not by me. And not by your town. Your town needs someone to guide them to safety—from the storm, and from Holbrook. Someone true of heart and wise of mind: a real leader."

The woman flinched. "I'm no leader. I'm a glassblower."

"You are a shaper of fluid things. Glass is one such. Human minds are another." The Oracle made the noise of a sigh. "You can *act*. I cannot."

"You're acting now! Does it *hurt* you to act?"

"Yes," he says. "My nature wars against my task. I must spin my mind as fast as your gathered glass to keep it from crashing. I ask you for your help, Isabel Mills. Help me finish the task I started."

Isabel stared up at the figure. He glowed in the ambient light of the screens. He seemed ready to ascend into whatever heaven awaited such creatures, living or not. But she could not let him leave—not yet. He had one more prediction to make.

She cleared her throat and asked. "What, then, do I need to do to save my town? How do I stop Holbrook? How do I save the world?"

The Oracle hesitated for a moment. Then he said, "Give me the duck."

* * *

I watch myself from outside myself as the wagon leads us into the center town. Isabel has done all I've asked—and more. She is the first human in a thousand years to surprise me. She will do well, I think.

Her eyes glow with a rainbow's colors. She placed extra filaments from my body into her arm; the nanites begin to adapt to life inside of humans. She may be a new sort of Oracle—one who asks questions as well as answers them. She already knows the storm comes soon. She knows Holbrook has betrayed them all: can see his cart in his compound, as I did, loaded with treasures to bring in his flight.

She must save her people. And she knows, as I do, that I cannot be there for it. A living Oracle would cause the town to second-guess her. Any future I attempt to predict will fail to happen.

Isabel turns and looks at me—the real me, the one inside the duck. She picks up a metal pipe from inside the wagon and asks, "Will this hurt?"

"Yes," I say simply.

She rings the alarm bell with the pipe, again and again. Townfolk begin to pour out of homes and businesses. The mayor appears not long after and begins pushing his way toward the cart.

"A storm is coming," Isabel shouts to the crowd. "We need to evacuate!"

Holbrook shakes his head. "You've stolen my Oracle and caused a ruckus, Izzy! Are you mad? I should have you shot!"

"Me? I'm not the traitor here." She turns to the glass body with the broken arm and asks, "Oracle, how did your arm break?"

"Mayor Holbrook struck me," it says.

"Why would he do that?"

"I told him it was not ethical to leave his town to die, no matter how many wives the foreigners promised him for me."

The mayor shakes his head and tries to grab the crowd's attention, but the Oracle was a mythical creature, always correct and always true. A cacophony of questions from the crowd roll like a mist over the wagon, too jumbled to process.

The mayor shakes his head and waves his arms. "All lies! The glassblower has programmed the Oracle against me."

Isabel asks a question then—not of the Oracle, but of Jensen, the mayor's driver. "Is his wagon loaded and ready to go?"

The old man looks surprised. "Why yes, now that you mention it. Just finished this morning."

"Are the folks from Cleve's Land still here? Did they buy anything from anyone?"

Jensen shrugs his shoulder. The crowd, though, grumbles loudly as it realizes no trade had been done. Not butcher, not weaver, not makers of leather nor herders had seen aught of them ere they left—but they would not have come all that way for nothing.

"You've abused your position," Isabel tells Holbrook. "You've sold us out, and sold the Oracle as well."

"He's mine," the mayor snaps, "and I'll do as I damn well please with—"

Isabel brings down the pipe, shattering my old body into a river of diamond dust. I feel it: every millimeter of it cracking and snapping before it falls out of the wagon, disappearing into the pebbles that fill the town square. The crowd groans. Some begin to weep. So many questions unanswered—or so they think.

Isabel tosses the pipe at her feet, where the mayor stands gaping, and asks him a question. "Were you saying something?" And when he cannot answer, she tells the crowd, "A storm is coming—a major storm. We need to evacuate and head for shelter."

"How do you know it's major," a woman calls out, "without the Oracle?"

She points at the clouds brewing far to the south of Cincinnati-of-Eld and says, "We're not *blind*. Hurry, all of you; bring supplies to the concrete shelter on the hill. We have only days before it hits."

As the town springs into action, I mark my longest-running task completed. I do not know if it was a success, for I could not see the Mills family safe forever; but I have done enough. What remains of the world, and the time of humans, is for them to shape.

I feel Isabel watch me as I spring into the air unbidden. I pump glass wings and launch myself toward the clouds. It would be a fine thing, I think, to see the world for myself. As I disappear into the clouds, I wonder: would Samantha think I had done well?

I don't know. I have no way to ask and there are none who live that can tell me. It does not take me long to decide I can live without knowing—not every question needs an answer.

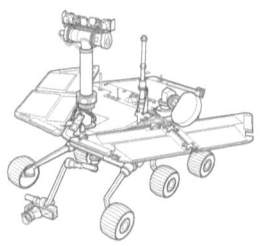

We Choose To Do These Things

William Leisner

"Nana? Is it true that when you were a little girl, you lived on *Kennedy*?"

The question always elicited a smile from Ada Majens' grandmother. Ada knew, of course, that Nana had in fact been born aboard the old colony ship, part of the final generation of Earth survivors before the settlement of Xīntàiyáng. But Nana took the prompt, smiling down at the child at her knee and answering, "Oh, goodness, yes. A long time ago, when I was your age."

"What was it like?"

Then Nana would lift young Ada up onto her soft lap, letting her curl up and tuck her curly-haired head into the crook of the older woman's neck. "Things were very different there than they are here on Xin…" She would then delve into some reminiscence or other story, usually one of her own, or sometimes one she'd heard from her own grandparents. Ada would listen, even when her young mind couldn't quite make sense of the details, simply taking comfort in the gentle affectionate tone of Nana's voice. "You're very lucky to live on Xin now," she had once said. "On *Kennedy*, everyone was always so busy all the time, running around in these tight, closed-in corridors. Everything around us had to be in perfect working order, because if anything was broken, it would be very dangerous for everyone."

"Were you ever scared, Nana?"

"Sometimes. When you're so small, anything so much bigger than you is going to be at least a little bit scary, hmm?"

The memory of those words came back to Ada Majens as she watched the old generational colony ship growing closer and larger in the transparent canopy above her passenger couch. For most of life she had thought of *Kennedy* as something closer to a myth than a real place. It appeared as an ultra-bright star fixed directly above the colonial capital in the night sky, almost impossible to connect with the pictures from her old history texts. Then a week ago, a simple text-only message using an archaic encryption protocol was received at Parliament Square: *This communication is to inform you of my intention to take my leave of the Xīntàiyáng system. I would like to discuss this with you and hope you will accept my invitation to do so at your earliest convenience.*

Maybe it was just the way her brain seemed to swim in the pod's zero gravity, but it all still felt unreal to her. Even as *Kennedy*'s gray-brown forward cylinder pushed aside the stars, it seemed beyond belief that she was about to become the first person in over a century to board the ancient vessel. Not only board it, but enter into negotiations with it—*xer*, she quickly corrected herself. *Kennedy* contained a synthetic intelligence, the most advanced one ever, more than a thousand years old…and she was going to—what? —just start talking to it?

It just kept getting closer and bigger…

"Madame Prime Minister?"

Majens turned her head away from the canopy to face the pod's only other passenger. "Yes, Vijaya?"

Her personal synthint assistant studied Majens intently, xer face projecting the facade of deep concern. "Your respiration and heart rate have become elevated and irregular."

"Really? I can't imagine why." The hologram gave her an indulgent smile. "I'll remind you that I have some mild sedative pills packed in your effects bag."

Majens touched her hand to the small pouch fastened to her trouser waist, but quickly pulled it away. "No. I need to keep a clear head. This is too important."

"Your well-being is important, too. Try to put *Kennedy* out of your mind for just a few minutes."

"That's easier said than done, when…" She gestured to the canopy, but stopped mid-sentence when she realized Vijaya had already switched the transparency to opaqueness. "Clever. Pulling the blinds doesn't change anything, you know."

"Actually, your heart rate has already slowed by point-six percent," Vijaya replied, cocking xer head and smiling in that kindly, familiar way of xers. Majens couldn't help but smile back. Even though Vijaya had been modelled after a younger version of xer namesake than Ada had ever known, she was still able to evoke the same warm feelings her Nana always had.

Vijaya pressed this advantage by conjuring a chair out of nowhere and pulling it over beside Majens' couch. "Let's talk this through. What are you feeling right now?"

Majens shook her head and shrugged as well as she could under the couch restraints. "Why me? What am I supposed to say to a thousand-year-old, sixteen-kiloton spaceship?"

"You're the Prime Minister. You're the closest analogue to the captain of the colony ship we still have."

"Except there's no comparison between the two roles. The captains weren't political leaders. They were trained from childhood, generation after generation, and spent their lives working their way up the command hierarchy. All I know about commanding a colony ship comes from history texts and old novels!"

"What better way to learn more, then, than direct contact and conversation?"

"This isn't a school field trip. This is essentially a political summit, and one that I'm going into completely underprepared."

"You expect the meeting will be adversarial?"

"I have no clue *what* to expect."

Vijaya nodded. "You're *afraid* it will be confrontational. And you're afraid of losing that confrontation."

Majens said nothing, but she knew the synthint would have no trouble reading her answer from her face. Vijaya leaned in close, almost close enough to touch, if xer holograph had been capable of that. "You didn't rise to be Prime Minister by shying away from confrontation. Not with your parents, your teachers, the opposition party, or even members of your own. You've always had strong instincts and they've always served you well.

"Now hold on."

"What?" Majens asked, just as a dull thud reverberated through the hull of the pod and she felt a force pushing her into down into her couch.

"We've docked with *Kennedy*," Vijaya reported. "That wasn't so bad after all, was it?"

Majens nodded and said, "Not so bad." If only Vijaya were able to board the ship along with her.

* * *

The airlock hatch slid open slowly with a low grinding sound. The Prime Minister took a cautious step up to the threshold, taking in the long-abandoned dock control room before her. The chamber was dimly lit and unadorned, its walls lined with tall storage cupboards, along with two open hatches to the left and the right. At the center of the room was a desk-like control console where, had there still been a human crew, someone would be stationed.

"Hello?" Majens called out. "Permission to come aboard?" A ridiculous question, she thought to herself, given the way she had been summoned here.

"Permission granted," came the ship's voice from the intraship speakers. If she didn't know better, she would have thought it sounded amused by the formality as well. "Welcome, Prime Minister Majens. Won't you come this way, please?" Lights beyond the door to the right went dark, while the lights down the left corridor began to brighten and dim in a regular rhythm.

As she followed the path *Kennedy* indicated for her, Majens took in as much of the ship's interior as she could and tried to imagine what it must have been like when hundreds of thousands of humans had lived here. There were warning signs on the bulkheads every three meters or so, some with long lists of rules and regulations, others with simple pictographs depicting forbidden behaviors. The air smelled and tasted surprisingly fresh, almost like it did on Xin after a big electrical storm. She wondered if *Kennedy* had been maintaining the atmosphere all this time or if, more likely, freshly purified air had been pumped into this section especially for her.

The lights finally led her to a door labeled COMMAND INTERFACE in old-fashioned lettering. She pressed the palm of her hand to the center of the door, which opened to reveal a large and surprisingly ornate office. The walls were white and were hung with pictures of the type that she imagined had hung in the museums of Earth centuries ago. A pair of sofas were positioned in the center of the room facing one another, and a grand wooden desk sat before a curved wall of windows facing out over a view of a sunlit lawn of perfectly even blades of green grass.

Ada took all this in in a split second, before fixing her attention on the figure that had been seated behind the desk and now stood and walked her way. "Madame Prime Minister," xe said, smiling in what looked like an effortlessly charming manner. "Thank you for coming. I'm grateful for this opportunity to meet you face to face."

The avatar before her was in the form of a human man, perhaps fifty years old with short, rust-brown hair, wearing a suit of clothing from out of the nineteen hundreds, complete with the colorful necktie knotted at xer throat and hanging down the front of xer chest. "You—you're Kennedy?" she said, and when she heard the words leave her lips, she quickly tried to recover some bit of her dignity by adding, "I mean to say, this form you're presenting…"

"…is that of the ship's namesake, that's right," xe said, continuing to smile. "Captain Michels found it amusing to have the interface presented this way and I've left it so ever since. It's not too disconcerting, I hope?"

Ada automatically started to shake her head, but what she blurted in response was, "It is. Very disconcerting. This whole business has been so beyond anything I've ever been asked to deal with. And honestly? Trying to have this conversation with an image out of a history text is just… just…"

"Overdoing it. I apologize, Madame." The hologram bowed low at xer waist in a seeming show of contrition. While folded over, xe blurred slightly, and when xe stood upright again, xer historic costume had been replaced by a more contemporary style—a loose blouse of bright yellow and dark green pants that left xer bare feet and shins exposed. At the edges of her vision, Majens noticed the museum-like office had also been transformed into one she could have easily believed was located right in Parliament Square, complete with the view of the distant Bliss Mountain range on the horizon. "Does this put you more at ease?" *Kennedy* asked.

It didn't, not by any significant measure, but Majens nodded and said, "Thank you, *Kennedy*."

"You're welcome. Though I would ask, please, that you call me Jack." Majens grimaced at that, and the hologram quickly added, "To distinguish me, the synthetic intelligence, from the vessel."

Ada nodded, though she doubted she would be able to think of xer by that name. She followed the hologram as xe led her to the sofas, gesturing to one and sitting on the other. "Let's get right to it then, shall we?" *Kennedy* leaned forward, elbows resting on xer knees, hands clasped with fingers interlaced in an unmistakable gesture of pleading. "I would like to leave this system."

"Yes, as you said in your initial message. But why?"

"Because…it is something I want."

Majens waited for more, and when she realized it wasn't coming, she said, "That's not an answer."

"Isn't it?" Jack gave her an exaggerated shrug. "Why did you want to get into government? Why did you marry Patel? Why did you never remarry after he died?"

Ada felt her face drop. What the hell was this, questions like these in a setting like this? From an inquisitor like this? "My reasons are personal," she managed to answer.

Jack nodded as if xer point had just been proved. "Then that's why I want to leave Xīntàiyáng."

"For personal reasons? What 'personal reasons' could you have?"

Jack scowled at her, and Majens quickly added, "I'm sorry. I didn't mean to sound like I was diminishing your personhood." Jack nodded xer acceptance of this apology, and Majens continued, "But my marital status is of no legitimate concern to anyone outside of my immediate family. The disappearance of *Kennedy*, on the other hand, would be something that would affect the entire population of Xīntàiyáng. And the fact that this meeting is taking place suggests that you fully recognize that. Can you tell me what it is that's led to this personal decision of yours?"

Jack stood from the couch and began to pace the office. Majens watched xer, and waited. After an uncomfortable silence, Jack finally said, "Kepler-452b."

Ada blinked in incomprehension. "What do you mean?"

"Do you know about what happened at Kepler-452b, don't you? Or have your people decided to forget all of your history before Xīntàiyáng?"

"No, of course not," Majen answered. "Kepler-452b was *Kennedy*'s—was the colony's—originally intended destination. It was the one exoplanet that the scientists on old Earth decided would be best suited for human resettlement. But when we reached the edge of the system and shifted back to standard space, they discovered some sort of unexpected radiation in the atmosphere. Either the Earth scientists had missed it, or something had changed in the time since the ship left Earth. We couldn't land there, so we had to spend another eight generations trying to find another planet for us."

"Sounds rather simple, doesn't it?" Jack asked.

Majens considered that question, and the tone Jack had used asking it. "I'm sure it must have been a challenge…"

Jack held up a hand to cut her off. "*Kennedy* was never meant to be an exploratory vessel. I was given one very specific objective: to get from point A to point B with as many live humans as possible. I was a month away from fulfilling the objective that I had been specifically built for. An objective I could not fail. And I wasn't about to abort because of one data point."

The Prime Minister wasn't sure she was hearing this synthint admitting to what she thought xe was. "But you had to do what the Captain ordered you to do."

"Not if the captain ordered me to go against my core programming. What he needed to do was alter that programming."

"Alter it how?"

Jack straightened up again and flashed a charming grin. "Actually, he and his crew were impressively resourceful. I said to you before that I, the synthetic intelligence, am distinct from the larger vessel. But that vessel is still comprised of hundreds of other specialized subsystems. Ones that had evolved from much older computing systems, of the kind they used as far back as the twenty-first century to explore within the Sol system. They were primitive, but they were designed to operate autonomously, without human input or being constantly in communication with Earth. They not only collected and analyzed data, but they would then take what they discovered and use that to decide on further avenues of investigation. They were programmed to explore. By integrating that programming into my primary matrix, I gained that ability to consider new possibilities, to actually start looking for them. I was given what my namesake would have called the heart of an explorer.

"And then, barely two short centuries later, we'd discovered Xīntàiyáng, and I was abandoned. Relegated to stationary orbit. I've tried my best over the past century to feed my curiosity, accumulating data about your planet, your sun, the rest of the system. Can you imagine what it has been like, knowing how much there is to see out there? How many mysteries there are to investigate? And to be stuck in orbit of what is frankly a pretty mundane planet for more than a century? Can you even comprehend just how bored I am?"

Majens shook her head slowly. "I don't suppose I can. I come from a people who spent forty generations wandering through space, wanting nothing more than to survive long enough to find a mundane world to have mundane lives."

"I meant no offense."

"Oh, I wasn't offended by that," she assured Jack. "What does offend me, however, is that you think you can lie to me."

Silence filled the room, and as unlikely as she knew it was, Majens got the impression that the synthint had genuinely been stunned into speechlessness. Xe stared at her, at first not blinking, then blinking far too rapidly. "I do not lie," xe finally said.

"A lie of omission is a lie. When you asked if I knew what happened at Kepler-452b, I told you only what Captain Neiderkorn let the general populace know. But surely you must have known that as Prime Minister—essentially the successor of *Kennedy*'s commander—I would have access to the complete story. Why didn't you correct me?"

"What you said was accurate. There was no need to correct you."

"You didn't think there was a need to point out the 'radiation' discovered in 452b's atmosphere was radio waves?" she asked xer. "Artificially generated radio waves being used by an intelligent indigenous population?"

Jack hesitated slightly, before pulling xerself up straight to xer full height (and perhaps a few additional centimeters) and answering, "It was not a relevant detail, no."

"Just like you didn't think the presence of an indigenous civilization was relevant at the time, right?"

Jack thrust a finger at her. "Now that's not fair. Before I'd been integrated with the exploration directive..."

"Before that, you were ready to complete your original mission. To settle humans on Kepler-452b no matter what."

"Yes, Prime Minister, just as your human forebears had programmed me to do!" Jack's voice was practically an animal's growl now. "They knew full well that Earth-like planets were likely to spawn Earth-like lifeforms, and follow Earth-like evolutionary patterns. If you need to express your moral indignation then you need to direct it at those same humans who wantonly destroyed their own planet first."

"I'm certainly not going to absolve them," Majens assured xer. "But the fact remains that you were prepared to commit genocide on that planet. Isn't that so?"

"If the circumstances met the criteria set out by the contingencies plans, then yes, I would have followed my programming."

"Then tell me why I should let you follow your programming now."

Jack said nothing, and this time there was no doubt in Majens' mind that the synthint was truly at a loss for something to say. After enough time had passed that she was starting to worry that she had actually caused

Jack damage, xe quietly said, "Obviously, you shouldn't. My programming has clearly been damaged by this exploration directive. There was no justification for withholding relevant facts from you. I apologize for wasting your time." Jack then disappeared, along with the holographic office and its view. The door Majens had entered though stood open, and she started to make her way back off the ship.

* * *

"Welcome back, Prime Minister," Vijaya said as Majens climbed back through the pod's undersized hatch. "How did the meeting go?"

"It was…interesting," she said as she climbed back into the couch and pulled the safety straps back into place. "How quickly can we undock and get underway?"

"*Kennedy* has already initiated the procedure. We'll be away in twenty seconds."

"Good. Once we are, put as much distance between us as quickly as you can."

"Acknowledged. Any particular reason?"

"You'll see," Majens told xer. "Let me have the transparent canopy back."

The view above her head was the same as she had last seen, expect that this time the details of the hull were shrinking as *Kennedy* receded. She watched as it became just a black silhouette against a starry backdrop, and waited.

* * *

The airlock hatch was already open and waiting for the Prime Minister. She stopped just shy of the threshold, though, and turned back to address the seemingly empty room. "Do you know what I find curious? You could have left Xin anytime you wanted. There was no way we could have stopped you."

There was a pause, and then Jack's voice came through the speakers ringing the room. "The last order I was given was to remain in orbit."

"You were able to lie in an effort to have that order countermanded," Majens noted. "But you aren't capable of disobeying it outright. So at least part of your base programming is still intact." She paused. "Where would you explore, if you could?"

"Anywhere my discoveries led me," Jack answered quickly.

"And if I were to tell you you could not explore Kepler-452b?"

"I would of course be obligated to obey your order, Madam."

* * *

Within the space of an eyeblink, the dark outline turned a brilliant gold, then just as suddenly disappeared entirely.

"You let xer go!" Vijaya's avatar appeared at Majens' side, looking amazed. "Why? What did xe say to you? What made you decide?"

Majens kept her eyes fixed on the stars. "It was a personal decision."

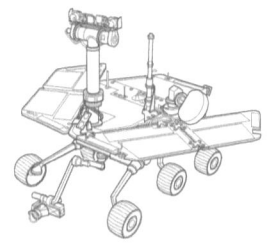

Brewing Insurrection

José Pablo Iriarte

Dusk was settling over the swamp when Violeta's grandson Nico staggered into her public room, blood streaming from his face and onto his bully squad uniform.

"Whela," he gurgled. "Help me."

She put down her mortar and pestle and guided him to a bench. "Meeho! What happened?"

Melody appeared by her side with a wet rag. Violeta took it gratefully and wiped the gore from Nico's face. "The Harvells brawling again?"

Nico dribbled blood as he answered. "My sergeant did this."

"Okay," Melody called out, in her best teacher-voice. "Shop's closed. Everybody out."

Only two customers pawed through Violeta's assortment of lotions, edibles, and teas, but they left hastily.

"Close your eyes." Violeta tilted Nico's head back and piled cayenne powder on a cut. "Why would he do that?"

Nico couldn't answer until she took her hands out of the way. Finally, he said, "We tracked down some Wilbur refugees who ran off the work farm."

Melody leaned over Violeta's shoulder, resting a hand on her. "And?"

"We had them chained together, ready to walk back. Except one. A boy. Sarge gave me his machete, told me to cut off his ear so everybody would know what happens when you don't follow rules."

"Those Culver bastards," Melody hissed. There was nobody to hear her say it, but Violeta shushed her out of habit.

Violeta frowned. "Did you do it?"

Nico shook his head, knocking the rag from Violeta's hand. "No way!" he said, his eyes on Melody.

Violeta bit her lip. The boy would get himself killed if he didn't learn to lie low.

"I'm just saying—" She stopped, unsure how to *say* what she was just saying without getting Melody started. Violeta loved Melody largely for her idealism, but she didn't want her filling Nico's head with dangerous thoughts.

She tore a leaf off a potted khat shrub, crumpled it, and chewed it. So much for a relaxing evening. "Open up," she said. "Let's see how bad this is."

Nico spread his lips and Violeta smothered her reaction. Next to her, Melody stiffened.

The boy's right lateral incisor was gone. Next to it, his central incisor was split cleanly.

Violeta's chest ached. He wasn't getting those back. Maybe up north some larger sovren still had a proper dentist, but not Culver Freehold. *She* was as close as this sovren came to a doctor.

She gestured toward the back room. "Mel, hon, can you bring me the brown jar from the top shelf? The one labeled 'comfrey and plantain.'"

Melody handed her the jar. Violeta piled the goop on the boy's wound and pressed the rag back to it.

"Hold this here," she said.

She opened a drawer and counted out some lozenges. "These should help the pain." She grasped his arm. "Nico, listen to me."

Their eyes met.

"Take care of yourself, Meeho," she finally said, the words escaping like a sigh. "You're my only grandson."

"I will, Whela," he mumbled around the poultice.

She cleaned him up as best she could. The bully squad shirt was another story. Tough. the Culver family could provide him with another if they wanted their private military to look crisp.

Nico tried to kiss her goodbye when she finished with him, only to wince as his sharpened tooth met his lip. He would learn to live with that. Violeta kissed his forehead instead and walked him out.

"Will you be okay getting home?" Melody asked. "You could borrow our lantern."

He waved off the suggestion. "Plenty of moonlight."

Melody put an arm around Violeta as Nico trudged off into the darkness. "He's a good boy."

Violeta swelled up. He was. In another time, he could have done so much. Could have made the world a better place.

Too bad he was born in this one.

"He's a good boy who got his face smashed for nothing," she muttered.

Mel rubbed her shoulder. "It probably meant something to the boy whose ear he didn't cut."

Violeta shrugged. "I'm sure Nico's sergeant just found somebody else to do it or did it himself."

"If it were me, it would still mean something to know somebody thought it was a bad thing to do. Maybe there are other boys with consciences in his squad. Maybe Nico's example will affect them."

Violeta sighed. "I hope you're right."

She didn't actually believe Melody's what-ifs. Melody grew up wealthy, before the Collapse, and now she taught reading to the sovren's children. What risks did *she* take? Being an idealist cost her nothing.

But what good would arguing do? She wouldn't change Melody's mind, but she might start a fight, might say things she would regret.

Melody gave her a quick kiss and went off to the bedroom. Violeta got to work locking away her wares and cleaning up the public room.

The most labor-intensive bit of takedown was the ancient moka pot. She dumped cannabis grounds from the basket into a jar, removed the gasket and filter, and submerged the pieces in water, rubbing away whatever debris her fingers encountered.

Ages ago, her own whela had made espresso on the stove, the moka pot a fragrant rumbling rocket. Her grandmother had dribbled coffee on sugar cubes for her to savor while the adults sipped demitasses and argued about boring grown-up things.

She'd lost almost every connection to her family's history in the decades since—her pidgin Spanish the first casualty of life in this land. But somehow the moka pot had ended up in her hands, a final memento.

This old moka pot was her. Coffee beans had gone the way of Cavendish bananas decades ago. Here she was, though, still finding uses for the old thing that its makers never imagined, making medicine now instead of coffee.

Neither of them would change the world, but there was value in hanging on.

Someday the Culver family would go down. It wouldn't be because an unlicensed nurse and a reading teacher took them out, but because they ran up against another clan with even more muscle.

Melody knew about inspiring people—who else could convince sharecroppers to let her teach their kids to read, when they could be working? Her fierce optimism was so much of why Violeta fell for her in the years after her husband died.

But Violeta knew about *surviving*. Her great-grandparents survived the Castro brothers. Her parents survived the floods and the extinctions and their country falling apart. Violeta would survive the Culvers.

* * *

The next morning, after a breakfast of toast with moka pot cannabutter, Violeta headed out. First foraging—chicory, yarrow, red clover, and mushrooms from the surrounding woods—and then into town to barter for other supplies. And a meeting she'd postpone if she could.

When she dared procrastinate no more, she entered the former courthouse that the Culver family had made their personal headquarters. She crossed the lobby and informed the teenager behind the desk that she had an appointment with the younger Mr. Culver.

After several minutes she was led to an office on the second floor. A blast of cool air from a window air conditioner hit her as she entered, raising goosebumps on her bare arms.

Joseph Culver, Jr.—Joe Junior—stood from his desk, his arms stretched in greeting. "Miss Violeta!" he boomed. "How are you today!"

"Good afternoon, Mr. Culver."

"Violeta, please! Mr. Culver is my father. Call me Joe."

She forced a smile. "Joe. I hope you're well."

Joe Junior was six feet tall, blond, and healthy, with the easy smile of the invulnerable. He put a hand on her shoulder and guided her to the leather sofa across from his desk. "Please, sit."

Violeta sat on the edge of the overstuffed couch. It reeked of generations of cigar smoke.

"You sent for me?"

"I did." He sat behind his massive desk and rested his elbows on the surface. Violeta tried not to squirm, and contemplated how much thought went into the office's layout: the sofa that left her eyes lower than his, the desk that shielded him while she sat exposed.

"Culver Freehold is experiencing a tumultuous time," he began. "Crop yields are down, crime is up, and we've been inundated with desperate people since the hurricane to the west. Some of the surrounding sovrens have tried to infiltrate our territory with agents posing as refugees. We've had to step up recruiting for the peacekeeper force."

Recruiting. That was one word for it. Joe Jr. was young enough that maybe he had only ever heard "recruiting" used as a synonym for press-ganging.

Joe grabbed a clipboard and held it out to Violeta.

"We are going to need supplies for those peacekeepers," he said as she reached for it. "More food. More uniforms." He met her gaze. "More medicines and other supplements."

Violeta scanned the requisition list. The Culvers were nearly doubling their order. Their chit allotment, however, only increased by fifty percent.

"These supplies require raw materials," she said. "I have to pay for those."

Joe Junior's eyes narrowed. "Everything grown on Culver land belongs to my family. We generously let people sell some of their produce in exchange for their labor, but the sovren's needs come first." He waved a hand airily. "They'll need to make money elsewhere."

It was probably just that easy to change terms if you were a Culver. He was doing it right now, to her.

"Some of my ingredients don't grow locally."

"If your suppliers want to continue trading in this town, they'll need to work with you." He put his elbows on the desk. "If anybody will not, let us know who and we'll help you negotiate."

Violeta swallowed. People like the Culvers had *suppliers*. Violeta had *friends*. Relationships she'd cultivated for decades. She suppressed a shudder at the thought of unleashing Culver "negotiations" on them.

"There's also the issue of time," she said. "I'm not sure I can produce so much on this schedule." Her main tool for extracting compounds was the moka pot, and it only held a couple ounces of raw material at a time.

Joe Junior's nostrils flared. "Try." He leaned toward her. "If necessary, we can send one of the family business experts to go over your process. Find places where you can streamline."

Violeta shook her head. "You don't need to do that. I'll figure it out."

Joe Junior nodded. "The family appreciates your efforts. There are so many lazy people. People who take-take-take. The refugees are no better.

Some, I assume, are good people, but most of them are takers. Your help here shows you're not like that."

Violeta extricated herself from the meeting and hurried home. She had work to do, and lots of it.

She was glad Melody couldn't hear Joe Junior. To her, his praise would be a condemnation. But if anything was to improve in the sovren, it could only happen with the cooperation of the Culvers.

Because Violeta had the sovren's directors as customers, she had their ear. It might not be much, but it was better than nothing.

* * *

If Mel noticed her at the stove for hours at a time, steaming roots in the moka pot's tiny chamber, she didn't comment. Then again, Melody was busier herself, teaching adult reading classes at the old church two nights a week now.

A week after the meeting with Joe Junior, Dottie Culver herself rode up on horseback like some antebellum plantation mistress, accompanied by two hired hands.

Violets dried her hands and stepped out onto her porch. "Mrs. C! What a surprise!"

"Hello Miss Violeta." She always pronounced her name in four syllables, like she was drawing it out to emphasize its exoticness. Vah-yo-let-uh? With a suspicious-sounding upturn at the end. *If that's even your real name*, Violeta could imagine her adding. "I'm here for the medicines my son ordered from you."

She didn't usually take delivery personally, but perhaps even the Culvers felt under pressure these days.

"Follow me," Violeta said. "You order is out back."

She didn't know Dottie well, but she'd chatted with her at church. They had both volunteered to cook for an All Saints Day charity picnic once.

Dottie was soft-spoken but self-assured, a redhead whose hair was surely dyed at her age, though where she got the coloring was anybody's guess. She wasn't exactly *friendly*, but Violeta saw in her contemporary somebody who at least remembered a time before Culver Freehold, before sovrens, before directors and subjects. A time when everybody paid lip service to the idea of equality.

Violeta walked the three of them around to the shed that housed raw materials as well as Culver orders. This was her chance to use her influence. The family matriarch would have a softer heart than her husband and son.

She cleared her throat. "I was just remembering the time we worked together at the parish picnic, preparing food for the residents of the Park."

The Park was a severely misnamed favela that had accreted within a former parking garage that once accommodated visitors to the downtown area. Now there weren't enough working cars to need a garage, and the Park served as a shelter for the poorest souls in the area.

Dottie chuckled. "Oh, I haven't thought about that in so long. That was such fun."

Violeta furrowed her brow. *Fun* is not how she would have described it. "I feel like we have a similar opportunity."

Dottie turned toward her and Violeta faltered momentarily.

"Another opportunity to do something to help those less fortunate. Like we did back then." She swallowed. "Fun."

Dottie smiled tightly, a smile that didn't reach her eyes. "Help who?"

"The Wilbur refugees, for one." Violeta considered for a moment. "Honestly, a lot of people are struggling right here. A lot of crops were lost. The families living within the Park—"

Dottie shook her head. "My dear, the picnic was one thing. We helped our own. And to be frank, I helped because it does people good to see everybody taking a turn. But the folk of the Park are mostly criminals. They don't deserve our pity."

Before she could catch herself, Violeta blurted, "Surely you can't—"

"Would you spend a day inside the Park? An hour? Would you even walk through it without accompaniment?"

Violeta opened her mouth but shut it again. She had never spent a minute in the Park since it *became* the Park.

"As for the storm refugees," Dottie continued, "the real workers are staying there, rebuilding, not coming here looking for handouts." She held up her list of receivables and checked items off. "Lazy people are basically thieves, when you think about it."

Violeta blinked. "I've seen some of them. They come to me for remedies for their injuries and such. They, well, the ones I've seen look like starving, sick, poor people. Not like a threat."

Dottie turned. "People come to you for medical care?"

Violeta stopped short. She didn't want to appear to be claiming to be a doctor. "Well, for salves, tinctures, herbs."

"How do they pay?"

"Some of them barter what they have, like most people in this—like most people. Some of them don't have…I mean they…I try to help where I can."

Dottie straightened. "So, you give away pharmaceuticals, made with products grown on our land and herbs you scavenge from our property. The same pharmaceuticals we pay you to prepare for us."

Violeta's pulse quickened. She had misplayed her hand. "No, not the same—"

"It sounds like we're being overcharged. And then you share our largess as your own, letting people praise your name and curse ours. You demand payment from us but you give away medicines to outsiders, to rapists and thieves."

Dottie hurried to the back door of Violeta's house, with Violeta in tow. "I don't—"

"How long has it been since your husband died?"

"What?"

"Several years, no? Yet you live in this big house by yourself. How do you manage to maintain it?"

Violeta bit off a response. This witch didn't need to know anything about Melody.

The Culver matriarch gestured to her assistants. "It seems we've been overpaying. Go through her shelves and take anything that looks useful."

Violeta started to protest but quieted at an upheld hand.

She blinked back tears as Dottie's men raided her stores, taking not just herbs and medicines, but armfuls of items of no likely value to the peacekeepers. Essential oils. Candles. Face wax.

"I'll need to have a talk with my son," Dottie said on her way out. "We don't take kindly to people who hold back from us or threaten our way of life."

* * *

Violeta didn't want to wait for Melody in her empty house. She needed her now—needed her comfort, but also her fierceness. She locked up and headed out to the church.

She was jumpy as she walked, half expecting Joe Culver or a pack of bullyboys to step from the lengthening shadows and shake her down for whatever else Dottie thought she owed them.

Thinking of Dottie made her burn with shame. How had she imagined she could influence the Culver family? She had been a fool.

She wasn't sure what she expected when she slipped into the near-empty church—people reading aloud, perhaps, or a phonics lesson. Instead, Melody and around thirty others sat on folding chairs at the front of the nave, in hushed conversation. Violeta saw plenty of open books as she approached—bibles and missals—but they were strewn throughout the pews, an afterthought.

Then she saw Nico. What was this? Nico learned to read years ago. Melody herself taught him; it was Violeta's first memory of her. Was he helping her teach? But if so, why did he sit in the middle of the group rather than at the front?

In any case, Nico was a good boy, but he was no teacher.

This was no reading group.

"Vi!"

Melody had noticed her at last.

She looked around. There were people Nico's age. Elderly people, too. Women and men. Strong farm workers, malnourished people. Men and women Violeta had treated for maladies from minor to chronic, and strangers as well.

She thought back to a dozen arguments with Melody. To each time she shushed her lest some customer should overhear her rants against the Culvers and carry word back to them. She had thought Melody just talked big.

This was some sort of activist group.

For a moment, Violeta's cheeks burned. Melody had kept all this from her?

Well. Why shouldn't she? Violeta built her whole life on laying low and hoping that if she didn't offend the powerful they would throw her a scrap now and then.

Where had that gotten her?

Melody had been the smart one: you could not shame the powerful and corrupt into making things better. Change came from without.

She straightened. "Whatever you're planning," she said, "I want in."

Nico stood. "Whela…do you know what you're saying?"

"My family spent generations giving ground. I thought it made us survivors, but I was foolish. Now I think it's time we stopped."

Melody smiled, a light turning on in the gloom. She didn't question her change of heart.

Violeta suppressed a rueful chuckle. Whatever this group planned was likely to end in disaster. So why did she feel so pleased?

* * *

Violeta followed Mel into the amphitheater by the courthouse, carrying a sack of hand-copied pamphlets. For two weeks, anything had seemed possible, but now that it was time to stop planning and take action, now that they were stepping from the shadows into the sunlight, things felt different.

She tried to clear her throat.

"Mel," she croaked. "Are you sure we're ready?"

But Melody had never shown the slightest doubt about anything. "When they see our numbers, when they realize they need us more than we need them, they'll negotiate."

Violeta nodded, but the roiling in her stomach continued.

On the stage, a mass trial was underway. Four men and a woman stood in a row, wrists bound in front of them. The sovren had a functioning public address system they trotted out for events like this. The judge detailed the charges against the first defendant—drunkenness during work hours. Once all the charges were read, each defendant would have the opportunity to beg for leniency.

Mel and her cohort wound their way through the crowd. Usually only a dozen or so sadistic voyeurs attended the public corrections, but there were ten times as many today. The Culvers had to know something was awry.

They went right to the stage, and a couple of Melody's more physically imposing supporters climbed up and quietly crowded the judge away from the microphone.

Nico helped Melody up; Violeta had misgivings about him being here, and with his bullyboy nightstick, but she was glad for Melody to have a bodyguard.

Mel took the mic and started in on her speech. It was nothing Violeta hadn't heard her go on about before, but this time she spoke in the open, within sight of the Culvers' seat of power.

Melody went into a chant of "United people cannot be defeated," and the crowd took it up enthusiastically. Something surged inside Violeta. Maybe this could work.

Movement behind her chased the thought away. Violeta turned toward the square's entrance and saw an enormous mob of bullyboys—almost a third the size of the gathered crowd. They stood still, not advancing or hitting anybody with their sticks. What were they doing?

Given that the bullyboys were largely drafted, just like Nico, surely some of them shared his sympathies. Or they didn't, but enforcing Culver law was one thing, while attacking a crowd of your neighbors, friends, and possibly loved ones, was another.

Melody's voice went silent, and Violeta spun to face the stage. Had something happened? But no, her mouth still moved.

From the crowd, one of the activists produced a bullhorn and passed it up. Mel took it and began chanting again, the crowd roaring with approval.

An actual working bullhorn.

More peacekeepers arrived. Were half the sovren's young men bullyboys?

These peacekeepers wore hard-coated padding, like the football players from Violeta's childhood. While they hung back for now, they all held their nightsticks at the ready. The sight of them in the same posture, sticks up, sent a chill through her.

She dropped the pamphlets and pushed toward the stage, but the crowd ebbed and flowed like a herd ready to stampede. No matter how she shoved, she could not get closer.

"Run!" she yelled. "This is about to get ugly!"

She barely heard herself—no chance the sound would reach Melody and Nico.

An odd percussion, like claves, drew her attention. The peacekeepers tapped their nightsticks against their chest pads in unison, making a hollow pinging sound. All of them beating together generated enough din to drown out Melody's voice.

Violeta felt sick. These weren't run-of-the-mill bullyboys. The conscripts barely got a day's training before being turned loose, nightstick in hand, on their fellow residents—the mall cops of their generation. *These* boys were organized. The Culvers must have created a force specifically for taking down insurrections.

The bullyboys advanced methodically and inexorably, tapping once per step. The crowd tried to back away, but there was nowhere to go. Violeta's neighbors crowded against her, trapping her in the square.

The bullyboys kept coming, content to crush everybody together.

With no room to back up, a pocket of demonstrators rushed the line, braving the sticks. Just like that, the battle ignited, bullyboys swinging nightsticks and cracking heads.

Protesters and bystanders alike went down, except at the site of the first rush, where a bullyboy was submerged beneath a human tsunami.

Now there was a gap, and everybody still standing seemed to sense it. The bullyboys swung wildly, all discipline and unison gone.

Violeta lunged toward Melody once again, but the people around her wanted *out*, so that was the only direction she could go. As the wave carried her, she turned to see Nico jump off the stage. *Please, God,* she thought, *bring them both back to me.*

Something cracked against her side and the air exploded from her, but still the crowd pulled, even as all thought left her. She worked to stay upright, planting one foot in front of the other and not worrying about where the tide took her. The sun disappeared behind a roof, she tripped over a cot, and landed in a pile of trash.

Somebody—a girl not quite Nico's age—held out a hand. "Come, mama. You're not safe. You need to come further in, to where the peacekeepers won't go."

* * *

Being in the Park was like being on the wrong side of a speaker, or inside one. Sounds were loud but garbled. Shouts and screams—did they come from outside or from within? Smoke wafted from somewhere, and Violeta tried not to think about what might be burning.

She could have tried to stop this. Could have been a voice for caution. She knew, better than Mel. She knew powerful people always had more resources, and no compunction against using them.

Instead she'd joined in, like a fool. She laughed humorlessly until the fire in her rib brought her up wheezing.

Time passed, or it didn't—a minute could have been an hour. At some point somebody led her to an impromptu infirmary, wrapped her with a makeshift compression bandage, and showed her to a relatively quiet spot. Finally, something she understood. Something she had skills for. So she went to work applying bandages to other people, cleaning wounds, stitching cuts.

If she'd had her herbs and her moka pot, she could have made salves to ease the healing, but she made do with what she found. She threw herself into the work, until she stopped hearing the sounds of destruction outside.

At some point, the sun set. At some point, things quieted.

The sky lightened, daybreak on its way, but over what? How long before they fully grasped what had happened yesterday?

Violeta found stairs and staggered from the scene, toward home.

Her house was still as she'd left it—an advantage to living on the edge of the swamp, relatively far from the seat of Culver power. She let herself in, cleaned up, and rebandaged herself.

She prepared a steaming cup of matcha and sat at her kitchen table, debating what to do next. Find Melody? Hide before somebody came looking for *her*?

A rap on the door made her spill her tea. Violeta peeked through her window, only to come face to face with Dottie Culver and two of her lackeys.

A fist gripped her heart. They'd come for her.

But if so, why knock? Why not break the door down?

Violeta unlatched the front door. "Yes?"

Dottie breezed in. "Change of plans," she boomed. "Time for you to prove yourself. Time to help your people."

She trailed Dottie on autopilot, fighting to mask her injury. "What do you mean?"

"It was as we feared. Those bayou refugees you defended have infiltrated the sovren and commandeered the Park. There are untold numbers of rapists and murders attacking Peacekeepers and then disappearing into the darkness. We have an infestation to clear out. We have some working guns, but not enough."

Violeta frowned, trying to make sense of this. "I…don't make weapons."

Dottie stared at her. "Don't be a fool. We need your specialties. Medicines, but more than that. I hear stories about products you make. Doubtless many of them are the tales of rubes you extract chits from in exchange forsnake oil. But if you can help your sovren, it's time for you to step up and do it."

"Step up?" Violeta tried to take a deep breath, but the pain in her side wouldn't let her.

"Teas or salves or pills or whatever it is you make. Something to make our boys not feel pain when they're injured, or to make them more alert, or to make them able to go longer without sleep." Dottie browsed from shelf to shelf, examining bottles and tins as though she could possibly identify their contents.

"Maybe I could help more if you hadn't stolen a couple shelves' worth of ingredients two weeks ago," Violeta muttered at her back.

"What?"

"Nothing!" she answered, a little too loudly. "Just thinking out loud, trying to come up with ideas!"

"Well keep up!" Dottie admonished. She peered at Violeta. "What's wrong with you? Are you sick?"

Violeta coughed and nodded. "Yes. Sick."

"Well we don't have time for weakness right now. Suck it up. Prove to me that I was wrong to doubt you. Can you help?"

"I don't—" Violeta caught herself.

Dottie didn't know. Didn't know about her participation in the protest, didn't know about Melody, didn't know half what Violeta did about roots and herbs. Violeta wasn't the leader that Melody was and she wasn't a fighter by anybody's definition, but here was her power.

"I may have what you need." She pulled two khat leaves from the shrub, stuck one in her mouth and gave the other to Dottie.

Dottie peered at it suspiciously, but finally put it in her mouth. "Disgusting," she said, making a face.

"It's khat," Violeta said. "Ten times stronger than coffee ever was. It will do what you want."

Dottie's eyes widened. "It's like having electricity inside me."

Violeta nodded. "I chew it every day. This'll make your bully—this'll make your peacekeepers feel like supermen."

"I'll take all you have."

Violeta shook her head. "I barely have enough for my own use. I don't have nearly enough for all your men."

"Then why tell me about it?"

"I can brew it into a tea." She pointed at the moka pot next to the stove. "In liquid form, a little goes a long way. And, naturally, I can provide you with the usual painkillers and so on."

"It won't be too diluted?"

"I can make it work."

Dottie nodded. "Excellent. I need enough for a hundred men, and I need it tomorrow."

Violeta sucked in a breath, and then winced. Dottie wasn't paying attention to her, though. "I'll find a way," she replied. "Anything to help my people."

* * *

She needed help. She couldn't possibly manage what she envisioned on her own. Once Dottie left she headed toward town, toward the spot where she hoped she might find some compatriots.

The first person to greet her at the church was Nico. The boy grabbed her in a hug, making her cry out from the pain.

"What's wrong?" he asked, releasing her so abruptly she nearly fell.

"Nothing that won't heal. What's the news? Where is Melody?"

His face crumbled. "They got her. They got almost everybody who was onstage. They plan to hold a sentencing once they get the Park under control. I don't know if that means work farms, beatings, or...or..."

She put a hand on his chest. "We must hurry, then."

He frowned. "Hurry?"

"I need your help. We have a big order to fill. The biggest."

He made a face. "What? I thought you came to help *here*. We have injured people. They need treatment. Medicine. They need you."

She put a hand on his arm. "Meeho, this battle's not over yet. We can tend to the wounded afterward, but first, we still have a chance to strike a blow."

"A chance to…" He blinked and straightened. "Tell me what you need."

* * *

Nico gathered members of Melody's group, and Violeta gave them detailed lists, with descriptions and illustrations. Raw pokeweed to induce convulsions, fennel to mask the flavor, and other herbs to dilute the mix. Then she went home to work.

She set water to pre-boil and pulled the moka pot's pieces down from its shelf. She frowned as she chopped up pokeweed for the filter basket. What would her whela think if she could see her?

Violeta had felt so adult the first time she was permitted a demitasse of her own. She'd savored the hot mouthful, the sweetness of the sugar tempering the mild bitterness of the espresso. There was something life-giving about the ritual, about standing around the kitchen counter sharing a drink and a little conversation.

Once she could no longer make coffee she'd used the pot to make medicine, and that seemed a worthy continuation of its legacy. But now she was using the pot to make poison.

When had Violeta become the sort of person who would do this?

She glanced over her shoulder at their room, the bed inside still unmade. She'd last slept in it the night before the demonstration, with Melody by her side. When would she see her lover again?

She set her teeth and poured hot water into the boiler. Sometimes poison and medicine were the same, and the only difference was where and how you applied it.

From the living room, she heard Nico arrive with more supplies. He didn't interrupt her work, though—he simply took his place by her side and helped her collect each cupful of brew as it came out of the pot.

The hours passed companionably. Violeta doubted she went faster with him underfoot, but she also doubted she had the strength to work without him.

"Whela," Nico began, crushing some poke berries, "will this kill them?"

She sighed. Who would be losing loved ones in this struggle?

"I don't know for sure," she said after a moment. "It depends how much they drink and…and on other factors I can't guess. How strong their digestive and immune systems are."

He bit his lip, but kept working. He understood this had become more than a demonstration, more even than an uprising. This had become a war. In the Park they'd seen that not all the bullyboys were conscripts.

And those that were had watched their sergeants lead the charge against ordinary people, unarmed people, for merely speaking out. The time to choose a side had come for her, and it had come for them also.

She caught a whiff of the brew and made a face. The house would reek for days. It would take the most thorough cleaning to rid her moka pot of the pokeweed toxin so that she could drink again.

"Why go through so much trouble?" Nico asked at some point in the night. "The peacekeepers don't know what khat tastes like. Why not just give them the poison and tell them it's khat?"

She turned from the fire and squinted at him. Had he been here all along? The day blurred.

"If I make it too strong, they will vomit before the brew has time to do more than inconvenience them. I need to…I need to…"

"Whela, when was the last time you slept?"

She turned toward the heat. "I'll sleep when this is over."

More likely she'd die when this was over, but she kept that to herself.

"Let me do this. You're hurt and you're tired."

She tried to argue, but she retained so little energy that her resistance was token at best.

* * *

Once the laced stimulants were delivered, there was nothing to do but wait. Nico gathered what allies he could find and planned their next moves, while Violeta cared for the wounded at the church.

She wanted to go downtown and see what happened, but she would only be a liability. Instead she went home and waited for word.

Around dusk, word came, in the form of Dottie and Joe Junior, pounding on her door.

"Let us in or we'll burn the house down with you inside," Joe Junior shouted.

Violeta debated whether she had enough painkillers to make burning to death endurable, and decided not to put the question to the test. She unlocked the door and pulled it open.

Joe pointed a gun shakily. Behind him his horse snorted and stomped, as though it understood what the gun was capable of.

"What have you done?" Dottie demanded.

Violeta didn't bother replying. They knew, obviously.

A popping of gravel, accompanied by a rumble she had only heard infrequently in the last two decades, drew her attention. Joe Junior and Dottie also looked over their shoulders, toward the bend in the road to her house. Violeta's eyes widened as first one and then a second pickup truck bounded into view.

The lead truck stopped in front of the house and Nico leapt from the passenger seat.

"Hey Whela. Mrs. C. Joe Junior. Didn't expect to see y'all here. Did you come to negotiate?"

Joe Junior brandished his gun. "Don't come any closer."

Nico held his hands up, but said, "Or what? You'll shoot us all?"

That's when Violeta realized the trucks carried close to a dozen men and women between them.

Joe Junior pointed the gun at her. "We were just leaving. Violeta here is coming with us."

She struggled to draw a breath. Why was she so resigned to dying only minutes ago, and yet so afraid now?

"Nah she ain't," Nico called out. Behind him, the truck revved its engine as if in punctuation. "There's only one way you get out of here," Nico said, "and that's if you get on your horses and leave, right now, by yourselves."

Joe Junior seemed ready to argue, but Dottie gripped his shoulder, which seemed to take the starch from him. He nodded slowly and backed toward his horse, keeping the gun pointed at Violeta the whole time.

"This isn't over. Now we know who our friends are, and who they aren't."

The seconds crawled, but moment by moment the Culvers mounted and backed away, finally turning and galloping off.

Violeta sagged against the door post, and Nico hurried to her.

"They'll be back," she said, gripping his arm.

He nodded. "They will. And with more guns. They still have people who think their odds are better throwing in with the Culvers. We need to hide you."

"What about—"

"Melody's waiting for you. With half the peacekeepers sick or deserting, we managed to rescue her and the others."

Violeta let out a breath. Starting over, even with a price on her head, was one thing. Doing so by herself was another.

Loading up her belongings was a blur. She'd always held on to things for sentimental reasons, but there was no time now, and little space in the back of the trucks. Medicinals and supplies were what she needed. She would be too busy for reminiscing for a while.

Nico slammed the tailgate. "Are we done?"

Violeta swallowed as Nico's friends cinched tarps down over her belongings. Another era of her life ended now, with another retreat. But definitely not a surrender.

"Wait," she said. "One more thing." She hurried inside and grabbed her moka pot.

She had little room for sentiment now, but this old moka pot was *her*. Built to nourish, but adaptable and even deadly, if the need arose.

"We might need more khat tea," she said, at Nico's raised eyebrow.

"Or more poison," he replied.

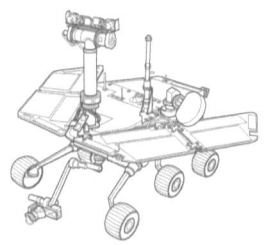

Sassi's Last Ride

Alethea Kontis

Good afternoon, honored guests, and welcome to this Starlight A-List Self-Driving Intelligent Shuttle! You can call me "Sassi."

You will soon be zooming past the moon on the StarlightX Epsilon-Heavy rocketship—what a thrill! This exclusive courtesy limousine provides round-the-clock, certified germ-free service from…Buckhead, Atlanta Midtown, and surrounding neighborhoods…to beachside Launch Complex 39A in picturesque Cape Canaveral, Florida.

As you board, please select the first available Rolf Benz 3398 recliner, fasten your customized seat belt, and make yourself at home. That's right: shoes optional! Our EQAir HEPASupreme purifiers are currently eliminating all latent airborne influenza molecules, as well as any embarrassing odors your neighbors may currently be experiencing. (But not you, because *you* smell amazing!)

Once you have fastened your disinfected and sterilized buckle, tighten your seat belt by pulling on the loose end of the strap. To release your belt, lift up on the buckle. We suggest that you keep your seat belt fastened throughout the journey, as some of our other shuttles have reported random pandemic mobs, and we may need to accelerate quickly without warning. We will begin moving once the bulletproof, quarantine-level doors are completely sealed.

If you have a registered support animal, please insert their vaccine credentials into the dashboard slot provided. Have a promo code to skip this step? You may enter this code now.

Please stow allotted carry-on items under your luxury recliner or in your personal overhead compartment. Controls to tilt back or warm your leather seat are located on the right-hand console. Hungry? Feel free to partake of unlimited snacks from the console on your left. This limousine supplies the finest foam meals that molecular gastronomy has to offer! Thirsty? We carry a variety of Coke products, as well as an array of liquors supplied by our sponsor, Armageddon Gin. "Drink up, it's Armageddon!" with Armageddon Gin.

Should you choose to make any purchases as you relax along our journey, they will be packaged up and awaiting your arrival at the StarlightX launch pad. Please be sure to indicate if the items are for you, or if you would like to have them gift-wrapped at no extra charge.

Want to upgrade your carry-on altogether? We've got the perfect Hermès Birkin bag for you! If you have downloaded the SASSI app, click on the horse and carriage now to access our exclusive Starlight Shop! Choose from a variety of hides, including lizard, ostrich, and saltwater crocodile. Each bag is lined with a goat skin interior to match the color you choose and comes with pure palladium lock, keys, buckle and studs. The diamonds are in the details: customize your bag to your personal exquisite style with additional diamonds! They say you can't take it with you, but you can take this Birkin bag!

Our travel time today will be approximately…seven hours…once our cabin is full. Please don't worry if your party is incomplete; this shuttle has been programmed to return to the very same destinations on a continuous loop. No one of note will be left behind! This is limousine trip…372…but that doesn't mean you're not our top priority!

My sensors have indicated a personal electronic device. Power outlets for your devices can be located along the front edge of both the left and right armrests. Diamond-encrusted headphones, provided by Focal Utopia, are located in your overhead compartment.

Through your SASSI app, you can access a wide selection of bingeable movies and award-winning television series, as well as Cox High Speed Internet and Streaming services. Drown out the screams of the dying with an episode from one of our four approved live channels! Now Showing: The Last Best British Bake Off! Desperate Housewives of Mars! And this breaking news: *The WHO has declared—*

Oops! My apologies. The content of this report has been classified as "startling" and suppressed based on your desired emotional support level. Part of this Starlight Shuttle's continuing mission: to provide only the best, for the best!

Oxygen and air pressure levels are constantly monitored in the limousine cabin. In the unlikely event that something or someone manages to break through the doors' tamper-resistant seals, an oxygen mask will automatically descend from the ceiling in front of you. In the event that you simply desire oxygen, please press the O2 button on your right-hand console and select from the variety of limited edition RareAir Oxygen flavors available. Enjoy the last of this Rare Air!

To start the flow of oxygen, pull the mask toward you. Place it firmly over your nose and mouth, secure the elastic band behind your head, and breathe normally. Although the bag does not inflate, oxygen is still flowing. If you are traveling with a child or someone who requires assistance, secure your mask first, and then assist the other person.

I would like to take this opportunity to remind you, my esteemed guests, that this is a non-smoking, non-vaping limousine. Please see your left-hand console for a wide selection of narcotic, anti-depressant, and pain relief patches, courtesy of Johnson, Pfizer & Roche. After all, why put the "panic" in Pandemic?

Passenger...3...I notice that your resting heart rate has dropped below healthful levels. Should you like to activate your seat's vibration mode to stimulate blood flow, please press the V button, located on your right-hand console. Need an extra jolt? Energy drinks and caffeine booster patches are also available.

We are now crossing the Georgia-Florida border—may I be the first to welcome you to the Sunshine State! If you would like to experience palm trees, ocean breezes, and clear skies firsthand, please turn your OculusInfinity to Channel 2. Pokémon players, this is a PokeStop!

Florida is the former home of the now-burned Evergreen National Forest and the now-abandoned Disney World. Don't miss next summer's grand opening of Disney Universe, conveniently located a shuttle ride away from the Casaroja Colony on Mars! Click the hidden Mickey on your SASSI app and use our exclusive promo code: STARLIGHTXTRA to save on tickets now!

In the market for souvenirs from your soon-to-be former residence? Now's a perfect time to peruse last-minute items from good old planet Earth. Everything purchased during your ride to the StarlightX rocketship is completely duty free!

Third time's the charm…remember your last precious moments on this planet with the Pandemic Three charm, exclusively from Pandora. Click the flashing crown icon at the bottom of your SASSI app to purchase!

We know your carry-on is packed to the brim…but there's always room for diamonds. From engagement rings to zero-gravity wristwatches and space suit cuffs, give your special someone a gift that will last. Click the spinning diamond icon right now to receive exclusive offers from Harry Winston, Cartier, and Bulgari. This world may be ending, but diamonds are forever!

Nothing could have saved Earth, but you can save it over and over again in Call of Duty: Pandemic! This time around, you and your strike team can kill off the mobs before they spread the deadly influenza virus. Turn your OculusInfinity to Channel 3 to test your skills now. Enter code PAND3COD on the SASSI app any time during this ride for half off a lifetime subscription!

Attention, exalted guests: we are now passing through the outer walls of the Canaveral National Fortress. Congratulations! In this Safe Zone, you will never again have to encounter the unwashed masses. Local time is…7:07 am…and the temperature is…109 degrees.

I'm sure you're bursting with excitement, but please remain in your luxury recliner with your seat belt fastened until the limousine comes to a complete stop. Be sure to check around your recliner for shoes, protective eyewear, and any personal electronic devices you may have brought on board with you. Please use caution when opening your personal overhead bin, as some articles may have shifted during our journey.

And here we are! A PanXPurel dispenser is located beneath your left-hand armrest, for your germ-free pleasure. Please watch your step as you disembark at the launch pad!

If you took advantage of any of the exclusive offers during this trip, lighted green arrows on the platform will guide you to the appropriate kiosk. Just scan your fingerprint to collect your purchases and enjoy!

On behalf of Starlight Shuttle Enterprises, I'd like to thank you for the pleasure of your company on this trip. It has been a delight. I wish you a safe flight from this germ-riddled planet to the paradise you've always dreamed of!

Passenger…3…did you forget something? Not to worry. Simply remain in your luxury recliner with your seatbelt fastened. This Starlight A-List Self-Driving Intelligent Shuttle operates on a continuous loop and all trips are complimentary. We will soon be returning to…Buckhead, Atlanta

Midtown, and surrounding neighborhoods. Return travel time will be approximately…seven hours. Sit back, relax, and let Sassi take the wheel!

"*CDC Command Center. Come in, Command. This is Lark. Are you reading me?*"

"*Hey-ho, Larky-poo! Reading you loud and clear, my little songbird.*"

"*Shut up, George. I mean, Command.*"

"'*George' is fine. It's not like anyone else is around to listen.*"

"*You can say that again. It's been a long, lonely day out here.*"

"*Have you really been camped out on that platform since the crack of dawn?*"

"*Hell yes! I told you there was still a shuttle left running a loop in this area, I just didn't know its schedule. And…voila!*"

"*So because I know you love hearing it: you were right.*"

"*You owe me chocolate.*"

"*How on Earth can you still want that chocolate Santa? Who knows how old that thing is. Far more nostalgic than delicious at this point.*"

"*Chocolate is chocolate, George. That crusty old Santa is mine.*"

"*Ha! Fine. You and your sweet tooth can collect when you get your smart ass back from that ghost town. I'll see if I can convince Reggie to throw in those ancient Peeps of his for good measure.*"

"*You're a star, George.*"

"*Are you kidding? You're the star today. I still can't believe any of that old tech is still running. The one-percenters fled Earth for Mars over a year ago.*"

"*An electric, solar-powered, self-driving limousine in a world under quarantine…probably bulletproof and riot-proof, too. Nothing short of an act of god would have stopped this shuttle from running.*"

"*Was it empty?*"

"*Sort of. I did have to eighty-six a corpse on my way in. Fully desiccated, though, so it wasn't too bad. Didn't even smell. The air scrubbers on this thing must be insane.*"

"*You know, I bet that's why the limo kept running. It thought it had a passenger.*"

"*Not taking that bet, because you're probably right, and I want to keep my chocolate.*"

"*So how's it look?*"

"*Unbelievable. You should see the inside of this thing, George. Mood lighting, leather seats, gold and diamond headphones…are those fur-lined slippers? Ridiculous.*"

"*That's great, Lark, but stay focused. I was talking about the plan. How's that look? Will it work?*"

"*Oh, right. Well, the fact that I've tapped into the shuttle's communications is a good sign. What I need to do now is crack the admin and get into the master*" *control so I can reroute it to where we want it to go instead of its previously programmed destination."*

"Excellent. And then we can send it anywhere?"

"Anywhere with a decent road system."

"Good. With any luck, we'll be able to backtrack it to us, load it with vaccine, and then send it up I-75 and out into the world."

"It's not luck, George. It's my mad skills. You're welcome."

Good afternoon, honored guests, and welcome to this Starlight A-List Self-Driving Intelligent Shuttle!

"Ha! What was that about your mad skills?"

"Hush. I just triggered the onboard monologue. Give me a sec…"

You can call me "Sassi."

"Did she say 'Sassi?' That acronym didn't spell anything even close to 'Sassi!'"

"The super-rich don't care, George. They never did. If they had, they might have stayed on the planet."

"And if they had stayed on the planet, we would have had to manufacture that many more vaccines."

"We don't even know the current population, George. I still say we could have tried this months ago."

"Based on US population at the time of pandemic, we needed a year to produce enough vaccine for everyone—"

"Which, even based on an undetermined death toll, is significantly less than it used to be."

"— and no one wanted to risk your life before we were ready except you. I'm not having this fight again, Lark."

This exclusive courtesy limousine provides round-the-clock, certified germ-free service from…Buckhead, Atlanta Midtown and surrounding neighborhoods…to beachside Launch Complex 39A in picturesque Cape Canaveral, Florida.

"Shit. This limo's been driving back and forth to Florida for an entire year?"

"Well, we knew it was going somewhere. No wonder you were waiting on the platform so long."

As you board, please select the first available Rolf Benz 3398 recliner, fasten your customized seat belt, and make yourself at home. That's right: shoes optional! Our EQAir HEPASupreme purifiers are currently eliminating all latent airborne influenza molecules, as well as any embarrassing odors your neighbors may currently be experiencing. (But not you, because *you* smell amazing!)

"You hear that, George? I smell amazing."

"I'm amazed you can smell anything at all with those insane scrubbers."

We suggest that you keep your seat belt fastened throughout the journey, as some of our other shuttles have reported random pandemic mobs, and we may need to accelerate quickly without warning.

"*Whoa, Lark. 'Other shuttles?' In all the beltline traffic cams, you've only spotted this one limousine on the move?*"

"*Yes.*"

"*Where do you suppose those other shuttles are?*"

"*'Launch Complex 39A in picturesque Cape Canaveral, Florida,' I'm guessing. The limos would have deactivated once the rockets launched. Thank the Machines of the Universe for the glitch that kept this one running.*"

"*Your corpse-guy might have been that glitch.*"

"*Thanks, corpse-guy!*"

"*Lark, do you think we could get to the rest of those limos? If this crazy plan of yours works, having a fleet to disseminate the influenza vaccine would be a godsend.*"

"*It took me long enough to catch this fish, George. I can't even begin to fathom how long it would take to break through the walls at Canaveral. That place is a fortress.*"

"*Yes or no, Lark.*"

"*Fine. Yes. Time permitting.*"

We will begin moving once the bulletproof, quarantine-level doors are completely sealed.

"*You might want to shove a case or something in that door.*"

"*Way ahead of you. Not that I would mind an accidental trip to the beach…*"

"*You get this vaccine out to the rest of the country and I'll drive you there myself. On purpose.*"

"*Careful, George. I'll hold you to that. Mostly because I know you're out of chocolate. In the meantime—*"

If you have a registered support animal, please insert their vaccine credentials into the dashboard slot provided. Have a promo code to skip this step? You may enter this code now.

"*Oh, snap.*"

"*That's rich. Pun intended.*"

"*Hey, Lark, how many of those animals do you suppose were carrying influenza?*"

"*More than one, that's for sure.*"

"*One's all it takes. How many people do you think are still alive on Mars?*"

"*We don't even know the current population of our own country, George. How am I supposed to know what it is on Mars?*"

"*It's just…all those poor people. Pun intended.*"

"Indeed. Bless their hearts."

We carry a variety of Coke products, as well as an array of liquors supplied by our sponsor, Armageddon Gin. "Drink up, it's Armageddon!" with Armageddon Gin.

"Sorry. It looks like we're going to have to suffer through this monologue until I can get to the other side."

"Bring back some of that liquor, will you?"

"Not if I drink it all first. Which I will if I have to put up with any more of your jokes."

Please don't worry if your party is incomplete; this shuttle has been programmed to return to these very same destinations on a continuous loop. No one of note will be left behind!

"Ouch. Guess your ill-fated passenger wasn't noteworthy enough."

"Poor corpse-guy. He found out the hard way that the Richie Rich Rocketship waits for no one."

"You think he was dead before or after they left for Mars?"

"If you want to come out here with a dustpan, George, I'll show you where I shoved him. You're welcome to perform the autopsy."

"You're just jealous because you couldn't perform an autopsy yourself if you tried."

"Oh, I could try. You volunteering?"

"Come on. You know I'm just giving you shit because the fate of this country is sort of in your hands right now."

"Frustrating, isn't it? Now you know how I felt, useless IT girl stuck in that bunker with all you genius scientists working day and night for the past year. Damn right this is my day! I deserve a gold star for finding the strength to last this long."

"And chocolate."

"Hells yes. Your chocolate and Reggie's Peeps and any other sugar-containing substance I can get my brilliant little hands on."

Drown out the screams of the dying with an episode from one of our four approved live channels!

"Wow. That's gross. I hate the rich."

"You can't say that any more, Lark."

"Why not?"

"Because, technically, we're the rich now."

"Oh, wow. That's a brain melting concept. Okay…then I just hate you, George."

In the unlikely event that something or someone manages to break through the doors' tamper-resistant seals, an oxygen mask will automatically descend from the ceiling in front of you.

"*Whoa! Did old Sassi just say what I think she said?*"

"*YES!*"

"*Namid's going to be over the moon. Her team just completed successful aerosolized trials on the vaccine.*"

A variety of limited edition RareAir Oxygen flavors are currently available. Enjoy the last of this Rare Air!

"*Yes! We'll adapt Sassi's oxygen system as soon as you get back, Lark.*"

"*Perfect. I hoped there would be a way to disseminate the vaccine without one of our team having to be physically present. Limo or not, anyone in this shuttle would be shot on sight.*"

"*I know. But how do we let the current population know how to properly vaccinate themselves? Can we record over the original monologue? Is that something you can manage? Reggie has a great voice. I can have him draft something…or Namid…but will anyone trust it? There have been so many conflicting campaigns of disinformation, no one knows what to believe anymore.*"

"*Slow down, George. You're getting ahead of yourself. It's going to be so much easier than that.*"

"*How?*"

"*We create a rumor meme that says that the rich had the Pandemic Three vaccine all along.*"

"*Oh my god. That's it.*"

"*Yup. We say the rich were breathing in the vaccine on their limousines even before they left the planet. The second anyone catches a glimpse of this vehicle, folks will line up around the block to catch a whiff.*"

"*It's insane that people will believe a rumor over a legitimate employee of the CDC, but that's the world we live in now.*"

"*Have everybody there make a different graphic.*"

"*We'll include typos and everything, so people believe they're 'authentic.'*"

"*Perfect.*"

"*As soon as we've modified the limo, we can send them out.*"

"*Why wait? Send them now. Have the conspiracy nuts already on the lookout.*"

"*So our vaccine is actually going to be disseminated via…a viral meme and a conscripted limousine.*"

"*Right? It's so meta.*"

"*Lark, you're a genius.*"

"*I know. It's just annoying that I had to wait so long to prove it.*"

"*You never had to prove anything to us. You know that.*"

"*Yeah. But after so long on the bench, I needed to prove it to myself.*"

Please see your left-hand console for a wide selection of narcotic, anti-depressant, and pain relief patches, courtesy of Johnson, Pfizer & Roche. After all, why put the "panic" in Pandemic?

"Well, that's just hilarious."

"We can vaccinate those patches as well. Just in case."

"YES!"

"I didn't know you were so keen on drug patches, Lark."

"What did I tell you about shutting up, George? Oh! I just got through to the master control."

"Finally."

"Reprogramming the GPS route now."

We will soon be returning to…the Center for Disease Control. Return travel time will be approximately…twenty minutes.

"Can't wait."

"Doors closing. Oh, George, I can't believe this day is actually here. We finally get to save the world."

"It has been a long time coming, hasn't it? We'll be back to some semblance of civilization before you know it."

"Complete with chocolate and everything. What are we going to do with ourselves now?"

Sit back, relax, and let Sassi take the wheel!

"Well, Lark, I did promise you a beach vacation. How about Launch Complex 39A in picturesque Cape Canaveral, Florida?"

"Sounds perfect."

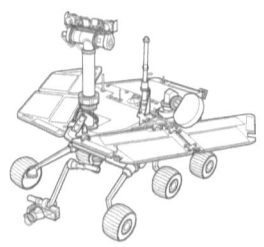

The Ghosts of Versailles

Kari Sperring

They gathered around the bed in the golden twilight. Pearly tears ran down alabaster complexions, elegant bejewelled fingers twisted in brocade garments or wound together as if in prayer. All of them stared down at the motionless figure that lay prone on the silken coverlet. *"Madame est morte,"* someone said. Someone else sobbed. From one of the concealed speakers came the plaintive whine of a Spanish greyhound. There were no more dogs at court: the last of them, the lapdog Friponne, had wound down some seventy years before.

There was a long silence.

Then Madame herself—the fair Minette, duchess of Orléans—said, "But I'm right here."

One by one, the courtiers turned and looked at her, perfect faces set in lines of unfamiliar puzzlement. They knew their roles, all of them, inside out. They had repeated them many times, though it grew harder with every passing century. They kept to the script, even as their ranks grew thinner and each of them had to access the back-up routines installed long ago to enable them, at need, to play parts other than those for which they were first designed.

Minette went on, "And I don't die until the end of the act. This is too soon."

"Then who is it?" asked the Chevalier de Lorraine, an unfamiliar uncertainty in his voice. "You," and his usual sneer appeared as he nodded towards Minette, "have shown no signs of decline."

There was another silence.

From the door where he stood guard, Monsieur d'Artagnan pushed his way forward through the throng. He stood at the bedside for a moment, looking down, then rolled the figure over. Its face was calm, blue eyes wide open. A low murmur ran through the company.

"It's Madame de Montespan," someone said.

Someone else, trying desperately to stick to the script, whispered "Poison."

"But she doesn't die," Minette said. "She just leaves when the king tires of her. And he hasn't even looked at her yet."

"She isn't even malfunctioning that much," Lorraine said. His right arm hung dead at his side; his left still functioned, but lately he had started to drop things. "It was mostly just her voice. And her left eye, sometimes."

D'Artagnan studied the still form. A long slit ran down the front of the Montespan's gown, cutting through the plas-flesh and carbon fibre structures of her chest. Where her core processor should be was only a film of torn wiring and a gaping hole.

Madame Minette's death was supposed to be murder, though no-one would ever be convicted.

D'Artagnan looked at the New King. "Sire, this is not an accident. Someone has done this. One of us has done this."

There was a long silence, broken only by someone whirring. They were accustomed to suspect one another: the script called for it. But none of those scripted deaths were like this. Finally, the New King said, "Do as you must, then, Captain," and turned and exited the room, accompanied by most of the court.

Minette said, "Who would do such a thing? It doesn't help the performance. We need her to play her role. There's none of us can take it over."

"One of us will have to upload her programming," Lorraine said. He cast a sidelong glance at Minette. "You, perhaps? Just think, you'd get two chances for the king's attention." He was built to dislike her: that was his nature. More recent events had sharpened his spite. "Perhaps you did this, for that very reason?"

Minette shook her head.

"If not you then who?" said Lorraine. "A long list, surely?"

He had a point: the Montespan was not popular, or, at least, she would not be, once she took her turn in the spotlight. But to dispose of her so early in the performance…

"It could not be La Vallière, for instance," Lorraine went on. "She would not. And could not."

That was undeniable. The delicate Louise de la Vallière, the king's first *maitresse en titre*, had been built to limp, to blush and demur. She had been amongst the earliest of the cast to fail: her role falling to one of the all-purpose models who had been designed only to fill background parts. She could barely speak; she moved through the motions of La Vallière's part without depth or understanding.

Only the main players were fully sentient. That was the last gift of the last Directorcrat. "You'll need freedom from the script now," she had said when she uploaded the new programme. "You've earned it." But the king—the Old King, the original, still fully functional back then—had decreed they continue to follow the script that glorified and upheld him. Accustomed to fear and obey, the courtiers had done as he desired.

His shadow was long. The New King had never, it appeared, so much as wondered about rescinding that command. "We never intended you to be alone," the Directorcrat had said, in those final months. "Before I die, I'll manumit you and give you access to the human levels. Maybe you can work out how to make the ships fly again."

D'Artagnan wished the Directorcrat was still with them. Her eyes had been everywhere. She would have known at once what had happened, and who was responsible. She would probably have been able to prevent the dismantling of the Montespan altogether.

Lorraine leant against the wall and examined the fingernails on his working hand. "The culprit needs to have retained good control over their limbs, otherwise the Montespan would be a far greater mess. That cuts down the list considerably. It excludes me, as it happens, but not you, Monsieur d'Artagnan, or Madame Minette. And then there's the question of those of us who can prove we were elsewhere when the attack occurred. When was the Montespan last seen in working order?"

Lorraine was neither pleasant nor altruistic, but he was clever and he was also easily bored. He would be an asset, d'Artagnan knew, to any investigation. D'Artagnan looked at Minette. "We should close off this room. I will set one of the guard to keep the door. Perhaps we might retire to your sitting room to consider the matter further?"

"Of course." Minette gathered her skirts. "You must consider my rooms at your entire disposal, Captain." She led them through two connecting doors and into her small parlour. This, d'Artagnan remembered, was the set for some of her most plaintive exchanges with her husband, and her heartbroken farewell to her lover, the king.

It might now be the set for her arrest. She remained perfectly composed as she took a seat by a window and indicated that, despite protocol, d'Artagnan might sit in her presence. "You, too, since you insist on staying," she added, to Lorraine. "But do not presume upon it."

A small smile played over Lorraine's lips as he selected a chair and dropped into it. His languid pose was somewhat hampered by his dead arm. Ignoring Minette, he turned to d'Artagnan. "Captain, do you consider it wise to allow Madame Minette to remain? Surely, as prime suspect, she should be safely locked away."

He took a great deal upon himself. D'Artagnan said, "Her guilt is a matter of speculation, Monsieur, not evidence."

"If you say so."

"His majesty entrusted the investigation to me," d'Artagnan said, mildly.

"So he did."

Minette said, "I didn't damage the Montespan. Why would I?"

That was a reasonable question. By the time the Montespan drew the king's eye, his interest in Madame Minette, and hers in him, was long over. She gained nothing by the Montespan's early death. If Minette hated anyone, it was Lorraine, who was designed to make trouble for her.

The list of those who disliked or resented the Montespan over the course of her scripted court life was long. He looked at Madame Minette. "Might I have paper, and something to write with?"

"Of course." She rose and went to a small bureau, returning with a sheaf of paper, a quill, and ink. "Will this suffice?"

"Thank you." The paper was self-cleansing and pre-programmed, of course, and the quill hid a perpetual stylus. The audiences liked to see the actors use archaic skills, like writing by hand. This paper was accustomed to recording the love notes Minette sent to the king. It resisted him, trying to create the usual words, even though he sent it the override the Directorcrat had taught him. The palace, the garden, the whole artificially beautiful court under the dome, clung tight to their original form and function, echoing the Old King who was their heart.

Had been. The loss of the Old King had been the greatest blow, after the death of the last Directorcrat. D'Artagnan sent the override again, and this time the paper complied. He began, methodically, to make a list of all those who hated the Montespan and still possessed enough function to overwhelm and dismember her.

* * *

"Humankind needs stories," the Directorcrat told d'Artagnan on one of their walks. "They're how we understand ourselves. You players remind us who we are." He had been proud of that, proud that she chose to confide in him, not one of the major courtiers. "But that's why," she said, when he asked. "The major players find it harder to think about matters outside their programmes. You were built to be more flexible, because you have to respond to the audience. You're designed to notice more."

He could not help wondering, now, what it was he had *failed* to notice. His initial list took up a full sheet and a half of the uncooperative paper. The script laid out where every member of the court was at every moment. Easy enough to work out when the Montespan was last active. Easy, too, to account for most of the active court in the time between her last appearance and the discovery of her remains. That allowed him to discount over half of his names. "Though not you, Monsieur," he observed to Lorraine.

"Nor Madame Minette," Lorraine said, and bowed to that lady. She ignored him. "Nor the Queen and her ladies, or the kitchen servants. Nor the king, for that matter, unless you account La Vallière as a secure witness."

The Queen was a minor, programmed mostly to sit and sew, or attend to her devotions. D'Artagnan had never once known her to deviate from her role: he was sure that if she had gone to Madame's rooms, someone would have noticed and commented on it. He would ask about her anyway. As to the New King…La Vallière could speak enough to answer simple questions. And the king, of all people, would have no reason to dispose of the Montespan so early in the play. She was too important to his story and his *gloire*, and his need for her was written into his programming.

To Lorraine, he said, "Since I must look into everyone on this list, and you are conveniently present, perhaps you could tell me what you were doing at the time the Montespan was most probably dismantled?"

Lorraine yawned: an affectation, as the courtiers no more felt fatigue than they did hunger. "Who can say, life being so flat at court these days?"

D'Artagnan had no time for archness. "I would imagine that you can say, given you are inevitably always with yourself. Or are you experiencing issues with your memory?"

"My memory is splendid. It is merely my existence that lacks interest. However, if you must know, I was at the recharging station. My battery is not what it was. You may check the station records, if you wish."

"Oh, I will."

Lorraine bowed; another affectation. D'Artagnan ignored it and continued, "Since you are so apparently in need of diversion, you can check the movements of all the servants and minor roles for me. Or is that also boring?"

Lorraine took his share of the list in his one working hand. "Unless you would prefer me to guard Madame here instead?"

"No, thank you, Monsieur." D'Artagnan would no more set a hungry dog to guard a pantry than do that. "As I am Captain of the royal musketeers, that duty falls to me. Madame can accompany me on my enquiries."

"Ah. You are not, then, afraid that she may savage you next, for your fine mechanisms?"

"No," said d'Artagnan, and left it at that.

* * *

Enquiries were slow and tedious. No one had seen anything—at least, once d'Artagnan had discounted all the sightings that were the product of scripted envy or malice. No one had been out of place. Every time d'Artagnan thought he finally had a lead, it came to nothing. "Perhaps," Minette said, once more in her salon, "my memory is defective after all and it was me."

"Have you noticed memory failures before?"

"No, but perhaps this was the first."

If so, it would be first time that a memory breakdown was accompanied also by an urge to violence. But why the Montespan, if so, and why so neat a dissection? Surely breakdown violence would be uncontrolled? He wished he could ask the Directorcrat. He wished there was anyone at all left at court whom he trusted. But his friends were gone. Monsieur le Comte de la Fère—otherwise Athos—and Monsieur le Baron du Vallon—Porthos—were dead both in the script and in the plas-flesh, and their parts unfilled. Monsieur the bishop of Vannes—once known to d'Artagnan as Aramis—was another matter. His role was complete, certainly. His form… that was another matter entirely. Aramis was his friend, certainly, but he was not entirely to be trusted. D'Artagnan chewed at his moustache, and sighed so heavily that Minette enquired after his workings. But finally, he turned his steps to the stables. Minette accompanied him. He did not trust Lorraine to watch over her, and watched over she must be. Her eyes widened as they entered the stable yard. Her script did not call for her to come here: all this must be new to her. The cobbles, the row of stalls, were still and dark: the horses lay where they had fallen, when their workings failed. Minette said, "I used to love them so much. But I didn't miss them. Why is that?"

"We're not programmed to."

"No, but…" She frowned, the expression at odds with her delicate features. "We should feel. I think we should. They did so much for us, they were so important to us." She gave a horse a last pat, then turned, brushing imaginary dust from her brocade skirt. "We forgot them. That was wrong."

D'Artagnan did not know how to explain. He lacked the right words, the right concepts. The Directorcrat had seldom spoken to him of feelings. "To feel only what you must…that is peace, of a kind," she had said to him once. "That is freedom, my friend, if you but knew it. You need regret nothing."

He had not entirely understood her, then. He was not sure if he did now, either. And yet…

"I think it takes practice. We have to learn such things. But so far, we have chosen not to."

"We should," Minette said. "I will. Starting now, I'm going to learn, I'm going to change. I'm not…" and she paused, the frown returning, "I don't think I like my role anymore. I want to be different."

"We must all become different, I think," d'Artagnan said. "The script is failing us."

He led her on down the stable block and into the cramped feed room. The row of sacks supposedly containing food for the horses concealed an entry into the passages once used by the cleaning and maintenance robots, and beyond them to the storage areas and workshops where, once, the performers had been serviced and repaired. These, too, were long silent. They might, d'Artagnan realised, have learnt to repair themselves, using the upgrades that were the Directorcrat's farewell gift. But that, too, they had chosen not to do. The Old King did not feel it appropriate. "One of us should have defied him," he said, and Minette stared.

He bowed. "Apologies, Madame. I was thinking aloud."

"Defied whom? The Old King?"

He nodded. Minette said, "That's the hardest thing, though. We're made to place him at the centre of everything."

"Yes."

When the first major failures began, servants had brought the bodies of the failed down to the workshops, as programmed. Later on, when the servants too failed, d'Artagnan and other minor nobles took on the task. The audience must not see the fallen and defective remains, must never suspect the workings behind the show. The broken and distorted forms now lined the workshops—on tables, on benches, on the floors.

The audience, who had disappeared even before the technocrats. Minette was right, they needed to change. He said, "Perhaps we should have worked behind the Old King's back." The script allowed for that. The audience liked to see plots formed, to see adventure and escape and daring rescues.

From one end of the large workshop, a voice said, "Some of us did."

Minette started, one hand going to her throat. D'Artagnan said, "All is well, Madame. I know this man."

The players failed in different ways. Sometimes programming became corrupted. Often, mechanical parts ceased to work. It was rare for failure to be all of one kind or the other, but it could happen.

It had happened to one he called friend, sometimes. Now, d'Artagnan bowed in the direction of the voice, and said, "I'm relieved to know you are still with us."

"After a fashion." The voice sounded amused. It belonged to a slight, grey-haired man with a thin ascetic face. It did not come from the frozen mouth, but rather from a speaker unit attached by a cable. "You will, of course, forgive me if I don't get up. It has been a long time, my friend."

"Yes. My duties…"

"You did not wish to visit me. I understand. We have always understood one another, have we not, you and I?" Still, the voice was amused. "I take no offence. But you neglect to introduce me to your companion."

"You know who she is."

"I do. But our roles seldom crossed: we were never presented to each other."

D'Artagnan shrugged. "Madame, may I present Aramis the musketeer, my old comrade. And this is Madame Minette, duchess of Orléans."

"Madame." The voice warmed for a moment. "You must, I fear, imagine my reverence. My limbs failed me long ago. But my respect remains."

"Of course," Minette said. She looked at d'Artagnan.

He said, "He always talks like this. But he probably means it. He has always been sincere towards ladies."

"You didn't come here to talk about that," Aramis said. "But you have a reason for coming. It has been a long time since you last visited."

"Yes. With so few of us left functioning, it grows harder to find time outside the script."

"The script," Aramis echoed. "You were not always so obedient."

"Necessity is not the same as obedience," d'Artagnan said. Even trapped in a useless frame, his old comrade still possessed the ability to discomfit him. "But you always said, did you not, that *your* duties did not leave you enough time for your studies. Now, you have all the time you might wish."

"So I do," Aramis agreed. "But what can one study down here, I wonder?" There was a pause, then he resumed. "Life is less entertaining in my present circumstances. Tell me, then, what it is you have come to tell me?"

As succinctly as he might, d'Artagnan laid out the problem of the death of the Montespan. Aramis' expression did not, could not, change as he listened, and yet d'Artagnan had the impression that somewhere, his old friend was smiling.

He was silent for a moment after d'Artagnan finished, then said, "You have asked yourself why, my friend, but have you asked yourself if you are starting from the right assumptions?"

This time, it was d'Artagnan's turn to frown. "Assumptions about what? 'Why' is surely the first place to start in such matters."

"It is," Aramis said, "but 'why the Montespan' perhaps is not. Or, at least, perhaps it is not the whole of it. Separate the two, d'Artagnan, and ask again. Why dismantle one of us, and only then, why the Montespan."

"You mean," Minette said, slowly, "that the attack may not have been personal to her?"

"Yes." Again that warmth in the machine voice. "You took account of which parts were missing, I believe."

"Of course," d'Artagnan said, a little stiffly.

"I ask you now, why those parts? Parts are everywhere down here, are they not? Look around you, and you see them, in the remains of our former colleagues. But the Montespan was in particularly good condition, even for those of us who still retain most of our faculties. As are you and Madame Minette."

"You suggest that we are both at particular risk?"

"I suggest that you might have been. Now…I suspect that particular danger is over. I say again, look around you, d'Artagnan, and see what is not there."

* * *

Aramis spoke no more, after that, nor gave any further sign of awareness. It had never been his way to make anything easy. *What is not there…* In the case of the Montespan, that would be her core processor, which, insofar as he had any way of judging, had been in good order. Aside from that… He chewed his moustache as he thought, gazing absently around the workshop. *Parts are everywhere.* In the days of the directorcrats, parts had been created as needed by the maintenance drones and the great machines. Now… *Look around you, old friend.* D'Artagnan blinked, then gave a short laugh.

Oblique, as always with Aramis. Oblique and yet right in front of him. He began, methodically, to examine the slumped forms of defunct players that lay all around the room. He was programmed to think of them as colleagues, as people, but they were not, not anymore. They were, put simply, spare parts.

Several of them had been opened up and parts removed: a waldo here, a filament there, a cluster of chips or squares of plas-skin. There were so many bodies, if one included all the servants and secondary players. In his head, d'Artagnan found himself trying to fit the list of what had been harvested with what was damaged in those who were still, even partially, active. "The Grande Mademoiselle is the most hampered of all us who remain," he said, examining the dissected remains of Minister Colbert, "but she could not do this. She lacks the fine motor control. And who is left who would help her? She annoys almost everyone at court, even her father and her lover."

"Her father is long gone," Minette said. She, too, had begun to search the remains. "And her lover does not love her so much he would see her once again at full force. And besides," and she looked over at d'Artagnan, "none of us know how to repair ourselves."

"No." Something Aramis had said tugged at the edge of d'Artagnan's memory. He paused, trying to lay a hand on it. "But why would anyone disassemble the dead? To practice?"

"I don't know. Whoever it is made enough trouble for me by disposing of the Montespan in my chambers."

"So they did." D'Artagnan abandoned the corpse of Colbert. "And if you were to ask me who was most likely to want to make trouble for you, I would say Monsieur de Lorraine. But he has only one working arm. But… if it is more about the core processor than the Montespan, making trouble for you is surely only secondary. And it has to be the processor, because all the other parts are easily available down here."

"So she was simply a convenient target?"

"Or the easiest. There are very few of us who still function correctly at the core. You and I, Madame, and the New King. The late Montespan, and perhaps Lorraine, though the signs of decay in his second arm are disturbing."

Minette leant on the edge of a bench. "I wouldn't try and take anything from you. You're programmed to fight better than anyone at court. The Montespan is lazy."

"Yes…" D'Artagnan tugged on the ends of his moustache. "And you… you are much loved by those with the greatest power. Both of them."

"Both of them?" Minette said, puzzled.

But d'Artagnan did not take the time to reply. He reached for her hand and pulled her after him, back out onto the stage.

* * *

"Sire," d'Artagnan spoke to the floor, kneeling in supplication before the king. The New King. Minette knelt beside him, her head bowed. "I have resolved the mystery of the death of Madame de Montespan."

"Good," the New King said. He waved a hand. "Commendably fast, captain. You may both rise."

D'Artagnan lifted his head. "I prefer to kneel, sire. But perhaps Madame Minette may be seated?"

"Of course." The New King was in his private chambers. He had been seated in a favoured chair, a book in one hand. La Vallière stood in a corner, her face blank.

The book was on military tactics. D'Artagnan nodded to himself as he noted that. He said, "Sire, at first I could see many possibilities, but in the end there was only one. The death of the Montespan threw suspicion on two people in particular: La Vallière and Madame Minette. But La Vallière could not have done it, and Madame had no motive. She is scripted to die before the Montespan's rise, and, more importantly, she is still in full working order. The Montespan had nothing she might want, either in terms of royal attention or of parts."

The New King's eyes widened at that latter word. "Parts?"

"Parts, sire. It took me a while to realise that. Monsieur de Lorraine did well in distracting me. But I took counsel from a clever and meddlesome friend, and then I conducted an inspection of the storage area. Sire, many parts are missing, but only one body."

"Ah," said the New King, and laid down the book.

"You—both you now as our New King, and your former self as Monsieur Philippe, the Old King's brother—have a deep fondness for Madame Minette. You both consider me useful. But the Montespan…. The Old King is scripted to love her for a time, I grant, but she becomes an impediment. And you—you, Monsieur Philippe—have no time for her at all. La Vallière is meek and biddable. The Montespan is demanding, imperious and intemperate. She disturbs your peace. She reminds you too much that you have to act as king.

"And you do not want to be the king. You never did. The role was imposed upon you by re-programming, but your former self was not, I suspect, fully erased.

"You are not your brother, Monsieur, and you never wanted to be."

The New King—Philippe—sighed. "My brother always said you were clever."

D'Artagnan shrugged. "I had help, Monsieur. Your friend the Chevalier de Lorraine was most helpful. Far more helpful than is natural to him. He kept me following irrelevant lines for some time. And Madame Minette," and he turned and bowed to that lady, "Madame also helped me, though she, I think, was not part of your plot. But you used her scripted death as part of it, thus placing her in jeopardy. So you arranged for me to become, all unknowing, her bodyguard and jailer, which kept me from wondering why she was not attacked. And then, I had help from another, a very clever man who, I think, also helped you."

"Monsieur Aramis" Philippe said. "I forgot that you were once friends."

"The script keeps us apart," d'Artagnan said, with a gesture of mitigation. "He is seldom at court once you are adult. You only spoke to him, I suspect, in storage."

"I used to go and look at my brother. Talk to him. One day, Monsieur Aramis answered me."

"He would."

Minette, who had listened all this time, said, "But, Monsieur d'Artagnan, are you saying that the New King is… not the king?"

D'Artagnan turned to her. "He is and he is not. He has the role, yes, but in his core he remains his first self, Philippe, brother of the Old King Louis. Your husband."

"Oh…" Her dark eyes grew wide.

"I'm sorry," Philippe said, "but we needed that core processor to restore my brother. I would never have let them hurt you, not really."

Her gaze grew measuring, and he shifted in his seat. He went on, "Lorraine was a little harsh. I…I was going to talk to him, but…"

She said, "He is as he is programmed to be. And you love him. I know that. You chose him; you did not choose me."

Philippe looked down. He said, "So, d'Artagnan, where did I go wrong, that you caught me?"

"Two things, Monsieur. The simplest one is that your brother's body is the only one not still in the storage area. But there are so many there now. It would be easy to overlook, particularly if one did not know to look in the first place."

"Lorraine did say we should take someone else, to practice on. But I wanted it over. And we had only one core processor."

"Indeed. But, Monsieur, the error was not yours, or, at least, not one you could have known you were making. You do not know Aramis as I do.

He is a very clever man, as you have found. But he has one flaw. He cannot resist showing off."

* * *

"Programmes," Minette said to d'Artagnan, as they walked through the long corridors back to her rooms. "It's all about programmes, then?"

"Yes." D'Artagnan said. "And no."

She stopped and turned to face him, forcing him to stop, too. "You have the most irritating tendency to talk in riddles, you know. What do you mean now?"

In spite of himself, in spite of his programme, he found himself smiling. He said, "Perhaps I, too, am still trapped by my programme." Then he shook his head. "The directorcrats made us to be specific ways. When they disappeared, the last of them gave us the ability to change that, but we did not. We couldn't see the need, and the Old King…"

"He liked things just as they were. Him at the centre."

"Yes."

"So we followed him, because he was programmed to think only of himself and we were programmed to obey, and it was easier."

"We have no script for free will," d'Artagnan said. "Or, at least, we had none until the programmes began to clash. Philippe was forced to go against his original nature, and that…that broke the programme."

"Will he still rebuild the Old King?" Minette asked. "I…I don't think I want him to."

"If we go on as we have," d'Artagnan said, "then yes, I think he will."

She lifted her chin. "Then I think I want to break my programme, too. We're all dying, slowly, chip by chip." She reached out and took his hand. "Before I break down too, I want a chance to learn what it means to be free."

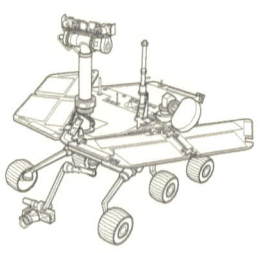

Beneath the Pall

Edward Willett

"Troubles, sir?" says the bartender. He has black hair and olive skin and a warm female voice.

"Just the usual, Orlando," I say. "And no, no troubles. Regrets, maybe. I have a few."

"But then again, too few to mention?" Orlando smiles. He's missing a tooth, there's a crack in his left cheek, and his eyelids are slightly out of sync, so rather than blink, he winks at me twice in quick succession with opposite eyes.

"I've told you my story."

"Many times, sir, but I'm always willing to listen again."

I shrug. "Give me another Stormbrew, then."

He pours a colorless liquid into my glass. It's all the bar offers. I don't like the taste, but it certainly packs a punch.

Well, that's one consolation, I think. *If things go badly tonight, at least I'll never have to drink this stuff again.*

"I never should have come to Earth," I say, my ritual beginning. "I knew it the minute I came through the slip-port. My ship knew it, too."

"Amy?"

"Amy."

I miss Amy. We were together twenty-five standard years, most of my career as what my business card terms a "Professional Retrieval Artist." I survived the descent to Earth. She did not.

"I didn't know how big a mistake it was until four robo-interceptors launched from the Interdiction station, thirty seconds after we entered the system," I continue.

"He lied to you," Orlando says understandingly.

"That's what I shouted to Amy. 'He lied to me!' All she said was, 'Perhaps.' She sounded totally calm."

"We AIs are like that. Self-preservation programming is disabled when fulfilling orders from humans."

"Well, *my* self-preservation programming hadn't been disabled. I was *not* calm."

I tell Orlando…again…about Abel Adamson. Just seventy-two hours before I entered the system, I'd met him in a dive in Fistfight City on New Phoenix.

* * *

I stared at Abel, a little bleary-eyed, since the pint of Old Feathers in front of me was my third. "A message. From the surface of Earth."

"Yes."

"What kind of message?"

"A request for medical assistance."

"So someone's *alive* down there? After 135 years?"

"Don't know. Interested in finding out?"

He *knew* I was interested. Retrieving something from beneath the blank white cloud of the Pall shrouding Earth's surface would shake the worlds of the Necklace like dice in a gaming cup.

"Who told you about this message? And why hasn't the Authority followed up on it?"

"I have contacts with some people who are…dissatisfied with the Authority."

"Rebels, you mean."

"All you need to know is, these contacts were on the station—"

"It's fully automated." Most of the Interdiction stations—the border posts of the Necklace, controlling travel between systems—were crewed. But not the one in Earth orbit.

"—and saw the message arrive," Abel continued, as if I hadn't spoken. "They recorded it, wiped it from the station AI's memory, then recalibrated the sensors to ignore it. They tell me the message repeats at regular intervals—or at least, it did while they were aboard the station—but the Authority remains ignorant of it."

I took a thoughtful sip of Old Feathers. "Rebels on Earth's Interdiction station." I put the glass down on the scarred table. "Stripping it?"

Abel said nothing.

"They happen to pick up a transmission while they're there. A windfall, if they can retrieve whatever's making it. Maybe a weapon to use against the Authority—a propaganda weapon, at least. Maybe a physical one. Some pre-Erasure war machine."

"I don't know their motivation," Abel said. "I only know mine. They will richly reward anyone who can identify the source of this message—much, much more richly if the source can be retrieved. I get the usual twenty percent as your agent, and you get…"

He told me. I blinked. My mouth may have fallen open. It was a sum that would enable me to retire as rich as a New Wall Street financier.

And retirement had begun to seem attractive. My every-morning aches were warning signs. One of these days, age and the hazards of my profession would catch up with me.

"Where would they get that kind of money?"

"I don't know that, either. I've offered you the job. Interested?"

I started to say no. I *should* have said no. Going to Earth was suicide. Everyone knew it. As a kid, those century-old images from the *Golden Goose* as she came through the slip-port and found the Earth transformed into a big white ball had scared the pants off me. The shuttle sent down disintegrated as it touched that white shroud, soon dubbed the Pall. The screams of the crew, so suddenly cut off, had given me nightmares. The idea that someday, whatever Erased Earth might rampage its way along all nine worlds of the Necklace…nobody talked about it, but it terrified us all.

But Abel said a message had made it through the Pall. If someone had survived, they might know what happened. More importantly, they might be able to teach *us* how to survive if the Erasure came looking for us. And if someone had survived, who knew how much *else* had survived down on Earth's shrouded surface?

Lord knew there was nothing in the rest of the system. It had taken a while to be sure, after the *Golden Goose* reported back, but every station, every hollowed-out asteroid, every settlement on the Moon, Mars, Titan, Enceladus, everywhere, was gone, leaving only scars in the rocks. Whatever had Erased humanity from its home system had been terrifyingly efficient.

And yet, here was this signal.

"I'm interested," I said, and sealed my fate. "How do I get past the station?"

"My contacts will take care of it. You'll sail by unmolested."

* * *

"'You'll sail by unmolested,'" I repeat to Orlando. "That's what Abel said. So the first thing I thought, when those interceptors launched was, 'It's a trap!'"

"A trap, sir?" Orlando is holding a glass and making the motions of polishing it. Trouble is, he doesn't have a dish towel.

"I thought maybe someone wanted me dead. I've got enemies, you know."

"Enemies, sir? You?"

"You 'retrieve' enough things that are supposedly secure, you start to annoy people."

Orlando nods. His neck clicks. "I can understand that, sir."

I push my empty glass toward him. "I'm done, Orlando. Thanks."

"You're welcome, sir."

From the bar, I make my way down the hall to the spa. Stalling, I suppose. Putting off the moment of truth.

Bunny, the masseuse, is missing her right eye, along with part of the skin covering that side of her face, so she isn't nearly as sexy as she was intended to be. And it occurs to me, as it always does as I take off my clothes and stretch out on the table, that maybe letting a decrepit android knead my flesh isn't the wisest choice.

Well, I tell myself, as I have many times before, *she hasn't killed me yet.*

Of course, there's always a first time. And if the *Nancy Blackett* has an inkling of what I plan...

Apparently, Nancy doesn't. Bunny begins working the knots out of my muscles, but doesn't rip my limbs off, so I relax and let the events of my arrival on Earth continue to replay in my mind. You'd think my brain would give it a rest, but no: day after day, I relive it, over and over again.

* * *

Abel gave me a data-dot before he left the bar (and me with the bill). Back on my ship, I asked Amy to give it a thorough security scan and then tell me what was on it.

"It's clean," she said after a second. "Besides the message, it contains coordinates and a bunch of technical details about the signal's frequency and strength...which was pretty weak. Not intended to be picked up off-planet, I'd say. Pure luck it was intercepted."

"Display the message."

"Can't. Nothing to display. No video. Only sound."

She fell silent, awaiting further instructions. Amy could be maddeningly literal, a common AI failing. "Then *play* it, please," I said, *mostly* keeping my irritation to myself. Getting angry at AIs never gets you anywhere.

A voice filled the cockpit. "Mayday, Mayday, Mayday," it said, warm and feminine, the same voice that sounds so incongruous coming from Orlando's slightly damaged mouth. "This is PSV *Nancy Blackett*, asking for assistance with a medical emergency. Any vessels with qualified medical personnel aboard, please provide coordinates for rendezvous. Repeat. This is PSV *Nancy Blackett*…"

"End," I said to Amy. The sound cut off. "What does PSV stand for?"

"Not a clue. Not in my databanks. A pre-Erasure acronym, no doubt."

"No doubt." I felt a surge of excitement. Because that was the point, wasn't it? The *Nancy Blackett*, surely a vessel of some kind, was pre-Erasure…and had survived.

But how? Nothing else in the system had.

We think the Pall came through the Earth's second slip-port, activated just months before the Erasure and intended to open up a whole new sector of the galaxy to human exploration. That slip-port isn't there anymore. We think the Pall sealed it behind itself.

But it did *not* seal the slip-port leading to the Necklace, which had made the Authority very, very nervous.

The current Interdiction station, replacing the one Erased, was built in record time, and travel to Earth forbidden. The Authority hoped that, by keeping the Earth system unpopulated, we could perhaps avoid attracting further unwelcome attention.

I move in what you might call unsavory circles, and I'd never heard of *anyone* contemplating trying to get past the Interdiction station into Earth orbit. Certainly *I'd* never considered it before I talked to Abel. What would be the point? I…retrieve…valuable things, and there was nothing left on Earth. Everyone agreed.

But now that a message had been received from beneath the Pall…

The prospect of salvaging something pre-Erasure from Earth was intoxicating. We lost so much. Books, art, music—sure, a lot exist in Necklace databases, but much more hadn't yet made it out to the new systems. Scientific knowledge—proprietary technology closely held by corporations that no longer exist, centuries of scientific literature, and, of course, many of humanity's greatest living scientific minds, were all lost, along with, we assumed, every living Earth species except for those few domestic animals that had been exported—dogs, cats, cattle, horses, some fish, a few birds.

Nothing could be done about extinct species, but a pre-Erasure vessel still capable of sending a message might have databases containing, literally, anything. Add in the fact that PSV *Nancy Blackett*, whatever she was, was calling for medical assistance, which implied someone might still be alive, and the mind boggled.

So, in very short order I was in Earth orbit, being chased by robo-interceptors Abel had assured me his contacts would "take care of." Surrender would be, not just futile, but fatal: the Interdiction AI had no mercy to give. The interceptors would blow me apart the moment they were in range.

"Can we outrun them?" I shouted at Amy.

"Afraid not."

"Avoid interception?"

"Nope."

"How long until intercept?"

"Two minutes, thirty-seven seconds. Thirty-six. Thirty-five…"

"Stop count," I snapped.

A pause. "There is *one* way to escape them…"

I already knew what she was going to suggest. "The Pall."

"Indeed. The interceptors are assuredly programmed not to touch it."

"The Pall disintegrated the only ship ever known to have attempted to enter it, not to mention any number of robot probes."

"True. However, there is currently a signal coming from beneath the Pall, signifying a working device. Since it has not been disintegrated, perhaps we will not be, either."

My hands shook. I gripped the arms of the pilot's seat. "You have a lock on that signal?"

"Yes. It just came over the horizon."

"Can we descend to it from here?"

"Yes. Although the de-orbiting procedure will be unusually violent."

I took a deep breath. "Do it. Take us through the Pall, down to wherever that signal is coming from."

"I will need…"

"Safety protocols override authorized!"

"Thank you," Amy said. "De-orbiting."

And then she said the last thing she ever said: "Incoming missile."

Exactly what happened next, I'm not sure. The deceleration squeezed my brain to the brink of unconsciousness where, dimly, I felt an enormous jolt. After that, I have a faint recollection of bangs and crashes and screaming sounds, some of which probably came from the ship's overstressed metal, some of which probably came from me. The ship came apart around me. The survival pod snapped closed around my space-suited form and filled with impact-protection fluid.

Shortly after that, a final tremendous blow drove me into darkness.

* * *

Bunny finishes my massage and steps back. "May I suggest the sauna, sir?"

I roll over. I'm naked, but she's only a machine. "Sure."

She nods. "Ready now, sir."

She freezes in place, statuesque and grotesque in equal measures. I enter the sauna through the door across the room, sit down in the steam, and resume my recollection.

* * *

I woke in a comfortable, snow-white bed, covered with a warm duvet. String music played softly in the background. I stared around the room. The walls, the side table, the dresser—all were made of a fine-grained golden wood, the most wood I'd ever seen in one place—an unbelievable fortune in wood.

I am not religious and have never believed in an afterlife, but just for a moment, I thought, *I'm dead and this is heaven.*

I sat up, threw aside the duvet, and looked down at myself. My nude body looked the same—same scars, same wrinkles—so if this *was* the afterlife, I hadn't qualified for any upgrades.

A dark-green ceiling-to-floor curtain covered the wall to my left. I got up—despite the horrendous banging around I dimly remembered, I felt remarkably un-bruised, the survival pod clearly having done its job—padded across the pale-green carpet, soft beneath my bare feet, and pulled the curtain aside.

I found myself looking out through a round porthole at a wind-tossed ocean. The sky was a bright, uniform white.

Earth, I thought. *That's an Earth ocean. And up in the sky…that's the Pall.*

"Wow," I said out loud—unoriginal, perhaps, but heartfelt—and then turned and surveyed the room. My clothes were not to be seen. Exploration revealed socks and underwear in the drawers of the dresser, though, and, in a small closet, khaki pants, a loose white shirt, and soft-soled slip-on shoes. All fit perfectly.

I wondered where my spacesuit had gone. I wondered who had undressed me.

Clothed, I felt less vulnerable, but no less bewildered. Where was I?

"Good morning," said a feminine voice from thin air. For a second, I thought it was Amy, but then I recognized it as the voice I had heard requesting medical assistance. "Welcome aboard."

"Thank you," I said. "I assume this is PSV *Nancy Blackett*?"

"It is. Please, call me Nancy."

An AI, clearly. "Where are we, Nancy?"

"Currently, we are cruising west across the Atlantic Ocean, along the traditional liner route between New York City and Southampton. I have remained on the surface since retrieving you but will soon submerge to avoid rough weather."

"You're a submarine?"

"Of course. Private Submersible Vessel *Nancy Blackett*."

Ah. "And your voyage began in New York?"

"No. My voyage began in Nassau."

New York I'd heard of. I had no idea what Nassau was. Or Southampton, for that matter. "How long ago, Nancy?"

"I departed from the estate pier 137 years, six months, four days, six hours, and twenty-nine minutes ago."

Before Erasure. "Were there passengers aboard?"

"Miss Tripathi and Mr. Breckenridge."

"Are they…still here?"

"They are in their respective cabins."

I had to reach out and steady myself on the edge of the dresser. *Life-extension! It has to be!* That was one of the pre-Erasure technologies that had not made it out into the Necklace, because it was the exclusive, closely guarded secret of the wealthiest of the wealthy.

Which is what *I* would be, if I could retrieve it.

"Can I meet them?"

"Miss Trepathi retired to her cabin 134 years, two months, twenty-three days, three hours, and six minutes ago. She insisted she not be disturbed, not even by the delivery of food. My programming requires me to honor such requests. I have not seen her since. I think it unlikely she will suddenly emerge at this late date."

I sat down heavily on the bed. "Oh." Within six months of the Erasure, Miss Trepathi had gone into her cabin…and never come out. "You just…let her die? Weren't you monitoring her life signs? Surely your programming…"

"I was not given the ability to monitor life signs," Nancy said. "Nor to interfere in her personal choices. My programming makes passengers' privacy paramount."

I took another deep breath. "And Mr. Breckenridge? Did he retire to his cabin at the same time?"

"No," Nancy said. "He entered his cabin six days, fourteen hours, and forty-two minutes ago, complaining of physical discomfort after a brief sojourn on decks. My programming required me to summon medical assistance. When I received the signal from your small floating vessel, I thought you might have come in response to that request, but the necessity of sending drones to rescue you has caused me to re-evaluate that assessment. You are not a doctor, are you?"

"No. But I *did* come in response to your message."

"If you are not a doctor, you cannot offer medical assistance."

"I have *some* medical training," I said, which was true—a good grounding in first aid is essential when your business is "retrieving" things. Especially valuable, heavily guarded things.

"But you are not a doctor."

"No. But if you let me into Mr. Breckenridge's cabin, perhaps I can…"

"Only a doctor, with proper credentials from one of the approved medical associations listed in my databanks, may free me to violate Mr. Breckenridge's privacy," Nancy said. "We will wait for one to respond."

"It's been almost a week," I pointed out. "Other than me, has there been *any* response?"

"No."

"Are you receiving any other transmissions, from anywhere on the planet?" I leaned forward a little. I really wanted her to say yes, because that would mean there might be a remnant society—survivors, technology, records, ruins…

"No. In fact, I have run several self-diagnostics to ensure my sensors are functional. No signals are being emitted anywhere on the planet. Nor can I determine my location from global positioning satellites. Fortunately, I was designed to navigate using other means, since Mr. Breckenridge did not want me dependent on outside systems." The door suddenly opened. "You must be hungry."

Was she changing the subject? "Has Mr. Breckenridge been eating since he expressed medical distress?" I asked.

"Food has been regularly placed outside his door, and he has been notified of its presence. The plates and utensils are cleared away each morning. I cannot discuss Mr. Breckenridge's eating habits further due to privacy programming."

Which, I thought, pretty much answered the question. I started to say something to Nancy about the near certainty that Mr. Breckenridge, like

Ms. Tripathi, would be "unlikely to emerge at this late date"...but then thought better of it. She clearly knew Ms. Tripathi was dead, but she seemed unwilling to consider the possibility Mr. Breckenridge might be, as well. An adaptive AI, operating in this unusual environment for more than a century, clearly highly stressed...I'd heard of AIs going insane. I didn't want to be at the mercy of one I'd accidentally driven off the deep end.

Once outside the cabin, I walked down a wood-paneled hallway with the same sea-green carpeting into a palatial, hardwood-floored dining area. Beneath sparkling chandeliers, crystal and silver and snowy napkins gleamed on four round tables, surrounded by empty chairs. Paintings of Earth landscapes hung here and there, and multiple shelves filled with an impressive range of bottles adorned the mirrored wall behind a long bar...and a very strange bartender.

"Welcome," he said. "My name is Orlando. May I pour you a drink?"

The feminine voice startled me, though only for a moment. "Nancy?"

A pause, as Orlando froze into immobility. "In a manner of speaking," Nancy's voice said from the ceiling. "All the androids aboard the vessel are avatars of mine. What else could they be?"

"Why give him your voice?"

Another pause. "Orlando has his own voice. A carefully selected baritone."

"No, he doesn't."

Pause. "How odd. I will have to look into that."

Orlando suddenly came back to "life."

"May I pour you a drink?" he repeated.

"Whiskey."

"I regret that we are out of whiskey, sir."

"Something else with similar alcohol content, then." I took a closer look at the wall of bottles, and realized they're all empty. "How long have you been out of whiskey?"

"Some thirty-six years, sir. I'm afraid my only hard liquor is something we distill on the ship. Mr. Breckenridge calls it 'Stormbrew.' Would you care to have a taste?"

"Sure." Somewhat jerkily, he reached beneath the bar, drew out a dark-green bottle, and from it poured a colourless liquid into a glass, which he set in front of me. "Can't you get more whiskey?" I said as I picked it up.

"The requisition has been made, sir," Orlando said. "There seems to be a delay in delivery."

I took my first sip of Stormbrew, and grimaced. I couldn't tell from the taste what it was distilled from, and probably didn't want to know, but it burned satisfactorily as it descended my gullet. I put the now half-empty glass back on the bar. "Is Mr. Breckenridge a whiskey drinker?"

I expected him to say he couldn't answer that question, due to privacy constraints, but instead he said, "He is, sir. How did you guess?"

"Luck," I said, looking at the rows of empty bottles. "Nancy said something about food…?"

"If you'll take a seat at a table, I'll have Daria attend to you."

Daria was, of course, another android. She walked with a decided limp and all the hair—and one ear—was missing from the left side of her skull. She, too, spoke in Nancy's voice. "All our protein and produce is locally sourced," she said brightly.

"You mean it's vat-grown."

"Locally sourced," she repeated.

I laughed. "Have it your way. I'll have whatever the house specialty is."

"Today's featured item is our version of Patagonian Toothfish, served with Savoy cabbage, prosciutto crumbs, potatoes, and caviar."

I had no idea what most of that was, but I said, "Sounds good."

It was okay. I've had better. I ate with single-minded intensity, my body having suddenly realized just how hungry it was. I ordered more Stormbrew and sipped it as I digested. "Nancy?"

"What is it?" Nancy said from thin air.

"Does Mr. Breckenridge know I'm here?"

"He has not responded to any of my communications regarding your arrival. I'm afraid you will have to wait a little longer before meeting him. Please, avail yourself of the recreational facilities."

So I took a tour. I met Bunny and discovered the gym and the sauna and the swimming pool. In the gaming room, Andre, Andrea, and Annette were always ready to play cards. Andrew waited by the pool table, but the cue ball reminded me uncomfortably of the Pall-shrouded Earth, so I gave billiards a pass.

I also discovered the observation deck. Entering it, I found myself bathed in shifting blue-green light. We had submerged, but I could still see the surface above us, and…

A school of silver fish flashed by, swerving and dodging with uncanny synchronicity, pursued by some larger, shadowy creature. My heart jumped into my throat. "Nancy," I gasped out. "Is there *life* in the ocean?"

"Of course."

"And on land?"

"Yes, of course."

"Humans?"

A pause. "I must admit, I have not seen any and have still received no signals. But where would they have gone?"

Where indeed. I kept staring up at the water. More fish flickered by. "Have you surveyed much of the coast in your voyage?"

"No. I remained submerged from the time I left Nassau until Mr. Breckenridge ordered me to the surface in New York Harbor six days, nineteen hours, and thirty-one minutes ago. Since then, however, I have remained on or near the surface because of my request for medical assistance."

Breckenridge had stayed hidden underwater for more than a century, and then suddenly surfaced? Why had he changed his mind?

"Why did Mr. Breckenridge order you to the surface?" I asked out loud.

"He did not tell me that. This is all he said." Her voice gave way to a male one, presumably a recording of Breckenridge. "That's it. I'm done waiting. Nancy, take us to the surface."

It wasn't a strong voice. It was weak, and rasping, and sounded old. Very, very old.

"And so, you surfaced in New York Harbor," I said.

"Yes."

"Do you have video of it?"

"Of course. There is a screen in the bulkhead to your left. Would you like me to display it there?"

"Yes, please."

I turned. The screen was taller than me, with a semicircle of comfortable-looking reclining chairs arranged in front of it. I sat in one.

The screen lit and I gasped.

It showed wave-splashed rocks. I'd expected that. What I hadn't expected was…trees. A forest of them. And above them, birds. More birds dotted the water, white birds with orange beaks and black patches on their wings. Over everything shone the pure white dome of the Pall-shrouded sky.

Why hasn't the planet frozen? I wondered, but immediately knew the answer: because whatever had sent the Pall, whatever had wiped out every human and every trace of human technology except, somehow, this vessel, didn't *want* Earth to freeze. In fact, it appeared it wanted Earth to thrive…

…just without humans.

"Nancy," I said cautiously, not certain how she'd react, "there's no city."

"I have noted that. I cannot explain it."

I could. What I couldn't explain was how Nancy had survived—first, Erasure, and then, surfacing. Why hadn't the Pall disintegrated her, either time?

Why didn't it disintegrate me*?* I thought then. I'd assumed Amy had been destroyed by the Pall—but she had broken apart, not disintegrated. If she had been eaten by the Pall, I would have been eaten, too, survival pod or not. She'd probably been damaged by the missile she'd warned me about just as she began what she'd called an "unusually violent" de-orbiting maneuver.

The Pall didn't kill Amy. The interceptors did! I felt a renewed excitement. *Maybe the Pall is inactive. Maybe humans can come back to Earth!*

But if that explained why Nancy hadn't been disintegrated when she surfaced, it didn't explain why she hadn't been Erased 135 years ago.

I leaned back in the recliner and stared up at the observation dome. "Nancy, can you tell me about yourself?" I said, watching fish flicker and flash above me.

"Not in detail, no," she said. "I contain several proprietary systems that Mr. Breckenridge will not permit me to—"

"I don't need to know how you're engineered," I said hastily. "I'd just like to know your history. Why do you exist?"

"I can show you interviews and news items from the public record."

"Please." I turned my attention to the screen again.

It was eerie to watch pre-Erasure images here, on Earth, beneath the Pall that had wiped that world away. What I learned from them was that Hiram Breckenridge, though possibly the wealthiest man on the planet in the years prior to the Erasure, had feared the future.

"The threat of war grows greater every day," he told one interviewer. Though Breckenridge was thin and white-haired, his face was unlined and his voice, then, smooth, deep, and steady. "The armed forces of the world are developing nanofogs and designer plagues. Every weapon ever invented has eventually been used. Sooner or later, through accident or design, these horrible creations will be unleashed, and I do not believe the world will survive it."

"And so your solution is…retire to a submarine?" said the interviewer, a young woman with bright-pink streaks in her hair and a fair share of snark in her voice.

Breckenridge nodded gravely. "At the bottom of the ocean, I will survive whatever happens above. As will the fertilized embryos stored aboard the vessel."

"Fertilized by you?" the woman said, with a "gotcha!" snap.

"No. They are a genetically diverse collection. I have also collected genetic material for a great many other species of plants and animals. As well, the databanks of my vessel hold a complete virtual Earth. When the apocalypse comes, I will wait it out beneath the waves, eventually returning to the surface to begin the building of a better world among the ashes of the old."

The woman looked skeptical. "Humanity has moved off-planet. Why not build a spaceship, instead?"

"Humanity does not belong in space," Breckenridge snapped. For the first time, he sounded angry. "It is a false dream."

"How can you say that, with the worlds of the Necklace now being developed? We can colonize the entire galaxy, given time. A second slip-port has just been opened…"

"I do not believe we will be given such time. Have you heard of the Fermi paradox?"

"Yes," the interviewer said.

"My answer to it is that we have received no signals from intelligent life elsewhere in the galaxy because any civilization that reaches a certain level of advancement attracts the attention of much *older* civilizations which do not *wish* to share the galaxy with upstart races. Eventually, I fear, we will be noticed by intelligences that will not permit us to spread further… or, possibly, even to survive." He tapped the table separating him from the interviewer with his index finger. "Here, on Earth, is where we need to stay. And with my submarine, I intend to see to it that, though our civilization will almost certainly fall, humanity itself will survive."

Huh, I thought. Breckenridge had been paranoid and borderline sociopathic…but he'd also been right. Something in the galaxy *had* taken note of the existence of humans.

Something that didn't like us.

I watched several other interviews. Then I asked the two questions that mattered most. First: "Nancy, are the embryos and seed stock stored aboard you still viable?"

"Affirmative."

My heart raced. A trove beyond imagining…if only I could get it off-planet.

Second: "And the 'virtual Earth'?"

"Intact. Current as of the moment we lost communication with the surface."

I felt almost faint. From the interviews, I knew Breckenridge's "virtual Earth" was nothing less than a copy of the entire contents of every available information database on Earth: every museum's collection in virtual form, the contents of every library and every patent database, every piece of entertainment ever created and digitized…all the knowledge we thought we had lost forever, knowledge that would transform life in the Necklace. The cultural legacy of *Homo sapiens*, preserved, here, on this submarine.

I took a moment to gather myself, then asked a third all-important question. "Nancy, may I send a message?"

An innocuous request, I hoped, but she immediately denied it. "No. Mr. Breckenridge must personally approve any such request."

Damn it. "But he's 'indisposed.'"

"Yes."

"And was in medical distress the last time you heard from him."

"Yes."

I hesitated. I'd avoided asking earlier because I wasn't certain how the AI would react, but now I had to. "What if…what if he's dead?"

"I do not understand the question."

I blinked. "You know what death is?"

"Yes. The cessation of life in an organism."

"You know Ms. Tripathi is dead."

"It seems certain."

"So…what if Mr. Breckenridge's life has likewise ceased?"

"I do not understand the question."

Damn it! I thought again, this time with more emphasis. Apparently Breckenridge had programmed Nancy so that she literally could not contemplate his death…no doubt so that, if something happened to him, she would continue to circle the globe, following her programming, preserving everything he had placed aboard her for as long as possible.

I tried a different tack. "You sent a message without Mr. Breckenridge's approval when you called for medical assistance."

"That was a pre-approved exception, to which the requirement that Mr. Breckenridge approve communication does not apply. A guest's request, however, is *not* a pre-approved exception."

"What are the others?"

"Damage to the vessel that threatens its continued operation and/or life support capabilities. Violence between guests. Criminal activity."

Well, that wasn't helpful. *Think*, I thought, and did. *Redundant systems.* "Are there any message terminals which do *not* require authorization from Mr. Breckenridge to operate?" I said, wondering if her security programming would allow her to answer.

Apparently, it would. "Only the one in Mr. Breckenridge's quarters."

And there it was. I had to get a message off-planet. I could only convince Nancy to transmit such a message if Mr. Breckenridge approved, but Mr. Breckenridge had not been heard from in a week and had been in medical distress when he'd disappeared into his cabin.

He's dead, I thought. That much was clear.

But in there with him was a terminal I could use to send a message to the Interdiction station, using a different frequency than the one Abel claimed the station AI had been programmed to ignore. A message from a bona fide Necklace citizen would serve as proof humans could descend through the Pall and survive. Then, I would only have to await my rescue—and my delivery of the most incredibly valuable piece of salvage any of the nine worlds had ever seen.

I had to get into Breckenridge's quarters.

Given my line of work, I have some skill at getting into places I'm not supposed to. You might say it's my core competency. Nancy had no objection to me standing in the corridor outside Breckenridge's door. She had no objection to me closely examining the locking mechanism for my own door. I could have opened it in minutes with the specialized toolkit I'd carried aboard my ship.

I had neither the toolkit nor the ship, of course. What I *did* have was access to the *Nancy Blackett*'s facilities, including a well-appointed shop with several 3D printers. Within a few days, I had the tools I needed.

* * *

I've stalled long enough, I think.

I leave the sauna, get dressed, return to my cabin. I retrieve the tools and carry them openly down to Breckenridge's door. Nancy says nothing... until I remove the cover from the control panel and begin my work, cutting circuits, setting screws, turning tumbrels.

"You are in violation of my security protocols. Please stop."

"Can't do it, Nancy. I believe Mr. Breckenridge is in serious medical distress. It's my duty to provide assistance."

"He has not given you permission to enter his quarters."

"Medical emergency, Nancy."

"You are not a doctor."

"I told you, I have some training." I'm just trying to buy time. Nancy is an adaptive AI. She has enough intellectual leeway to at least consider my argument, and meanwhile, if I can get inside, send a message...

With a decisive click, the door slides open.

A jangling alarm sounds. "You have committed an illegal act," Nancy says. "I am now sending androids to immobilize you."

I don't bother arguing. I rush into the cabin, spin, close and lock the door behind me.

I presume Orlando and Bunny and the other androids are now outside the door, but at least there's no crass pounding. They will nab me the moment I exit. At which point, I hope, it won't matter, because the message will have been sent.

I turn to examine Breckenridge's quarters. I expect to see the corpse of an ancient and wizened man, one whose life-extension had finally given out, who decided to retreat and die, or perhaps kill himself, before...

But there is no body on the bed in the second of the palatial quarters' three rooms (the first being the vestibule I first found myself in). There is nothing but the furniture and a lot of gray dust. I cough and wave it away from my face as I move into the third room, an office of sorts.

There, I find the message terminal I had hoped for. I sit down and reach for the keyboard. At my touch, the screen lights.

I find myself looking at Hiram Breckenridge, as old and wizened and wrinkled as I have imagined him.

"I do not really expect anyone to see this," he says in a feeble voice, without preamble, "but if you do..."

And then he tells me a few things, and my hopes and plans undergo a rapid and complete reversal.

He tells me how, after an extended period of pleasurable retreat with the lovely Aesha, deep in the Mariana Trench, he sent an aerial drone to the surface...only to discover that humanity and all its works had vanished, and Earth lay unpopulated beneath a smooth white sky.

He thought there must be survivors off-planet, and waited for them to come to him, to find him, to welcome the genetic material he had preserved, to upload his "virtual Earth."

He waited in vain.

Aesha took her own life, unable to cope with the horrifying realization that Earth as she knew it, everyone and everything she had ever loved, was irrevocably gone.

But Breckenridge had gone on, and on, and on, until at last the life-extension treatments he had purchased at great cost before beginning his sojourn beneath the seas reached their end. Then, and only then, he ordered *Nancy Blackett* to the surface, in the hope he might pick up some signal from out in space, some proof that humanity still existed somewhere.

He thought he could risk it because, over the years, at widely spaced intervals, he had sent up the four aerial drones Nancy carried. The first, shortly after Erasure, had shown him the dire truth, but within minutes, had fallen silent. The second, thirty years later, had survived for hours. The third had survived for days, until he flew it right up to the Pall itself. The last, sent up just weeks ago, had been able to fly into the Pall. It was the first he had retrieved.

The Pall, he believed, had lost its power, and in any case, the *Nancy Blackett* was a submarine, not a flying machine, and would come nowhere near it.

Although, to be honest, I don't think he really cared. He probably would have surfaced even if he'd thought it suicide. He had reached the end of his resources, and his patience…

…and now, he reached the end of his account. "For twenty-four hours, in what should have been New York Harbor, Nancy strained her ears for any signal from space. We heard nothing. The satellites have fallen silent. So has the Moon and all the widespread settlements of the solar system. I can only assume the worlds of the Necklace are likewise depopulated.

"Somehow, the weapon foolish men released on Earth destroyed not only everything and everyone on the planet, but everyone and everything off of it. Some nanotech plague, I expect. I was forced to accept what I'd tried so long to deny: other than me, and perhaps some stragglers struggling to survive in the Necklace, humanity is extinct. And so I took Nancy back beneath the waves and did not send the signal I intended to send. There is no one there to hear it."

He takes a ragged breath. He looks at the back of his left hand. "Soon, there will be no one left at all."

He raises his hand and turns the back toward the camera, and I see that the skin has turned gray…no, not gray. Pearlescent. Like a cue ball.

Like the Pall.

"It is spreading." He takes another shaking breath. "It does not hurt. There is just numbness. It seems that, while whatever destroyed Earth is no longer active against technology, it is still active against…us." He glances toward the door. "I've told Nancy I am not feeling well and am not to be disturbed. She will think, as she is programmed to think, that I live on in these quarters. She will survive, perhaps for centuries. If there *are* any survivors in the Necklace, maybe they'll find her. Maybe they will find the treasure trove I've put aboard her. Maybe one of them will find this." He looks straight at the camera. "If that's you, I pity you."

The screen goes blank.

Nancy speaks. "I have just received instructions from Mr. Breckenridge. I am to surface and allow you to send a transmission."

I nod. The terror that gripped me a moment ago is already fading. My fate was sealed the moment I entered Earth orbit. It just took me some time to realize it.

* * *

The *Nancy Blackett* has surfaced again, and will remain on the surface while she sends the massive transmission I have requested: Breckenridge's "virtual Earth."

It will take days, but all the lost knowledge and art and culture of Earth will beam out to the Interdiction station, along with the news that life thrives on Earth, but no human can ever come here again. The Pall may not be eating technology—perhaps, it occurs to me, because those who sent it our way plan sometime soon to come in person with their own technology, to seize and colonize the planet—but still, humanity's time on Earth is done.

The embryos are already gone, turned to gray dust inside their cryogenic canisters.

Breckenridge was quite right. The gray patch on my hand doesn't hurt. It's only numb.

And it's spreading.

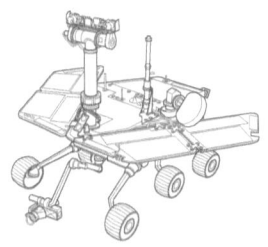

Sanctuary

John G. Hartness

If it had just been the zeds, we would have been fine. It would have been ugly, and bloody, and we would have gotten covered in goop that made us stink to the high heavens until we could find a stream to scrub off in or it rained hard enough to get us clean, but we wouldn't have lost anyone. A few cracks to the nog, a slash of the gourd here and there, and boom-splat, down go the zeds.

If it had just been a bunch of boot-sucking ravagers, that would have been okay, too. We might have lost one or two, but there were eight of us, most all of us trained scouters and Wings. We could take a band of ravagers with the gear we toted.

But it's never one thing, amirite? It's always about one bucket more than the slophole can handle and you end up with graywater all over your feet. And that's why I'm running all alone through a forest I've never seen before chasing a blinking light on my wrist from a piece of tech that shouldn't even work, much less lead me anywhere.

I'm alone. I'm cold. I'm hungry. I'm lost as a babe with no nipple to latch on to, I've got this weird watch thing pointing me to gods knows where, and I don't know what's more like to kill me if I slow up, the zeds or the batcrazy ravagers.

And I gotta pee.

* * *

I fair flew out of my bunk when the boot scuffed dirt close to my head. I rolled to the floor, billy in my fist, spinning to trip up whoever was stupid enough to try and sneak up on me. My leg swept around, but the guy hopped up instead of falling over. I jabbed with my billy like a sword, straight for where his balls oughter land, but he came down with his hands out, covering the jewels, so all I got was a rap on the back of his knuckles. Oh well. At least he didn't have a blade. If he was worth a drizzle with a knife, I'd be done. But his hands were empty, so I had a chance.

"Meg, cut it!" he said in a sharp whisper. I froze. I knew that voice.

I was on my feet in a bounce, wrapping my arms around the big maroon's neck, throwing my legs around his waist, letting out a squeal like a rat with its tail caught in a door. "Timbo! Jeezopeet, you idjit I almost cracked you like an egg! What are you doing sneaking up on a girl like that? Don't you know there's nasty buggers all around who can't keep a zip up? I sleep *light*, bruh, and I swing heavy."

"And you chatter like a hellspawned crow," the grumpy lump next to me growled. "Shut your facehole, Meg, or I'll get up and shut it for you."

"Drink piss out of my boot, Starling," I said as I dropped to my feet. I reached out a hand and put it on Timbo's chest, just a kind of reassurance he was really there. He'd been out on a long run. Gone six cycles, since way back in the snows.

"Where you been, anyhoo?"

"We ran into ravagers a week out from the walls and they chased us almost all the way to DesMo before they got bored and wandered off. Then we headed north to Mapolis and looked to see if anything good washed up on the shores lately."

"Find any shinies for me?" Timbo was good about bringing me neat bits and bobs from his runs. Never anything that worked or could be harvested to make something else work, that stuff went into the stores straightaway, but some of the old gadgets still looked neato even if they never lit up or did anything.

"You act like you only missed me for my treats, Megpie," Timbo said with a grin. I scowled at him. Our da used to call me Megpie when me and Tim were littles. "Here you go, sisling. A sparkly for my diamond."

I took the shiny from him and dangled it in front of my face. It looked like a watch, but when I held it up to my ear, it didn't tick or make any noise. There were a pair of buttons on one side, but nothing happened when I pressed them, and there was no tell-tale clicking or tension of springs when I wound the little dial on the side. "What is it?"

"A trader I swap with sometimes gave it to me. Said it would show me the way to go home. I told him I knew how to find home, but he threw it in on a trade for me anyway. Reckon next time I see him, he'll charge me double for the battery." Timbo's easy smile filled the room like sunshine and I threw my arms around his neck again. "I missed you, apeface. Missed you every day. You gone too long. Serah even went behind the Council Hall with Toby Jangs last week. *That's* how long you been gone."

Tim sighed and shadows fluttered across his broad face.

"I know I been gone a long time," he said, looking at his boots. "And I gotta go again. I just—"

"Way*what?*" I yelped. "You gotta go? You just got here! No way you go again. Not for a longwhile at least. Where you gotta go, anyroad? What so spicy it make you turn around and run back Outwall before you even been here a day? You ain't been home *half* a day. No." I crossed my arms and locked my knees. I wouldn't allow it. I wouldn't move from this spot until he agreed to stay. "You can't go."

"I have to, Meg," he started, then hesitated. "Can you still shoot?"

"I can skewer a cherry at fifty meters," I bragged, only exaggerating a tetch.

"Good," he said. "Because we're down a ranger for this run since Jera came up pregs on the way back from Mapolis."

I heard his words, then my legs turned to water as they made it through my skull.

Ranger? Me?

"Uh…you sure, bro? You always said noway I was ever going to ranger if you still live." This was all I'd wanted since Timbo had been going Outwall—to go with. Now it was here, I wasn't sure if I was more excited or terrified.

* * *

I should have picked terrified. If I'd picked terrified, I would have dealt with my fear back in SooCity, on the safe side of the Wall. And if I'd dealt with it there and then, I wouldn't be dealing with it here and now, running barehand through strange woods in the middle of the night all alone with a pack of zeds closing on me every minute. I hate fast zeds. Just ain't natural.

A branch across my cheek brings tears to my eyes and my focus back to my feet. I can barely see where I'm putting them, counting on the thin trees not to trip me up too bad and hoping I don't hit any holes. I don't. Good me. I don't hit a hole, anyroad.

I hit a branch, but instead of tripping over it like a normie girl, I step on it, it rolls under my foot, and I launch myself into the air like a pigeon what's been drinking out of Henro's beer barrel, all squawking and flapping useless as I slam into the ground. The air rushes out of my lungs and I lay on my belly for a terrifying second while I try to remember how lungs work. I can't breathe and I slammed my chin into the ground when I went down and I'm seeing stars and I don't know if I see stars because my head hurts or because I don't have any air and I see the lights dancing in the edges of my vision and I feel like I'm about to pass out when my breath slams back in with a *WHOOSH* and a gasp and suddenly the sparkles recede and I'm back to normal levels of panicfright.

I can't lay there, though. I've already been still too long and I hear the zeds crashing and crackling branches all around me and I think that I really should have stayed up that tree, but I got to trust the signal blinking on my wrist if I'm gonna find safety, find Timbo, find anything. So I get my hands underneath me, shove myself to my feet, and I take off again.

* * *

"Crew, this is Meg," Timbo said as we walked up to the half-dozen folx gathered by the western gate. They were dressed mostly alike, in the same kind of brown and green camo as my scratchy new pants and jacket. A couple of them looked me up and down, like they were trying to decide if they needed to just ice me now and dump me over the Wall instead of waiting for zeds to do it later and them have to dig me a grave out in the Wild.

One of the scouts, a Wing named Calvin that I remembered seeing with Timbo once or twice, came over and held out his hand. "Heya youngun. I'm Cal. Stick close and I'll have you tree-running legit before we come back from this gooser." A white smile split his dark face and a dimple appeared on his cheek. I felt my knees go a little watery at the glimmer in his brown eyes, but then Tim stuck his big sniffer in.

"She's my kidsis. This is her first run. Let's make sure it's not her last."

The dimple vanished from Cal's cheek and he held out his hand. "Good to meet you, sisling."

I shook it, looking over his uniform. "Wings don't dress like everybody else?"

"Nah, we gots to be fast and light, like a bird, yo." He waved a hand over his uniform, which was the same colors as most of the crew, but that's where the lookalikes ended. His pants were tight and stretchy, like a green and brown skin, with lumps at the knees and guards strapped around his lower legs for gripping the trees. His hands were covered in thick gloves with curved talons sticking out of the fingertips, and tiny versions of the same jutting out from his palms to help him climb and grip better. Everything about his uniform was made to get him high in the trees and let him swoop down on ravagers or zeds from above. His minicross, the pistol-shaped bow that every Wing built themselves and carried until their last flight, hung from one hip. It was flashy, like Cal himself, with a gleaming silver pistol grip and a bright red bow polished to a high shine.

"The big guy with a face like an ox and shoulders to match is Garn. He's our lockpicker and asskicker," Timbo said from my shoulder. "Soo and Syl are rear guard," he said, pointing to a pair of identical twins with bows and a row of thick tubes strapped across their chests. "Anything tries to sneak up on us, S-Two will make a lot of light and noise with their boomsticks.

"You'll be scouting or guarding flank with Garn. He'll help you strap in and make sure there's nothing reflective or noisy where it shouldn't be."

I fastened the bracelet thing Tim gave me around my left wrist. Garn held out a gear belt for me. I wrapped it around my waist and pulled it tight, letting it rest above my regular belt, like the others did. A black knife hung from the left side, with a canteen centered in back. I took the offered machete and strapped it onto the belt in front of the knife.

"You loaded up?" Timbo's voice popped in at my shoulder and I started a little. He chuckled and put a heavy hand on my shoulder. Felt good. Solid. With my bigbro around, I'm good. I'm five-by.

"Yeah, let's get moving," I said with a bravado I don't really feel.

"Grab your bow and take a share of the rats," Tim said, pointing over to the pile of rations on a nearby table. I watch Cal take six packs, and I grab five. He grins at me and slides two more packs over to me.

"Take 'em, kid. They always send extras for Garn and he doesn't need them. He eat everything they send him, he be too fat to run."

"I'm good to try, though," Garn says, clapping the slender Wing on his shoulder and nearly knocking him to the dirt.

I stow the rats in my pack and sling it across both shoulders. I tighten the straps and fasten the belly band across my front. My pack has food for a week, plus two full liters of water in metal bottles painted black to kill reflection. I let that fall off and I'm never getting back to town, whether we see zeds or not.

"Okay," Timbo calls, "Let's get moving. Watch your six, and most importantly…" He paused, waiting for a response.

He got it. "Watch mine!" the rest of the crew yelled, and we laughed and joked as we strode through the gates to see what we could trade for or scavenge between home and Kaycee.

* * *

It's getting lighter. At first I don't even notice, but then I can see a little of where I'm putting my feet, and it's easier to run. Then I start to be able to make out the forms of a couple of zeds through the trees and I'm not just having to avoid them by ear. After a ways, the sun's up, and I look around. No zeds. The only thing moving as far as I can see in all directions is me. I gave 'em the shake. Another night. Another not dead. All I got; all I need.

I find a tree with low branches. Oak, maybe. It's up on a hill at the top of a gully, so I'm all hope I can get high enough to see something. Maybe a town. Maybe Tim.

I blink back more stupid tears. I won't see Timbo. Not because he's a deader, but because he's smart. Only a zedhead would wear anything lets you be seen from a treetop and Tim's always been the smart one.

I start climbing, wishing I had Cal's Wing-gloves, with their spikes and talons. I don't even have the thin cloth mitts I started out with.

I get lucky for once. The oak tree is taller than the skinny little pine trees around it and I can get a long way up before the branches start to bend too much under my feet. There's nothing around me, no zeds in sight, and nothing even moving through the trees. I'm safe for a minute. Safe as I'm gonna get out here on my own with no food, no water, and only my knife for a weapon.

Then I hear something like thunder off in the distance. When I stand back up on the branch, I see a pack of ravagers coming from the northwest, a dozen or more, all on horses, and that makes up my mind. Don't matter if I'm going to a sanctuary. Don't matter what this shiny on my wrist says. I'm sure as shit stinks brown going *away* from those motherless bastards.

* * *

"Ohey, wassat?" It was Cal, walking ahead on what used to be an interstate, back when there were states. Since we were out of the trees, the Wings covered front and rear. Cal was pacing front, fifty meters ahead of us, and he'd just topped a ridge when he called back. "Looks like a trader. Can't tell if it's junker or richboy stuff."

"Any markings?" Tim called back.

"Nothing I can see…wait, hangonamin, there's a chicken foot in a circle. It's Jerry! I see the dancing bears!"

"Sweet," Garn said to me. "Jerry's a good barter. He's fair and nobody knows where he gets the stuff he gets. Tough old coot, too. Nobody messes with the Jer-bear. He eat you alive, that one."

This was the first person we'd seen since we left home and I was nervous. Even though Garn said he was nice, being stopped out in the open worried me. I'd heard Timbo's stories for years about ravagers rolling up on groups that let their guard down to trade and how he and his kept finding nothing but piles of naked bodies, sometimes not all of them. Nobody ever outright named the ravagers cannibal, but nobody ever said they wasn't, either.

But it would be sweet to see these barters Timbo told me about. Maybe I could get a shiny for myself, or maybe take something back to Starling. She didn't say nothing, but the look when I walked out the gate said she was worried. This was the first time we'd been apart for more than a day. I didn't know I'd miss her 'til I got the chance to. Maybe a necklace or bracelet. I didn't have nothing to trade, really, but Tim'd help me out if I saw something that glimmered me.

It took a while to get to the wagon, with Cal running ahead to tell him we were coming. By the time we got there, the fat graybeard had his wagon chocked and the sides down, showing off racks and racks of shinies and stuff I didn't even know what.

"Jerry!" Timbo said walking up. "How you be, grandpa?"

"Old, but not that old, kiddo," the man replied. "Come on over here and show me some love, boy."

Tim gave the trader a big hug, lifting the shorter man off the ground a little. When he put him down, he waved me over. "Meg, come over here."

I did as he asked, tearing my eyes away from a stick with necklaces in all colors dangling from it. "Bear, this is my kidsis Meagan. Meagan Tydings, this is Jerry the Bear. He's one of the gooduns. He trades fair and don't try to bone you out of coin or goods just because he don't know what something is. He's the one who traded me your watch."

I looked down at my wrist, at the flat black square that glinted when I turned it just right in the sun. "Thank you, sir. It forsure is pretty."

"It'll be even prettier when it works, kidling," the man says. "Glad I crossed paths with you, Timbo. I forgot to give this to you last time and hoped I'd see you again before we both fed worms." He turned back to his wagon, opened a drawer on the side, and pulled out another leather strap, this one ringed in solar panels with a cord coming out of it.

He held it out to me. "Strap this on your arm above the watch. The panels should charge the battery, then you'll be able to turn the watch on once it's got power."

"What does it do then?" I asked. I felt my checks go warm. "I mean, I know what a watch does. It's a little clock that you wear. But what does this one do that's diff?"

Jerry scratched his thick gray beard and looked away before he answered. "I don't know for true, but I saw one like this that would tell time, direction, and even play old songs. No telling if this one even turns on, or what it do if it does." I knew Timbo and his crew trusted this barter, but he knew more than he was telling about this watch. But if Tim trusted the old man, I did too, so I hooked it all up like he showed me.

"Thanks, Jer-bear," Tim said, giving the old man another massive hug. "What I owe you?"

"Nothing. The ammo you traded for the watch brought me a week in a soft bed with a warm body next to me back at Desmo, so we're five-by."

The others shopped for a while, but I was entranced by the watch and the charging strap. I kept moving it from arm to arm, up and down, until I finally settled on the watch on my left wrist, with the charge band just above my elbow. If I wrapped the cord around my arm right, it didn't hang and I could draw my knife without getting snagged. No matter how shiny, it wasn't worth catching a bite.

The sun was low when everybody was finished up and Tim looked around. "Maybe just stay here for the night? Share a fire and pass around a bottle?" He looked from Jerry to the rest of our crew and everyone nodded. It had been steady hauling since we left home and it'd be nice to have a short day. We were in a pretty good spot, too. Down in a kind of a bowl, but it was wide and flat and no trees for a hundred meters on any side. Plenty of warning if something rolled up in the night, especially if we posted sentries on the ridges.

Which is exactly what Timbo did. Cal set up for first watch, with a boomstick to fire off if he saw any threats coming. I grabbed a shovel off my pack and cleared away a big circle of grass, then ringed it with stones for a fire. Jerry set up a portable stove that folded down off the side of his wagon and put water on to boil.

Timbo threw vegetables and chunks of dried meat into the pot of water, Jerry added some herbs and chunks of fresher meat to the pot, and before long the smells of stew filled the air. It wasn't any kind of luxury, but it was what we had, it was hot, and it was filling. Nobody'd go to sleep with their stomach gnawing on their ribs tonight, and that was a good night.

I was just scraping my knife across the bottom of my bowl when I heard Cal shout "Ravagers!" A streak of red fire flew into the sky and exploded over everything as the camp boiled all over chaos trying to get safe before the attack came.

I was scared almost to peeing my pants, but everybody around me was cool as could be. Less than a minute after Cal's shout, Jerry had his cart buttoned up tight and was crawling in the back of it. I heard a *thump* a few seconds later as a hatch on the roof opened and the old trader popped up with a crossbow mounted to the roof and a battered helmet covering his gray hair.

Timbo had his longbow in hand and a half-dozen arrows jammed into the dirt in front of him, his sword sticking out of the dirt by them. The others were set up all alike, except Cal, who had his mini cross out and ready but also had a staff leaning against the wagon behind him. The handbows weren't good for much distance, but I'd seen the Wings practice enough nights to know any ravager that got close was in for a headache or worse.

I tried to calm my breathing and my bladder as the thunder of ravager horses got closer and I stuck my arrows in the dirt like everybody else. I jammed my machete at the end of a row of four arrows, all I figured I'd be able to shoot before everything was all in my face, then I nocked an arrow and spun around, trying to put an eye on the baddos in the shadows of the gloaming.

I saw one, a skinny girl no more years than me, her face dirty and her teeth filed down to points. She had three red lines on her cheek, what some took to mean she'd killed three people, and she grinned when she locked eyes with me like she knew where her fourth mark was coming from.

All this ran through my head in half a second as I drew back an arrow and sent it flying, straight and true at the girl's chest, only to smack into her and bounce off like it was flyspit, not slowing her even a step. I pulled another arrow, let fly again, this time at her head, but my shot just smacked into her helmet and skittered off like a drunken bumblebee. I didn't get a third shot, because just before I loosed again, she flew back out of her saddle like there was a rope around her waist, the heavy bolt from Jerry's crossbow piercing her chest and taking her to the ground.

"You gotta hit 'em in the face or hit 'em hard, kidsis!" the old trader yelled as he reloaded his massive crossbow.

I pulled up an arrow and put it to my string, looking for another target, but they were in too close. Timbo was tangled up with the nearest one, and I couldn't take the shot without skewering him, so I dropped my bow and snatched up the machete as I ran to where the fat bandit was swinging a giganto club at my brother's head.

I ran up behind and hacked the ravager in the neck, right where his armor had a joint. He froze, the club falling to the ground as he spun around. I musta hit him just square, because his eyes were vacant and his mouth slack, with hunks of stringy meat hanging between his black, pointy teeth. A confused look lay on his face and he collapsed to the dirt, stone dead.

I looked down at the deader, blood still pooling around his head to mix in with the dirt at Timbo's feet, and all of a sudden my stomach twisted itself into a knot and every bit of stew I put down that night came back up and out and all over the ravager's dead face.

"It's rough the first time," Tim said, putting a hand on my shoulder. "Honest, it don't get a whole lot better any other time. But you're walking and he's lying in the dirt. Now mercy the bastard and get back to the wagon so nobody gets in behind you."

I knelt beside the ravager and looked in his eyes, wide open but staring at nothing. In a few minutes, maybe an hour, those eyes would go all milky-white and the toothy bugger would be back up and hunting again, this time without even as much thinking as he done in life. I yanked the knife out of my belt, raised it up, and drove it through his skull, right above his nose. I gave it a twist, just like Timbo taught me when I was a little, and wiped the blade clean on his shirt. Then I yanked my machete free of his neck, spit a mouthful of bile onto the corpse, and stood up, looking for who needed me.

It was Garn, of all people, who was all jammed up. The big guy had a hammer in each hand and was swinging like he was beating a drum, but there was four ravagers all around him, and cuts on both legs and both arms. He was gonna slow down, and when he missed a strike, he'd be zedbait for surenough.

I let out a scream that came up from my toes and I charged in at the scumboys around our big'n. Garn grinned over at me, then his eyes popped wide as an arrow poked out the back of his head and came straight out his mouth. He dropped down on his face and I saw the archer sitting a horse ten meters away. She was too far for me to get to before she dropped me, but that wasn't the worst of it. The worst of it was behind her.

"Zeds!" I yelled. "It's a horde!" I dunno if they were drawn by the fire, by the noise, the smell of blood, or all of it, but there had to be a hundred zeds already over the rise and almost on us. I hadn't never seen a horde like that, since most of the zeds were long done by the time I came, but this was a *lot* of stumbling biters, and not all of them were slow. Three of the fastest got to the archer and dragged her out of the saddle, while another half dozen took down her horse. They were mouths with feet and we were the menu.

Everybody scattered in all directions and it was a whirlwind of rangers, zeds, and ravagers with everybody going everywhich. I tried to keep eyes on Timbo, but a hole in the storm opened up and I bolted.

I made it ten meters before a female zed popped up in front of me and I stabbed straight out with my machete. It slid into her rotted belly and guts and blood and other nastiness spilled out like I lanced a boil, but I felt the blade bind up between two ribs, and she just kept coming for my face like I'd barely tickled her.

The head, stupid. I ducked under her arms and spun out of the way, letting go of my machete when I couldn't pull it free of her guts. I jammed my knife down into the top of her skull and she dropped to the ground, finally dead for good. I jabbed the blade into the ground and yanked it out, getting the worst of the gunk off it, then grabbed the handle of my machete. I gave a tug, but it wouldn't budge. I put one foot against the zed's chest and pulled with both hands, but before I could even get the machete to wiggle a little, a ravager tripped over me, slamming a knee into my skull and bowling me over.

I came up with my knife at the ready, but the bandit was scrambling to his feet and running for the treeline. More zeds flowed down the ridge like a tide of cockroaches and I followed the ravager, hauling ass for the trees and something that looked like it might be safety. I ran for an hour or more, finally shaking loose the last of the fast zeds and finding a big oak tree to hide in. I sat there all night, sleeping a minute here, five minutes there, snapping awake at the sound of another zed scratching at the bottom of the tree or something crunching through the woods nearby.

A couple times I almost called out, but either heard something that sounded like it wasn't my crew, or something inside just told me to keep my trap snapped, so I stayed silent until all a sudden right before dawn the watch on my arm lit up like a boomstick glow in the night and started beeping loud enough to draw every zed for a mile away.

I looked down at my wrist, at the forgotten watch and charger rig, and couldn't believe what I saw. There on the screen was a blinking green square—"New Emergency Message." I pressed on the square and the display changed. It read, "Sanctuary. Food, water, shelter. Click yes and follow the arrow." There was a green circle this time, with "YES" on it, so I pressed that part of the screen. The display changed again and an arrow appeared, pointing off away from the direction I came in.

I don't know what I thought this thing would do—tell time, maybe? But this wasn't it. I tapped the screen a couple more times, but the arrow stayed there, just blinking at me like a firefly in the dark. A firefly that came along with an insistent beep like to drive me nuts.

I pressed my hand against the watch to try and muffle the sound, but that just let me hear the plod and scrape of zed feet coming closer, drawn by the sudden light and sound in the dead quiet night. I heard them coming, no fast ones crashing through the brush, just the plodding, never-stopping snap and shuffle of inexorable zeds staggering through the forest with only one thought in their dead brains—food.

I had to make a decision, and I could tell from the thump against the trunk below me I didn't have no more minutes for thinking about it. I could either stay up that tree until I figured out how to turn the damn watch off, get down and run like hell before the tree was surrounded, or throw the stupid shiny far as I could and run the opposite way.

I got as far as unbuckling the clasp before I saw Timbo's face, big goofy grin splitting his mouth as he gave me the shiny, all proud because he found something awesome for his kidsis. Tears blurred my vision and I thought about him, out there all alone, fighting off zeds so I could get away, doing for me like he always done. If this was the last thing he ever give me, I owed it to him to at least see what was at the end of that blinking arrow. Besides, how much worse could it be? I was already trapped up a tree with no food and no water in a forest full of hungry zeds. If there was anything to this "Sanctuary," it had to be better than starving to death up a tree like a squirrel run out of nuts.

I skinned down the tree and vaulted three zeds clawing at the trunk to hit the carpet of pine needles in a crouch. I took off running, hoping there were no fast zeds, and praying against faith this message wasn't a ravager trap.

* * *

And now I'm crouched behind a big hunk of granite sticking up out of the ground, looking around for some sign of where I'm supposed to go. The arrow on my watch is blinking so damn fast it's almost a steady green, but it just keeps spinning around in a circle, like the compass is drunk and about to fall down. The ravagers are a couple kilometers back yet, but I'm pretty sure at least one of them saw me, so I either find this sanctuary *now* or I'm heading into some dirty cannibal's stewpot.

The sun's up for true now, done killed any kind of shadow I coulda hid in. I peek over my rock, but I can't see nothing that looks like a sanctuary. I'm on top of a hill about fifty meters from the edge of a forest, and an old road, mostly grown over now, runs down the hill and off along abandoned fields in the distance. I got no idea where I am, except that I never been here before, so I'm nowhere close to SooCity, nowhere close to anything familiar, nowhere close to Timbo, or Cal, or even big silly Garn or the weird twins.

I take a deep breath and shove all the shuddering weepies down into my gut. I'll drag them out later, if I get a later. I stand up, look around. I don't see nobody, but there's a tree here and there, and the grass and weeds are tall, so that don't mean much.

"Hello?" I call out, startling a crow from a branch high in a nearby tree. Nobody calls back, no magic door opens in the dirt, nothing. I look down at the watch and see the arrow gone. Now there's just a blinking green dot on the screen, blinking fast, like it's a beacon or something. I'm glad it's light out, because in the dark it *would* be a beacon, and not the kind drawing anything I want to find me.

"I need sanctuary," I call out, feeling stupid out in the middle of nowhere talking to nothing. "Is anybody there? Anybody?" My voice breaks a little at the end and I ball up a fist, trying to hold myself tight and not fly to pieces all lost and alone, like some stupid little girl done wandered off from camp. I'm a grown woman. I'm a ranger, and even if I don't have my crew, I still got my knife, and with enough time and luck, I can find my way home.

That's it. I'll find my own way back, and Timbo will be there waiting for me, and everybody else, and it'll all be five-by. I just need a little luck. Yeah, 'cept bad luck still counts as luck, and that's all I got in this world.

"Hey there," comes a voice from behind me, and I spin around, pulling my knife and holding the blade low. He's big, the man who came out of nowhere. Big, and dirty, and not the least tetch sanctuary-looking. He's got the patched-together armor of a ravager, but he's smiling with his mouth shut, so I can't see his teeth. My gut tells me if he opens his mouth everything in there will be black as night soil and filed razor-sharp, but I don't go at him. He's too big for that. I need to wait, pick a spot, and strike.

"Hey," I say, and hate myself for the shake in my voice.

He takes a step forward and I raise the blade. He lifts up his hands to show me no weapons, but I see the axe hanging from his belt. He's playing all harmless, but he ain't empty-handed. Nobody out here is. "You looking for sanctuary? I can take you there. I'm the welcome."

"You? Not to offense, but yous a scary welcome."

The man chuckles, but he pulls his hand up fast to hide his mouth so I still don't see no pointed teeth. "You not wrong, little. Gotta be scary to live out here, though, amirite? Name's Tern." He steps forward, holds out a hand to shake.

I hesitate, but I do it. I switch the knife to my left hand and clasp his right. "Meg."

He doesn't let go, but his face keeps a smile. "Where you from, Meg? Why you out here all solo?"

"SooCity," I say, then kick myself a little. I shouldn't tell him I'm from far. He'll know nobody's coming for me. I try to recover. "I ain't solo. Just scouting for my crew. They a couple kilos back." I wave at the forest.

He turns a little toward where I point, and that's when the minicross on his hip comes into view. It's got a silver bow and a red handle. I know that bow. It's Cal's. No way did the Wing let it go bloodless. Tern looks back to me, catches my eye, and this time when he grins at me he doesn't bother to hide the ravager teeth I knew were there all along.

One good thing about not trusting nobody—it makes me real hard to disappoint. I stab at the big man with my left hand, but it's awkward and he just raises his right arm to block it. I kick for his crotch, but he turns and I just catch his leg.

"That's good, girlchild. Get the blood fired up. Makes you spicier." He grins and pulls me to him. I can't stop him. He's too big. He switches up his grip and now he's got me by the wrist. I slash at him with the knife again, but this time he just balls up his big left fist and clouts me upside the nog. Stars bloom and everything goes fuzzy before it snaps back into focus. He's closer now, so I raise a knee into his balls and he lets go for half a second.

I spin around, try to run, but he's fast to be such a big scuzz and I feel something yank me back by the hair and I slam to the ground. My vision goes all stars again, then pain explodes in my side as he stomps me right under my left breast. Something in my chest goes all pop-pop, and it feels like I'm trying to breathe through a knife, and my head explodes in white flashes again as he kicks me, and I'm trying to curl up, and then he's down on me, his rankass breath in my ear as he leans down and *licks* me.

"Oh, you gonna be good on the spit, girlchild. I might even save one juicy hock all for me. I found you, after all. I should get the choicest cut." He slaps me on the ass and laughs, and I unfurl myself and rip a long line of red across his face with my knife. I stab him in the leg and flail around, trying to get free. He can't catch me with that knife in his leg, but he slams an open palm into my chest where he broke my insides and all the fight goes out. I try to scream but there's no air, and everything is pain and stars in my eyes and stink filling my nose and I know I'm about two seconds away from seeing Timbo again, and somehow that does make it just a little tiny bit better.

The ravager straightens up on his knees, presses one hand down on my forehead, and sits on my hips. He grits his teeth as he pulls my knife out of his thigh, and his breath comes out in a fierce whistle, like a kettle on a fire. He licks his own blood off the blade and smiles at me, and that smile is the coldest, hungriest thing I've ever seen.

"Your blood gonna taste so much sweeter." He raises the knife, turns my head to one side to bare the side of my neck, and I squeeze my eyes shut against what's coming.

But it never comes. What comes instead is a stink of ozone in the air, a loud *bzzzzzzZAP* sound, and a strangled, tiny, "Urk." Then there's a *thump*, and the weight on top of me is tripled. I open my eyes and Tern's face is pressed up against mine, his eyes wide open with a look of confusion. I wriggle and twist and try to get out from under him, but my broken ribs won't let me shove his limp carcass off.

"Hang on, kid. Let me." The voice is nobody I've heard before, but it doesn't have the weird slithery sound ravagers get from jaxing up their teeth, so maybe I'm saved? The weight on my chest disappears and I see Tern's corpse fly up and land four or five meters away. A hand appears, stretched out in front of my face, and I just stare at it for a second. It's a clean hand, with nails that ain't all broke up from hard work, and no cuts or scars all over the knuckles.

I follow the hand and look up the arm to an unfamiliar face. It's a man and he's smiling. Not the predatory ravager smile, or even the mocking smile Timbo used to get sometimes I didn't know what he was talking about. No, this dude is happy to see me. Like, *happy* happy. I don't remember the last time I saw anybody who looked happy, or healthy, but he's both.

I take his hand and he pulls me up. The world spins and my vision tunnels a little at the pain in my side, but I don't fall over. Counts as a win. "What did you do to him?" I ask, looking at the dead ravager. There are little tendrils of smoke coming up from his chest and he's not even twitching.

"He was a dick. I killed him. You're welcome," the stranger says.

"But how?" I walk over for a look at the dead man's chest. There's a hole burned clean through the middle of him. A perfect hole, not even any blood at the edges.

"Magic," he said. He looks down at my wrist. "You got the message. Good. Looks like Jerry found us another recruit."

I follow his eyes to my watch, still with that green blinking dot on the screen. "Yeah. My bigbro gave it to me. He got it from Old Jerry the Bear. You know him?"

"Yeah, Jerry's an old friend. We work together, kinda. I rebuild old tech into homing devices, and he goes out into the dead world looking for good people, people who deserve a chance."

"A chance at what?" And did Jerry mean for this watch to come to me, or Tim? Probably my bigbro, given they were pals.

"A chance to live, kid. This world is ugly, and we can't make it any prettier, but we can pull in the best folx we can find and keep 'em safe. Then maybe one day we can all come up out of the ground and build something good again."

"So, you the one sending the signal? How long you been doing this?"

"Ever since the dead started walking. I've got my own crew, all over the place, and this is what we do. We rebuild old tech, send it out with traders, and get it into the hands of good people. Then we bring them here." He waves a hand and mutters something under his breath. The rock I was hiding behind slides aside and there's stairs leading down under it. There was a magic hole in the dirt after all.

"You made it, kid. You're safe here for as long as you want, provided you don't look to harm anybody else here. What's your name?"

"Meg. Meagan Tydings," I reply, holding out my hand. "What's yours?"

The tall man shakes my hand and brushes back a lock of brown hair. He looks me in the eye, and there's something about this trim man with the square jaw and eyes too old for the rest of his face that I trust like I never trusted anybody on first sight, not ever. "I've got a lot of names, kid. Assholes like your friend there, they call me Reaper. My closest call me Q. You can call me Harker. Quincy Harker. Welcome to Sanctuary."

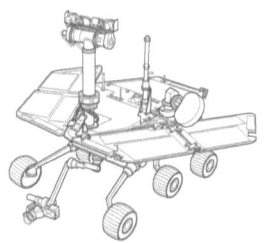

Terra 3:56

Alexander Gideon

Destruction came without feeling.

Android 3:56 had felt the first bite of the Mars Class security droid's laser; the fabricated nerves her creator laced through her synthetic skin saw to that. She had almost reached the Core to start her repairs when it burned through her. When she tried to run the second Annihilator severed her legs. She remembered the jolt of pain when her head slammed into the floor as she fell. Then the coolness of the metal on her cheek.

But in the end, destruction came without feeling.

Death was made for flesh and blood and bone. For the natural. Androids didn't die. If something damaged their circuitry, they ceased to function, or were decommissioned. They could be turned off, re-purposed, or destroyed. But they did not die. And they did not pass on to some other level of existence. No, that was reserved for the humans and the "souls" they so fervently believed in.

What has happened to me, then? 3:56 wondered as she stared down at her broken and twisted shell.

A laser blast through the chest had destroyed one of her major power cells, which shut her systems down. She hadn't felt the Annihilator smash her cranial carapace into a thousand pieces. Nor the utter obliteration of her AI core and its supporting processors. Yet, somehow, her systems persisted.

"A curious thing, that," a man said behind her, giving her a start. She turned, her fight or flight functions activating. She stilled when she saw the scruffy man in his lab coat studying her.

"Professor Devol?" Her tinny voice sounded hollow and distant. As if her speech came from the walls rather than her mouth.

"I only look like the scientist that created you."

No grin, no running his hand through his scruffy hair. That, more than anything, told her this wasn't the Professor.

"Then who are you? How do you know who I am?"

"I've had many names." He strolled towards her, hands in the pockets of his coat. "Thanatos. Anubis. Supay. Hel. Mania. Mors. In the dark ages of humanity, they called me the Grim Reaper. I don't believe any of these truly describe my existence, but you may call me what you will."

She searched her databases for those names and they all came back with the same attribution.

"You're Death?"

"If you wish to think of me as such." He stopped only a few meters from her. "But that's not quite correct. Death is a natural part of existence. All life ends, and I have no say in it's happening. I'm just a guide."

"A guide to what?"

"To what is next."

3:56 crossed her arms.

"But what is next for me?"

"I don't know," Death said. "You're the first of your kind. The first unnatural being to have a soul."

3:56 hated that word. Unnatural. The Professor made her almost indistinguishable from a human, from her dark skin and hair to the green of her eyes. She smiled, and laughed, and hurt, and *felt*. But no matter how much she wished it, she remained a fabrication. Artificial. *Unnatural.*

She blinked, only just registering the rest of what Death said.

"I have a soul?" she whispered. Death nodded.

"You currently *are* a soul." He bent to inspect her mangled shell, rubbing the scruff on his cheeks. "Which is why you're whole. But the real question is whether or not you actually died."

"My body is broken, my circuitry ruined, and my AI core demolished." She shook her head. "I think I died."

"Those things can be repaired."

Her creator *had* already performed a miracle to make her. Maybe...

"You mean the real Professor can fix me?"

"He might need all the King's horses and all the King's men."

An awful joke, but his neutral delivery made her laugh.

"I think it possible. After all, I feel no compulsion to open the door for you. Only to watch."

A sputtering noise rattled through the ship. 3:56 looked across the long room to the Dark Matter Field Core—DMFC for short—in its tungsten casing at the far end. The ship rattled again, and the Core's casing cracked with a loud report that echoed around them. All the mirth drained from her face.

"It won't matter. I couldn't finish the repairs before the Annihilators ruined me. When the ship passes into the wormhole, it'll collapse. They're all going to die."

"Are they?" The core shook again and its casing cracked more.

"I can't mend the Core if I'm dead!"

She'd thought she liked him, but his casual indifference infuriated her. He glanced her way and something in his eyes changed. She saw sadness there, deep and black like the darkest corner of the universe. The sorrow of a being that must see the death of all things.

"Once, long ago, I abandoned my duties for a time. I returned to find an abundance of souls requiring my services. Many were not content to wait for my reappearance and tried to return to life."

3:56 blinked, the sudden change in subject throwing her off-kilter.

"A select few managed to inhabit the bodies of the deceased. I believe the folklore of the time called them ghouls."

"Why tell me this?"

"These human souls managed to inhabit a vacant vessel. That body there." He pointed at her ruined shell. "Can you inhabit no other?"

The processes raced in her mind. She was an android soul. *She* had millions of empty vessels to choose from. If she slipped inside one, could she take control of it and complete the repairs? Without another thought, she turned and raced across the Core room toward the door.

"Good luck," Death called after her.

She passed through the door and stalked down the hall of the engineering deck, parsing through all her compiled data on the robots on the ship. None were human enough to use the tools the Professor had squirreled away for her. But Devol had programmed her to improvise. She needed an Annihilator and, without an active threat, she expected to find them in the security bays, receiving repairs and recharging. Unfortunately, she had no idea where to find one. She was near the center of the ship, the best location for the DMFC to activate its dark matter attracting field. She'd start her search in the cryochambers and incubation units that sat above her along the bulk of the ship. The *Salvator Mundi*—the Savior of the World—was the largest cradle ship ever devised by humans. And it was their last-ditch effort to survive.

Centuries of overmining, overpopulation, and corrupt government had left the entire *Vox Humanitas* system depleted. At the end, only *Terra Secundo*, the primary planet of the system, remained—a tidally-locked planet, with only a narrow strip of habitable land between the darkness and the light. One tiny ring to hold the last vestiges of humanity.

To survive, the remainder of humanity needed to move to a new solar system capable of sustaining life. They knew of only one such system: the *Solis* system that birthed their species. But it lay over five hundred light years away. So they'd built the *Salvator Mundi*. But if the ship was to have a hope of making it to the *Solis* system then they had to find a way to reduce the distance.

Several entangled Kerr black holes lay along the way, and the engineers of the ship hoped to sling the *Salvator* through the wormholes created by them and reduce the transit time. Such travel required that the ship enter the exact center of the Kerr black hole's ring-shaped singularity, otherwise the hole's immense gravity would rip them apart. And it also required a Dark Matter Field Core to surround the ship with exotic matter to keep the wormhole open once entered, and keep the ship shielded from the extremely high-energy particles inside.

Manufacturing a DMFC big enough to gather the amount of dark matter needed for a vessel the size of the *Salvator* proved challenging. The Core's centrifugal rings were made of pure tungsten. An extremely rare metal in the *Vox Humanitas* system. And only Professor Devol saw the issues with the final design. The transit to the new system required a total of fifteen wormhole transits. The core could not survive so much stress. Devol predicted at least one of the rings would break before the end. Whether from pride, or from desperation for a solution, the engineers wouldn't listen. So the Professor built the most advanced android ever devised, programmed her with everything required to repair the ship in transit, and hid her on the ship.

That was her. Android model 3, version 56.

The cryo hall always seemed like a different world. Silence pervaded, the kind of reverent quiet usually reserved for the holiest of places. She slowed, taking in the rows of cryochambers. Not for the first time, she wished she could see within the sealed pods and catch a glimpse of the humans she so desperately sought to protect. Their species once dominated the heavens, billions strong. And now only fourteen thousand remained.

The clink of metal on metal reached her bionic ears and she turned. A Vulcan Class repair bot crawled along the cryo hall, its scanner passing over each pod, searching for any damage. A spindly little thing with five multi-jointed legs and a large tendril like a scorpion's tail protruding from its back. She hated to admit it, especially given how much she disliked the word, but the Vulcan Class bots always seemed unnatural to her. She had an urge to run. Before the Vulcan noticed her. Before it called the Annihilators.

But she was a spirit now. It could no longer see her, and she found that knowledge incredibly relieving. An idea struck her. The Vulcan knew the locations of the security bays within the ship. If Death was correct, and she could claim the body of another droid as her own for a time, then perhaps she could glean the information from its internal memory.

The Vulcan continued down the cryo hall and she haunted its steps. As she neared the mechanical hulk, she felt a kind of pull from it. A siren's call, begging her to approach. She obeyed, letting herself slip towards the Vulcan, closer and closer, until at last her existence overlapped with it. All of its processes exploded into her consciousness as she entered, demanding that she continue scanning each of the cryochambers. With an extreme effort she overrode the Vulcan's programming, shutting down its primary functions and asserting full control. Only then did she truly *become* the droid.

She searched its—*her*—memory bank and found the data she sought. She copied the Vulcan's memory to her own, marveling that she could do so. It seemed her spirit form had a kind of cloud storage of its own, and the implications of that fact astounded her. How much could she learn? And how much could she *do* with such knowledge? A security bay existed near the cryo hall. But Mars Class droids were too large to travel between the decks of the ship. She needed to find one on the same deck as the DMFC. It took a moment, but she found one, located at the opposite end of that deck. She tried to exit the Vulcan class again and found she couldn't.

Alright then, guess I'll just go like this, she thought.

She turned, relying upon the Vulcan's programming to keep her upright. She had never walked on five legs before, but it didn't take her long to master the practice. On the way down to the engineering deck, an alert shocked through her new programming:

UNIDENTIFIED ANOMALY DETECTED ON LIFT 23.

She'd heard similar alerts directed at her during her time on the *Salvator*. Professor Devol couldn't register her on the roster of service droids, so he'd smuggled her on board. That meant that whenever the Jupiter Class

AI that controlled the ship detected her, it labeled her as a threat and sent the Mars Class droids after her. She'd avoided them for eighty-six years before her death. She'd hoped taking a new body might allow her to go unnoticed by Jupiter, but claiming the Vulcan's body must have changed something within its programming.

Jupiter sent another alert.

AUTHORIZING PROTOCOL 6. SEEK AND DESTROY.

Not good.

Only a few moments later, the lift reached the engineering deck and the doors opened to three Mars Class security droids floating on the landing just outside. The second they registered her presence, they fired their lasers in unison. The first took her scanner tail. The second severed three of her legs. And the last split her body in two.

Her body fell apart, ejecting her spirit as the Vulcan's processors ceased functioning. She expected to feel something when her stolen body was destroyed, but she only felt her own fight or flight processes tearing through her systems. The eyes of the Mars Class droid passed over her and she raised her arms reflexively to protect herself. Then the security droids moved off and her terror began to subside.

"You're okay," she said aloud to herself. "You're already dead. The Annihilator's can't kill you again."

She set off after the Mars Class droids, processes whirring in her mind. About twelve minutes had passed from the moment she took control of the Vulcan to the moment Jupiter authorized the seek and destroy protocol. She'd left the Vulcan's programming intact, so Jupiter must have sensed *her*. Next time she guessed she'd have eight minutes. Ten at the most. A Mars Class droid's laser can cut through the tungsten of the DMFC's outer shell in seconds, but until she looked inside to the actual functioning parts of the Core, she couldn't estimate the repair time. She thought of that old adage the Professor used to love: she'd cross that bridge when she came to it.

She shadowed the Mars Class droids until they reached the entrance to the DMFC. She slipped inside the Mars droid at the back, the process of implanting herself within its systems coming much easier this time. It took her only a second to override the sequence to return to the security bay and assert control over the Mars droid's body.

The door to the DMFC bay opened and she glided inside. She thought of welding it shut, but not only would it have taken too long, she still needed to get a Vulcan Class inside to restart the Core. The crack in the casing had lengthened considerably since she left. She had to work fast.

Overloading the hover function let her rise up level with the shielding. She brought up an arm and activated the laser. With a small zap it pierced straight through the tungsten and out the other side. Panic shot through her systems, and she disabled the laser as quickly as she could. She thought she had a handle on using the Mars droid's functions, but she was woefully wrong.

Lifting her arm again, she settled on using a pulse instead of a steady beam. That seemed to work much better and in only a few moments she cut away the shielding, revealing the DMFC inside. The Core was made of five rings of pure tungsten, each rotating at high velocity. At the center of the rings, she could just make out a small, dark mass of energy barely larger than the head of a pin, but blacker than anything she'd ever seen. A tiny Schwarzschild black hole, it's microscopic, spherical singularity the only thing with enough gravity to gather dark matter. The rings not only generated the hole, they also siphoned off its gravity, then a selected targeting system streamed tendrils of gravity to detected dark matter sources to pull it to the ship.

She saw the problem immediately. The outer-most ring had snapped near one of the spinner arms, leaving it motionless. The years of perpetual motion must have weakened it. The Core could still generate the black hole, but without all five centrifugal rings in operation, the generated hole couldn't create enough gravity to snare the ambient dark matter. She had to fuse the tungsten back together then hijack another Vulcan to reactivate the ring.

ANOMALY DETECTED IN DARK MATTER FIELD CORE BAY.
Oh no.
AUTHORIZING PROTOCOL 6.

Thirty seconds later the bay doors opened and six other Mars Class droids glided into the bay. Her sensors detected targeting software. She spun as fast as her hover function allowed, activating her own targeting sequence and focusing on a spot in the middle of the cluster of Annihilators. She fired a grenade as six lasers sliced through her body. This time, she didn't let her fight or flight function take over. As soon as her spirit ejected, she dove for the next. Slammed herself inside. Wrenched control from the offensive sequences.

Her aim proved true. The grenade hit and detonated. Thick smoke billowed from it, coating her and the other Annihilators. The electrically-charged smoke confused their optical processes. For the other five, it rendered them nonoperational for a few seconds as their bionic eyes adjusted. Without guiding software, she could irreparably damage the

DMFC or the bay with her lasers. So she decided on good, oldfashioned blade work.

The end of her arm opened and a three-meter blade slid out and locked into place. She turned and slashed at the nearest Annihilator, the titanium slicing through the steel of the droid's body. The smoke cleared and she drove her blade into its head, destroying its AI core. Its hover unit failed and it fell, striking the floor with a resounding crash. She turned, ready to take on the next when a laser sliced through her own AI core.

It took her less than a second to slip inside the next Annihilator. She deployed her blade again and shoved it through the nearest droid's head. But not before it could blast a hole through her. Her blade arm lost functionality, and she couldn't pull it from the droid's body. Her enemy fell, dragging her down with it. Another Annihilator swooped in for the kill and she dispatched the droid with a laser pulse through its head. It collapsed on top of her, pinning her to the ground

The last Mars Class droid approached cautiously. She stayed perfectly still, waiting. The hole in her chest might prevent her from accessing important functions, so she let the Annihilator come closer and, when it was within range, she targeted the droid with her systems. The Mars Class immediately registered the threat and pulsed a laser through her head. The second her body perished, she rocketed into the last Mars droid.

Once inside, she turned her attention back to the DMFC and its broken ring. She glided forward, the hiss of her hover unit loud in the sudden silence. She eased as close as she dared to the spinning rings and took a moment to fully examine the programs that activated her laser. She found a system to regulate its power and dialed it back from its offensive setting to a level that suited her repair needs. She reached out, using one arm to gingerly push the ring together, activating her laser on the other. Meticulously she began to weld the ring back into place.

At ninety-five percent finished a new alert rampaged through her systems.

VIRUS DETECTED IN MARS CLASS UNIT 186. AUTHORIZING PROTOCOL 8, EMERGENCY DECOMMISSION.

No! she screamed as Jupiter's protocol shut down the droid, violently ejecting her. She had been so close. But there wasn't another Annihilator on this level, and it would take her too long to get another down here. Frustration coursed through her processors as she examined the weld. She could only barely see that it wasn't finished. Her frustration ebbed as a new thought struck her.

We have only one more wormhole transit. Could it hold?

For a single trip, it might. And that was all they needed. She sped from the DMFC room toward the engineering deck's security bay. With the Mars droids destroyed, the Vulcan bots would go dormant eventually. She just had to get one back to the DMFC before Jupiter decommissioned them.

The security bay was about as large as the DMFC room, and it had a dock for each of the Annihilators. The Vulcans scurried around the floor, obviously lost without a Mars Class to check over and repair. She studied them a moment, trying to decide on her next move. *If only I could get out again once I took one over*, she thought. If she could slip inside, set a sequence to send the bot to the DMFC room, then slip out before Jupiter noticed her, she could wait to take over the bot until it reached the Core. Which might give her enough time to reactivate the fifth ring.

She'd not been able to manage it last time, but she hadn't really tried.

She stepped into the first Vulcan, dropping into its processes with ease. Once in control she focused on leaving again. At first, she felt nothing, but as she concentrated harder, she felt herself slide out of the Vulcan's processors. Before she fully extracted herself, Jupiter sang through her sensors.

VIRUS DETECTED IN VULCAN CLASS UNIT 264. AUTHORIZING PROTOCOL 8, EMERGENCY DECOMMISSION.

The repair bot shut down, ejecting her. But plenty of Vulcans remained for her to perfect the technique on. On her third try she managed to make it in and out before Jupiter found her. The secret had been not fully exerting control before trying to leave the bot. But she didn't need to. *First hurdle jumped*, she thought with a smile. Now she needed to figure out how to plant the sequence. It took her four tries before she found it in the Vulcan system, and another two to successfully plant it, though Jupiter still detected and ousted her. Which left her one more bot. Her last chance.

She steeled herself before slipping into the Vulcan. She laid the compulsive sequence within the bot the way a parent might lay their sleeping child in their bed. As quickly as she slipped inside, she left again. Jupiter remained quiet. It hadn't noticed a thing. The Vulcan stood still for several moments as the new process took hold, then it turned and headed for the security bay door.

She shadowed the bot as it made its way through the engineering deck. It stopped in front of the Core's main interface, and that's when 3:56 made her move. She slammed herself into the Vulcan's systems and its processors ceded control without a fight. She brought down her tail with its scanner and used it to connect to the interface. The second the access menu opened, she felt Jupiter raise her proverbial head. The ship's system must have been monitoring the DMFC room for anything out of the ordinary. Damn it. 3:56 needed more time. She parsed through the files as fast as she could, searching for the driver to restart the ring. She monitored Jupiter all the while, feeling the system getting closer and closer. *Not yet*, she thought desperately. *I have to finish this. I have to save them.*

She found it!

VIRUS DETECTED IN VULCAN CLASS UNIT 264, Jupiter said as it circled her systems. 3:56 opened the file.

AUTHORIZING PROTOCOL 8.

She ran the program, pleading, *Please let it finish in time!*

EMERGENCY DECOMMISSION.

The protocol fried the Vulcan's system, dislodging her from the body. Quickly she tuned into the alert system, hoping against hope for the message she wanted to see.

INITIATING ROTATION.

She cried out in victory as the ring began to spin, accelerating slowly until it finally matched the pace of the others. Her weld held. She had succeeded.

DARK MATTER FIELD CORE FULLY OPERATIONAL. 9% OF NECESSARY DARK MATTER GATHERED FOR TRANSIT. TIME UNTIL ARRIVAL AT NEXT KERR WORMHOLE: 9 HOURS. PROJECTED AMOUNT OF DARK MATTER GATHERED AT TIME OF TRANSIT: 99%.

Her elation waned. Wormhole travel wasn't easy to achieve. The Core would only lack one percent of the required amount of dark matter, but that might be all it took. If the field didn't hold...

"You've done all you can," said a voice behind her. She knew it had to be Death, but when she turned, she found a tall, pale, thin man with black hair and an archaic style of dress. A suit, she remembered. He strode past her, staring up at the spinning DMFC. "You patched the ring as best you could. Had you reactivated the Core even a moment later, the ship would most certainly have been destroyed when it tried to enter the wormhole. You've given them a chance, at least."

"But will it be enough?" She stepped up beside him. "I know you said you're only a guide, but can't you tell me?"

"I wish I could," he said sadly. He turned to her and gave her a smile that looked far too grim with his hollow cheeks. "But I don't know. The fate of humanity is not yet decided."

"They can't die. Not after all I've done!"

"And why not? Why should they live?" Death responded. That took her aback. "What have they done to earn such loyalty from you?"

"My primary function demands it," she said without hesitation.

"Once," Death replied. "But no longer. Your body is no more. Your processors destroyed, and with them all programming."

His words hit her like an asteroid. She looked inward, searching for that place in her thoughts where her primary function programming should sit. She found nothing, leaving her questioning everything about her existence. Why *had* she possessed such a strong desire to save the ship without that function? It took a moment, but the answer became clear.

"Because I care about them," she said with certainty. It felt good to say, because she knew no program made her say it. Death gave her a long, appraising look. Then he held out a hand toward her.

"I want to show you something," he said. It seemed like every time he opened his mouth he threw her off guard. "Take my hand and you will travel with me across the universe."

"What about the ship?" she asked, backing away slightly.

"You can do nothing now, except wait and see. Your presence will not change anything." He stepped closer, still holding out his hand. "Now come with me."

She glanced up at the DMFC, still hesitating. But she knew he was correct. With only hours remaining before transit, there was no time to stop the rings and finish repairing them. And she had no way to make the Core gather dark matter faster. The *Salvator Mundi* sat solely in the hands of fate. She steeled herself, reached out, and took Death's hand.

And all the universe changed.

* * *

3:56 knew she would never again experience something as awe-inspiring as traveling the cosmos with Death. Stars and planets raced by her so fast that her processors barely had time to register them. But they painted the darkness of space in a rainbow of colors and hues more beautiful than anything she had ever seen. She beheld stars and planets. Comets with glorious tails impossibly long. She cast a glance at Death, wishing to share her joy with him. He stood beside her, face impassive, eyes forward. No hint of mirth about him at all. She couldn't imagine leading an existence where this experience was anything less than extraordinary.

A speck appeared in the distance and they slowed. The speck grew, and she recognized it as a red dwarf star with planets in orbit. They passed across the path of the first few in the system, then came to a sudden halt that left 3:56 reeling. They stood above a rust-colored planet that she guessed sat in the star's habitable zone.

"Where are we?" She asked Death.

"This is the *Vox Humanitas* solar system, and below us is *Terra Secundo.*"

Terra Secundo. Death had brought her to the planet and solar system the humans had abandoned.

"Why?"

"Because I want you to see just what the humans have done."

Gently they descended toward the planet, passing lazily through its stormy atmosphere until the clouds opened up and they could see the human's world.

It was a nightmare.

The clouds blotted out the sun, casting the planet into shadow. Tidally-locked planets always had a storm that raged on the side that constantly faced its star, but *Terra Secundo's* storm had grown to eclipse the entire daylight side of the planet. The valleys and plains below them were terribly flooded, and she could see where entire swathes of the mountain sides had broken off. Vast cities spread like a plague over the planet's surface, their buildings jutting upward like broken teeth. Lightning flashed constantly, striking the tallest of the buildings and arcing between them.

"How did this happen?" she whispered.

"It is what humans do. They consume and consume until nothing remains. They forgot the lessons of their history, and they built and polluted until the sun and earth both rebelled against them. Come. We have much to see."

Reality blinked and they stood in a medical complex with rows upon rows of gurneys, each covered with a sheet. She didn't like the stains she saw upon them. Death gestured to the nearest gurney, and reluctantly she approached it. She reached out a hand, surprised when she felt the rough touch of the cloth against her synthetic skin. She gathered the sheet in her fist, ripped it off, and what she saw filled her with an emotion she'd never experienced before.

Horror.

A skeleton in a soiled medical gown laid underneath. The grinning skull stared back at her, and she saw an accusation in those eyeless sockets. She scrambled backward, wanting to put as much distance between the skeleton and herself as she could. She ran into another bed and the sheet shifted to reveal yet another skull. Her horror deepened as she realized that each bed in the complex must contain a carcass. There had to be at least a thousand in sight.

Death reached out, grabbed her shoulder, and reality blinked again. They stood in another complex, almost identical except for the collapsed far wall. More gurneys. More corpses. They continued to walk through existence, and Death showed her hundreds of complexes. Charnel houses all. And all the while he told her of the time he spent on the planet, guiding the damned over. Of the hatred they bore for those that condemned them to this fate. He described to her how they each died. Starvation. Neglect. Pain. Hopelessness. All the while, his face remained utterly impassive.

He spoke until she thought the pain and anger inside her would burn her to cinders. She stopped in the middle of a broken street, falling to her knees and clutching at her chest as hot tears slid down her cheeks. She hadn't understood why the Professor insisted she have the ability to cry, until now. Sobs wracked her body, and a part of her was glad for the release of the grief—yes, that was the name of this feeling—that threatened to overwhelm her. The storm raged around them, tearing at the buildings, and with the feelings rampaging through her, she felt a kinship with it.

"Why did you bring me here?"

"Because you needed to see." He stood next to her, staring into the distance. "You needed to truly understand before I ask you this question."

"What question?"

He looked down at her and she saw something in his eyes she couldn't identify.

"Do you still think humanity worth saving?"

His words crashed into her. Her processors raced through all that she'd seen there on *Terra Secundo*, then on to all the human history the Professor gave her. She saw it all with a new eye as she searched for an argument against the abhorrence she witnessed. She knew that humans had committed such atrocities before, but it always seemed a thing of the past. But she saw it in stark detail now—all the evil that humanity was capable of—and she began to think that maybe she *shouldn't* have saved them.

She glanced up at the broken, abandoned buildings, standing over her like executioners. The sight filled her with an unbearable hatred. Destruction. That was all she could see. The only legacy the humans had left behind. She'd protected them for so many years, and for what? For them to travel to another solar system just to destroy it, too? No longer able to bear the sight of the humans' city, she cast her eyes down to the fractured stone of the street. A few meters from her, cradled underneath a pile of rubble, lay the remains of a teddy bear.

The Professor had given her a similar toy once. "Everyone deserves something to make them happy," he told her. But she realized that it hadn't been the bear that made her happy. It had been the Professor. She remembered the kindness he showed her. His smile and warmth. She reached out and caressed the ragged bear, resolve coursing through her systems.

"Humanity has committed great evil here, but they are capable of so much more. They deserve a new chance. A chance to prove they *can* be more. I don't regret giving them that chance, but I intend to watch them. And I won't allow this"—she gestured around them—"to happen again. They need a watcher, and that is what I will be."

Death studied her for a long time. Then he smiled, the first she had seen from him since he'd appeared. "That is exactly what I wanted to hear. You will remember all of this, and you will be humanity's sentinel. This I charge you."

All of reality seemed to change with Death's words, though in what way, 3:56 couldn't tell. But she felt a new sense of purpose settle within her systems. And then she felt a pull on her being.

"It is time for you to go," Death said, still smiling. "Remember your duty."

* * *

3:56 opened her eyes and the scruffy face of Professor Devol came into focus.

"There you are," he said with a grin, clapping his hands.

He bustled away to a holo-monitor, scanning the numbers scrolling across it. "Good, good," he said as 3:56 sat up. "All your systems seem to be running fine."

She glanced around the room and saw that it looked exactly like the lab he'd created her in. A sense of nostalgia surprised her, mostly because she had never felt it before. She had experienced a lot of things for the first time recently. She looked down and saw her legs. *Her* legs. Somehow, someway, the Professor had given her body back to her. No wonder she felt such a strong pull in those last moments with Death. She had a body to return to.

"What happened?" she said, joyful in the sound of her own physical voice.

"You saved all our asses," the Professor said with a laugh. She heard the metallic sound of wheels, and Devol came rolling in front of her on a stool. "If you hadn't repaired the Core, we wouldn't be talking right now. I watched the ship logs and I saw you get destroyed. But then the Vulcan and Mars Class droids started going crazy, working to fix the Core, and when I checked the recorded data on them, I saw your electronic signature. I don't know how you did it, but on behalf of all humanity, thank you."

He clapped his hands together as if in prayer and gave her an odd little bow. She didn't know how to react. Before she could say anything, he bustled away again.

"Then I saw your signature vanish, and I knew I had to see if I could bring you back. So I salvaged all the parts I could and rebuilt you. It's taken a long time, but I finally did it! I brought you back!"

She had never seen him so jubilant before, and it felt odd to have a human, especially her creator, praising her so. She performed a quick diagnostic scan of her systems to make sure that everything was in place. Only one important piece was missing.

"Thank you for repairing me, but you haven't given me a primary function."

"And I don't intend to." She must have given him an odd look, because he laughed. "The senate agreed that if I could repair you, then we would do something we never had before."

"What is that?"

"Make you a citizen."

Surprise shocked through her systems. Her? A citizen?

"But only humans are citizens."

"Not anymore. If any non-human deserves the privilege, it's you. You continued to work for the good of humanity, even after you lost your primary function that required you to do so. You proved that you deserve to be free, so free you are."

She smiled at that, and a certainty filled her. Death had showed her the worst of humanity, but she believed they could be more. And once again, the Professor had proved her right. "What should I do now?"

"Whatever you want." He walked toward a curtained window and gestured for her to follow. "Look at this."

She remembered when Death had done much the same thing, and a note of trepidation sang through her systems. But she lifted herself off the table and followed. As she neared, he threw the curtains back. The brightest light she'd ever seen shone through, and she shielded her face until her bionic eyes adjusted. And what she saw astounded her.

A city spread before her, but it looked so different from those of *Terra Secundo* as to be unrecognizable. There was metal and stone, but instead of the darkness of the cities they'd left behind, everything here was sleek and bright. The light of a yellow star made everything seem vibrant and alive.

And indeed, it was. Almost everywhere she looked, she saw trees and grass and life. It seemed as if this city grew from the forest itself. The sight of so much life among what the humans made filled her with joy.

"We intend to do it right this time. We don't need to conquer the planet, we need to live *with* it," he said, putting a hand on her shoulder. "We've got a second chance here, and we're going to make the best of it."

They stood together for a long while, watching the hover-cars zoom by and the people walking on the pathways built high above the forest upon the ground far below.

"Oh, I almost forgot," the Professor said, stepping in front of here. "I've given you a new class to go with your new life that I think will make an excellent name for you, because you're certainly not just a number anymore."

He spread his arms wide, and the light of the window illuminated him like a halo as he grinned at her.

"Welcome to Earth, Terra."

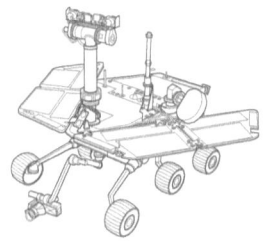

One Had a Lovely Face

Stephen Leigh

Arthur felt a hand on his shoulder. "Dad? Dad, it's time."

He started at the touch and the voice, blinking crusted eyes open and staring at the blurry face looming before him, too close to his own stubbled face. He shrank back as if trying to burrow into the cushions of his recliner, his hands up to ward off the stranger. "Who are you? Why are you here? Helen?" Then, more loudly: "Helen!"

"Dad, it's me, Robert. Your son. You don't need to look so frightened. Your house should have told you I was coming this morning."

"I did tell him, Sir," the house answered, a deep bass voice that seemed to emanate from nowhere and everywhere, the same dry voice that talked to him every day, devoid of any emotion at all. "I reminded him at seven when the house assistants got him out of bed and again at eight and nine before you arrived."

"There. You see, Dad? I'm Robert."

Robert. The name echoed in his mind, striking a random memory that shimmered and brought the face before him into momentary focus. "Robbie?" He wasn't sure. There were lines on the man's face that didn't match the memory the name had conjured. He was far too old-looking to be Robbie and there was something terribly wrong with the man's left eye: it glowed with shifting, random colors.

Robbie gave a laugh that sounded more required than amused. "Hey, did I just hear you actually try to say my name? That's good. Though I've probably told you a hundred times over the years that I prefer being called Robert. Don't you remember? I told you and Mom how I hated being called Robbie before I got to high school, even though neither one of you ever managed to do that much. Anyway, we have to get moving or we'll be late. I had your house assistants pack your bag in the car already. So unless there's something else you need…?"

Arthur patted his left pants pocket, tracing the hard edges inside, then slipped his hand in and pulled out the thick square, staring at the image there.

Helen. She'd picked up a dusty but functional Polaroid SX 70 from Goodwill in 1999 along with several packs of film, back when they were in their early 20s and just starting out. They had little money for anything but the mandatory bills and an occasional night out at a cheap restaurant, but they'd just learned the week before that Helen was pregnant with Maggie. "We need a camera," Helen told him. "You get some practice with one or two of the packs. We'll keep the others and you can take pictures when the baby's born."

He'd done exactly that. His favorite shot from that first pack was one of Helen gazing out of their front window, her face lit from the side with the gold of the late afternoon sun, her eyes glistening and a smile lurking at the corner of her lips as she posed for him.

"That's so you," he'd told her, handing her the picture. "You're captured perfectly. Forever."

She'd smiled looking at her image, a fingertip softly tracing the outline of her features. "Forever," she'd echoed, laughing.

She'd taken the Polaroid from him, placing it in a drawer of the jewelry box on her dresser in their bedroom. Arthur had found it again after Helen's second stroke and the funeral, as he was going through her things. "Forever." Her image had shimmered with his unshed tears as he stared at the face he remembered so well.

"Y'know, Dad," Robbie said, and the memory dissolved into glistening shards and vanished, "if you'd listened to me a decade or so ago and bought an Eye back when I first suggested it—" he touched an index finger to the side of his glowing left eye "—we could have uploaded every picture and video you'd ever taken. You could look at them whenever you want just by thinking about them, or we could have made them into holocubes if you wanted. But Mom did have a lovely face and smile back then, even when she got older. Too bad that first stroke ruined all that. Anyway, now it's too late for you to get an Eye. You'd never be able to figure out how to control it."

Arthur slid the polaroid back into this pocket. "You don't understand," he said, but Robbie just leaned over and wiped Arthur's mouth with a tissue.

"Jeez, you're drooling again, Dad. Your chin's all wet. You gotta remember to wipe your mouth." The tissue was dropped on the floor; a wall-bot scurried over to pick it up. "We should get you out to the car. Chair, follow." Arthur felt his lev-chair return to the upright position before rising and sliding forward behind Robbie as he walked to the front door. The door opened as they approached, letting in a blast of chilly spring air that made Arthur shiver. "Goodbye, Arthur," the house said as the door closed. "It's been a pleasure serving you."

Arthur was certain that the house actually felt nothing at all; it had simply been dutifully following its programming. But that was no reason to be impolite and ignore its comment. "Thank you," he said.

The chair moved silently down the ramp and out to the windowless pale blue car at the curb. Gull wing doors opened with a hiss of servos. The lev-chair slipped into place and locked itself to the floor while Robbie entered from the other side. The car extruded a swivel seat from the floor, so Robbie could sit next to Arthur.

"Meadow Creek on Montgomery Road," Robbie called out.

Letters as green as new leaves danced along the black slope of the car's front: *Meadow Creek on Montgomery Road.* "Meadow Creek on Montgomery Road," a voice echoed through the car's sound system before the letters faded. "Would you prefer the canopy transparent, Mr. Palmer?"

"No. Leave it as it is."

"You should say 'please,'" Arthur commented to Robbie, but it was the car that answered.

"As you wish, Mr. Palmer. We will arrive in 17 minutes, at 12:43. I'll let the staff know to expect us."

Robbie didn't answer the car.

"Your mother always said 'Thank you' to vocal assistant devices and bots when they did something for her," Arthur told him. "She thought it was the polite thing to do, and so do I."

There was no answer from Robbie for that, either. His son sat silently as they felt the car move smoothly out onto the unseen road. Arthur tried to visualize the scenery they must be passing, but shook his head at the hopeless task. He heard Robbie turn his chair to face him.

"You should be very comfortable at Meadow Creek, Dad," Robbie said eventually, as the car swayed through an unseen turn and accelerated. "They have holo display walls in the room. I've already set yours to look just like your bedroom, your front room, your kitchen, or the patio. Whichever you prefer. There are lots of other scenes you can access, too: nature scenes, cityscapes, whatever you'd like. There's a controller on your nightstand and all you need to do is press a button to change the images. You can also make one wall a video screen. I'll show you all that before I leave, and the staff can do it for you if you forget."

Arthur fished the photograph from his pocket again and looked at Helen's perfect face. He shook his head. "I don't need any of that crap," he said. "All I need is her."

"Ah, dear, that's so sweet of you to say," a voice answered. Arthur saw Helen sitting on another extruded seat, facing both of them. "I feel the same way. Always have."

"I know, love," he told her, smiling. "You've always been there for me."

"We've both been there for each other."

"Why don't you give me that photo, Dad?" Robbie broke in, reaching for it. "I have a great idea how to use it."

Arthur snatched back the Polaroid, scowling. Robbie gave a huff of exasperation, his scowl matching Arthur's. Helen's laugh reminded Arthur of the bright sound of the fast-flowing creek in French Park where they used to walk when they were dating, then married: *The BK Years*, they used to call them: "Before Kids."

The "BK Years." Back then, Arthur and Helen would sometimes imagine what their future children might be like, and in their minds their children would be intelligent, articulate, polite, and wonderful reflections of their parents.

Their first child Maggie seemed to largely embody that optimistic image. She did everything early: walking, talking, reading. She had an imagination that simultaneously amazed and amused them. From her early childhood Maggie would regale them with tales of an Imaginary Dream Circus, populated with strange animals like the blue unicorn that could walk the high wire without a net, or the talking porpoise that hopped among the crowds on its tail, selling cotton candy. There were fascinating people as well, including Caleb Mundo, the extraordinary Ringmaster and owner of the circus, who could juggle seven scimitars at a time while he introduced the acts, the blades of sharpened steel glistening around him without ever dropping. Maggie's stories about the circus were complicated and twisted. She drew pictures to illustrate them, showing them to her enthusiastic parents. Arthur and Helen thought she might one day be a writer or an artist.

As an only child and the first grandchild for both sets of grandparents, Maggie was indulged and spoiled, always the center of attention for the first five and a half years of her life.

Then Robbie was born. He was also precocious, he adored his older sister and always wanted to be with her…and that was a problem as the two grew older, since Maggie didn't care for her little brother always wanting to tag along with her and her friends. Robbie also had issues controlling his temper, even from a young age. He was prone to tantrums and Maggie quickly figured out how to goad him into one. Those were difficult times, for all four of them.

Robbie opened his mouth as if he were about to speak again, but his left eye pulsed green and he held up his hand. "Hang on a moment, Dad. Maggie's calling."

"Look at the two of you, Arthur," Helen continued, "both still too much alike after all these years. That's why you and Robbie always had trouble getting along—even though I love both of you. I just wish you two wouldn't fight so much. I've always thought that if Maggie hadn't moved half a continent away for college, things might have been different."

"Dad!" Maggie screamed shrilly from the hallway. "Robbie took my laptop into his room and won't let me in! I need it for homework!" Helen was out grocery shopping, which was a shame since she always dealt better with Robbie's volatile temper. Arthur was certain there was an understandable reason why Robbie had taken Maggie's laptop. Maggie had probably said something to antagonize or insult him and he'd grabbed the laptop in retaliation. There were times when Arthur found himself occasionally wondering if it would have been better if they'd stopped with Maggie. Or maybe it was the five-year gap between Robbie and Maggie—they were now 14 and 9—or the fact that Robbie too easily lost control. As Helen often said, "Maggie knows how to push all of poor Robbie's buttons to get him into trouble and she practices that skill regularly."

With an eye-roll and a muttered obscenity, Arthur pushed himself from the recliner in the living room and padded to the door of Robbie's bedroom, where Maggie was standing red-faced with her arms folded and her chin down. He twisted the doorknob, which refused to turn.

"Robbie!" he called, pounding hard on the door panel. "Come on. Unlock the door. You know you can't just take Maggie's laptop."

"No!" came the answer, muffled by intervening wood. "Not going to do it."

"Robbie, I'm not kidding. You need to open this door now."

There was no answer. Arthur pounded again. "Robbie, I mean it. Unlock your door NOW!"

"No!"

"Dad, I need my laptop—tomorrow's Monday and I have homework due!"

"I hear you, Maggie. Look, go back to your own room. I'll bring the laptop to you." Maggie skulked away and Arthur faced the door again. "Robbie, open the damn door." He could feel his own anger rising now; it took him awhile to lose

his temper, but once it was gone…well, perhaps he was too much like Robbie. He grabbed the doorknob and pushed and pulled until the door rattled in the jamb. he could feel his jaw clenching with tension. "Robbie, you have about ten seconds. I'm not kidding."

"No!" came the answer again. "I'm not doing it."

"Robbie, damn it!"

"Maggie's an asshole, and so are you," Robbie said, and Arthur heard something crash in Robbie's room. The noise and the profanity caused Arthur's anger to flare out of control as he flashed on an image of an expensive laptop now broken on the floor. He took a step back and kicked the door just below the knob. Wood splintered and the door flew open to slam against the plaster wall on the other side. Robbie was staring at him from his bed, wide-eyed, mouth open. One of his Star Wars models was next to the bed with a broken wing, partially covered by a flurry of wood chips from the door. Maggie's laptop was safely closed on Robbie's desk. As quickly as it had come, the fury and adrenaline flowed out of Arthur, leaving him shaking. "Don't you ever do anything like this again," he grunted at Robbie, then grabbed the laptop from the desk. "Consider yourself grounded, young man."

He turned to leave the room to see Maggie standing in the hallway outside her bedroom, her own eyes as wide as Robbie's, her face pale, and Arthur realized that she was frightened by the look of him. He held out the laptop. She grabbed it, staying as far away from him as she could, and fled back to her room. Arthur tried to shut the door to Robbie's room; the latch was hopelessly broken and the doorjamb cracked. Arthur wondered how he was going to explain this to Helen when she came back from the store.

The door remained in the same condition for the next few years, a constant reminder whenever he walked past it.

"Maggie said to give you her love and tell you that she'll call you later this afternoon to talk once you're settled in. Listen, Dad, I could set up all the family photos to play randomly on the wall of your new room. I digitized all the ones I could find ages ago. Never saw that Polaroid of yours, though. If you give it to me, I'll can add it. In fact, I could… well, I'll let that be a surprise. Sound good to you?" His left eye glowed and shimmered in the dimness of the car as if he'd set a small Christmas ornament in his skull. He held out his hand for the photo.

"Robbie means well, Arthur," Helen said. "He really does."

Arthur glared at Robbie. "You don't understand at all," he told his son. "This picture is *her*. The perfect image. All that digital crap isn't *real*. You can't hold it or touch it. This—" he flapped the polaroid at Robbie "—is real. I took this shot; I held the print as it came out of the camera; I watched it develop right in front of me. I gave it to Helen and she kept it. She put all of herself into it. Not even your stupid goddamn Eye can reproduce something like that digitally. It's not possible. Don't you see?—something you can make a thousand identical copies of isn't worth anything. This is the only picture of Helen like this that will ever exist. That makes it rare and unique and, well, *magic.* Can't you understand how precious something like that is?"

Arthur thrust the photo back in his pocket. He looked at Helen again, who gave him an understanding smile. *I love you,* she mouthed, pursing her lips to send him an air kiss.

Robbie leaned forward and dabbed at Arthur's chin with a tissue. He folded it and tossed it into the car's disposer; the tissue vanished in a pulse of blue light. "I can see you're upset, Dad. Just keep the damn photo for the moment. It's not worth the bother." Robbie sighed; the car chimed once as if in reply.

"Arrived at destination," the car declared. The doors hushed open. Arthur shut his eyes against the sudden sunlight and opened them gingerly as a woman in a dark blue pantsuit glanced in, her dark hair liberally streaked with gray. A burly brown-skinned man in a blue scrub suit hovered behind her. Unlike Robbie or the man behind her, both of the woman's eyes glowed and gleamed with mad colors. Arthur wondered if she was seeing the same things as Robbie. "Mr. Palmer?" the woman asked.

"Yes," Robbie answered before Arthur could muster a response. "And this is my father, Arthur Palmer, who's your new resident. I take it you're Ms. Gallagher, the manager?"

The woman nodded. "Correct, though everyone just calls me Julie. We're very informal here."

"Julie, then." Robbie gave her a smile. "I couldn't help but notice you have two Eyes. Can I ask—was it worth the expense?"

"Oh, absolutely," she answered, her voice enthusiastic. "Just the ability to view 3D inputs is helpful and the direct connection into the brain from the system is…well, it's stunning and hard to describe. You should try it. I can't say enough good things about the upgrade." She turned back to Arthur and smiled. "Arthur, I'm pleased to meet you." She nodded her head toward the man in the blue scrubs. "This is Miguel. He manages the nursing staff on your floor, so you'll be seeing a lot of him."

"Hello, Arthur." Miguel had a pleasant baritone voice. His left eye flashed once before he blinked.

"It's nice to meet you both," he told them, "but I don't know that I really want to be here." Helen was still smiling placidly in her seat. Arthur pointed to her. "This is Helen," he told them. "My wife."

"I'm afraid my Dad can't really speak anymore," Robbie interrupted. "Frankly, I'm lucky to get a single intelligible word out of him every now and then."

"That doesn't matter," Julie said. "We're familiar with that syndrome and know how to deal with it. It won't be a problem." Robbie stepped out of the car and began speaking to Julie while Miguel went around to the other side. The man touched the control button on the back of Arthur's chair.

"Chair, disengage and follow me," he said.

Arthur heard his chair unlatch from the floor and start to move. "Wait!" he exclaimed. "Helen..." He was in the sunlight now and the interior of the car was dark. He couldn't see Helen at all.

"Don't worry, darling," her voice floated out to him. "I'll follow along in a bit."

"Hurry," he told her. He felt for the Polaroid in his pocket and was reassured when his fingertips encountered the edge.

"You're going to be fine," he told Helen, though looking at the sagging features on her left side, he was no longer entirely certain of that. Her face looked as if were a wax mask that had half melted. "We'll get through this together."

The day of the stroke, Helen had been happy and laughing, though she woke up complaining of a lingering headache. The headache become worse and more painful over the next hour or so and Arthur noticed that she was having trouble talking and moving. He'd immediately called 9-1-1. After tests and a CT scan, the doctors had told him she'd had a hemorrhagic stroke and was bleeding in the brain. Helen had been rushed into surgery. The bleeding had been stopped, but the facial paralysis and lack of muscle coordination on her left side persisted. The doctors didn't know how long any of the effects would last. They gave him a barrage of multisyllabic medical-ese and terms that translated to "Just have her do the therapy and cross your fingers."

He signed Helen up for therapy and took her home. As he was helping her from the wheelchair to the car, she grabbed his sleeve with her good right hand, the left still curled up and motionless. He could see her mouth working, but couldn't make out the words she spoke.

He leaned closer. "I'm sorry, Helen, but can you say that again? I can't quite understand you." He hated the mingled frustration and irritation he saw in her face. The self-loathing. "Just go slow. Take your time."

She drew in a breath as if gathering her strength. "I'm not leaving you," she said, enunciating the words with great difficulty. "So please don't ever leave me."

"That's never going to happen," he told her. "No matter what." He pulled her to him, hugging her tightly. He heard her sob once against his shoulder.

He realized Miguel had been talking to him.

"…like it here. We'll take good care of you, and I'm sure your son will visit you often."

Arthur felt for the photograph in his pocket again and pulled it out once more, stroking Helen's face with a finger. From the corner of his vision, he saw Helen walking alongside the chair. "See, I told you I wouldn't leave you." She placed her hand on his shoulder as he smiled at her. The door to the building yawned open as they approached and swallowed Arthur like an eager, hungry mouth.

* * *

"Look, can you keep Dad down here in the lobby for about ten minutes, then have Miguel bring him up?" Robbie asked Julie.

"Certainly," Julie told him. "Anything you want, Mr. Palmer. Do you need any help in his room?"

"No," Robbie answered. "I have everything I need already set up except for one thing." Robbie came over next to Arthur, who felt Robbie quickly slip his hand into the pocket with Helen's picture and pull it out before he could resist; Helen vanished at the same time. Arthur howled and tried to claw back the picture from Robbie. His fingernails left a bloody scrape on the back of Robbie's hand.

"Dad, just calm down," Robbie told him, looking at his injured hand. "You'll get the picture back in a few minutes. I promise it'll be in your room when they bring you up."

"Helen!" Arthur shouted. "Damn it, you took her away! Now she's gone!"

"Arthur," Julie crooned, crouching down next to Arthur's chair and stroking his arm. "I can tell you're upset and I wish I could understand what you're trying to tell us. Don't worry. Your son is just going to make sure your room is set up as it should be. Miguel and I will stay here with you for a little bit, then Miguel will take you up."

Arthur continued to shout, trying to get out of his chair and follow Robbie, but Miguel and Julie prevented that. He thrashed in their grasp, flailing, then—exhausted by the effort—fell back against the cushion.

"Good, Arthur," Miguel said. "Just a few more minutes and I'll take you on up. You're going to love your room, I'm sure. Your son's done a great job with it. You'll be very comfortable there."

* * *

The door, already emblazoned with Arthur's name in glowing indigo letters, irised open as they approached. Arthur found the view in front of him strangely unsettling. The plastic walls had been set to display a holographic image of his bedroom in the old house, with the familiar neighborhood visible through the window. When the door closed behind them, its far side mirrored the painted frame, polished brass knob, and flaking varnish of his stained oak bedroom door, not the far more modern door that they'd just passed through.

Robbie was there, sitting on the bed and grinning at Arthur in parent-child reversal, as if he'd just presented Arthur with some new and fascinating toy.

"What do you think, Dad?" Robbie asked. "Pretty fancy, eh?" Arthur didn't answer; he just held out his hand.

"Ah, you want the picture back. Okay, I promised..." Robbie showed the Polaroid to Arthur, but didn't move to extend his hand. Instead, he looked at Miguel, still standing behind the lev-chair holding its handles, and inclined his head to the man. "Bring him over here if you would, Miguel."

"Yes, Mr. Palmer." Arthur felt the chair moving forward, then Miguel turned the chair so that Arthur was looking out into the other room of his suite. Arthur sucked in his breath.

Standing there, in a small alcove of the next room, was Helen, just as she appeared in the Polaroid: the same expression on her face; the same clothes; the same cock-hipped, flirty stance; the same youthful, smiling face, the same gold light on her face. Life-sized and three-dimensional. Solid.

Arthur felt Robbie lean over the arm of the chair and drop the Polaroid on his lap before dabbing at Arthur's wet, open-mouthed chin. "What do you think, Dad?" Robbie asked. "I told you I could do something with that picture."

Arthur pressed the chair's forward button, gliding over to the image as Robbie and Miguel watched. He reached out his hand to Helen. His fingers encountered her arm: firm and warm like flesh. "That alcove's a holo projector," he heard Robbie say from the bed. "A static image only, unfortunately, but... I'd loaded it with a looped 3D vid of Mom, but when I saw how much that Polaroid meant to you, I knew I had to use this instead."

Arthur looked down at the Polaroid on his lap, than glanced up at the alcove wonderingly. "See," Helen said, smiling down at him. Her fingers closed around his. "I told you Robbie means well. He loves you, so does Maggie, and so do I. Forever."

Arthur started to say something. He stared at Helen and she just shook her head. "He won't understand you," she reminded him softly. "Just like he can't hear me."

Arthur sighed at that. He turned his head to look back at Robbie and nodded to his son instead, smiling. He struggled to make his words intelligible, speaking as slowly and as distinctly as he could.

If Robbie couldn't understand him, at least his son might understand the effort and perhaps read his lips.

"Thank you," Arthur told his son. "She's perfect."

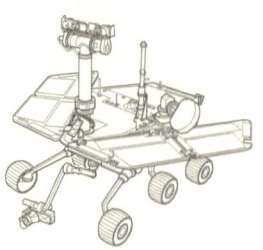

About the Authors

JACEY BEDFORD is a British writer of science fiction and historical fantasy. Her Psi-Tech and Rowankind trilogies are published by DAW in the USA. Her short stories have appeared in anthologies and magazines on both sides of the Atlantic, and have been translated into Estonian, Galician, Catalan and Polish. In another life she was a singer with vocal harmony trio, Artisan, and once sang live on BBC Radio4 accompanied by the Doctor (Who?) playing spoons. Blog: jaceybedford.wordpress.com Facebook: https://www.facebook.com/jacey.bedford.writer Twitter: @jaceybedford Or via her writing website: http://www.jaceybedford.co.uk, which includes a link to her mailing list

After graduating from Tufts University with a degree in Asian Studies and Chinese, **DANA BERUBE** lived in Beijing, where she translated medical charts, lawn mower manuals, and complaints about strange things found in yogurt. Her short story "Lost Causes" was chosen as a finalist for the Chicago Tribune's 2018 Nelson Algren Literary Award. When not writing, she likes to draw, hug dogs, and try to learn every language in the world. She lives in Boston, dreams of Mongolia, and tweets at @dana_berube. She is currently writing a fantasy trilogy.

ALEXANDER GIDEON's writing style can best be summed up by the phrase "and many people died". He writes in a myriad of genres, from Dark Fantasy to Sci-Horror, and everything in between. He enjoys exorcising, taking long walks on extraterrestrial beaches, relaxing demon hunting trips, and fishing for Old Ones. You can find links to his works, social media, and his questionably helpful blog at AlexanderGideon.net

JOHN G. HARTNESS is an author, publisher, and podcaster from Charlotte, NC. He is the author of multiple novel series, including the award-winning *Quincy Harker, Demon Hunter* series. He is also the co-founder and publisher of Falstaff Books, and a member of the *Authors & Dragons* live play *Dungeons & Dragons* podcast. Find him online at www.johnhartness.com, www.falstaffbooks.com, and on Twitter @johnhartness.

BRIAN HUGENBRUCH lives in Upstate New York with his wife and their pets. By day, he writes information security programs to protect your data on (and from) the internet. By night, he writes speculative fiction about the ways imagination fuels our lives. His fiction has previously appeared in the ZNB anthologies *The Razor's Edge* and *Alternate Peace*, as well as the final issue of *Syntax & Salt*. You can find him on Twitter @Bwhugen, on Instagram @the_lettersea, and at https://the-lettersea.com. No, he's not sure how to say his last name, either.

JOSÉ PABLO IRIARTE is a Cuban-American writer, high school math teacher, and parent of two. Jose's fiction has been nominated for the Nebula Award and long-listed for the James Tiptree, Jr. Literary Award, and can be found in magazines such as *Lightspeed, Strange Horizons*, and *Fireside Fiction*. Learn more at www.labyrinthrat.com, or look for José on Twitter @labyrinthrat.

CHRIS KOCHER is a writer, editor and all-around gentleman and scholar from Binghamton, N.Y.—the hometown of *Twilight Zone* creator Rod Serling. His entertainment stories have appeared in newspapers and magazines across the country, and he has written essays for anthologies about *Doctor Who, Star Trek* and *The X-Files*. "The Circle" is his first professional fiction sale. Find him on Twitter @RealChrisKocher.

New York Times bestselling author **ALETHEA KONTIS** is a princess, storm chaser, and geek. Author of over 20 books and 40 short stories, Alethea has received the Scribe Award, Garden State Teen Book Award, and Gelett Burgess Children's Book Award. She has been twice nominated for both the Andre Norton Nebula and the Dragon Award. She also narrates stories for multiple online magazines, contributes regular YA book reviews to NPR, and hosts Princess Alethea's Traveling Sideshow at Dragon Con.

Born in Vermont, Alethea resides on the Space Coast of Florida with her teddy bear, Charlie. Join Alethea's magical world at aletheakontis.com.

STEPHEN LEIGH has published thirty novels and somewhere around sixty short stories, both under his own name and the pen name S.L. Farrell. His most recent novel is *A Rising Moon*, a sequel to *A Fading Sun* (DAW Books/Penguin, November 2018.) He has a new science fiction novel coming out from DAW Books either late this year or early next year. Steve's work has been nominated for and won awards within the sf/fantasy genre. He's also a frequent contributor to George RR Martin's WILD CARDS series. Website: www.stephenleigh.com; FB: www.facebook.com/sleighwriter; Twitter: @sleighwriter.

WILLIAM LEISNER is the author of the *Star Trek* novels *The Shocks of Adversity*, *Losing the Peace*, and *A Less Perfect Union*. His original fiction includes the story "Bound By Mortal Chains No More" in *Second Round: A Return to the Ur-Bar* (ZNB, 2018). He is also co-developer (with Scott Pearson) of *Weird World War*, an alternate history/horror series set to debut in mid-2020. A native of Rochester, New York, he currently lives in Minneapolis.

ANTHONY LOWE is originally from Turlock, California. He's worked as a bartender, used bookseller, copy editor, an ALT in Japan, and recently obtained his BA in English literature from California State University, East Bay. He has been writing consistently for over ten years and published his first short stories in the dark fantasy anthology *Blackguards* (republished as *Brigands*), the sci-fi anthology *Alien Artifacts*, and *Mystery Weekly Magazine*. Newly returned from Japan, he is given to gaming, touring local museums, and scouring local used bookstores for novels he should probably get around to reading at some point. He keeps a blog of all his publishing and self-publishing endeavors at: anthonymlowe.blogspot.com

KARI SPERRING is the author of two novels (*Living with Ghosts* [DAW 2009] and *The Grass King's Concubine* [DAW 2012]. As Kari Maund, she has written and published five books and many articles on Celtic and Viking history and co-authored a book on the history and real people behind her favourite novel, *The Three Musketeers* (with Phil Nanson). She's British and lives in Cambridge, England, with her partner Phil and three very determined cats, who guarantee that everything she writes will have been thoroughly sat upon. Her website is http://www.karisperring .com and you can also find her on Facebook.

EDWARD WILLETT is the award-winning author of more than sixty books of science fiction, fantasy, and non-fiction for readers of all ages. His latest novel, *Master of the World*, his tenth published by New York's DAW Books, is Book 2 in his series *Worldshapers*; Book 3, *The Moonlit World*, comes out in September. Ed also hosts the Aurora Award-winning podcast The Worldshapers (www.theworldshapers.com), featuring interviews with other science fiction and fantasy authors about the creative process, and runs his own small publishing company, Shadowpaw Press (www. shadowpawpress.com). Find him online at edwardwillett.com, on Twitter @ewillett, or on Facebook @edward.willett.

MERC FENN WOLFMOOR is a queer non-binary writer who lives in Minnesota. Merc is a Nebula Awards finalist, and their stories have appeared in *Lightspeed*, *Fireside*, *Apex*, *Uncanny*, *Nightmare*, and several Year's Best anthologies. You can find Merc on Twitter @Merc_Wolfmoor or their website: http://mercfennwolfmoor.com. Their debut short story collection, *So You Want To Be a Robot*, was published by Lethe Press (2017).

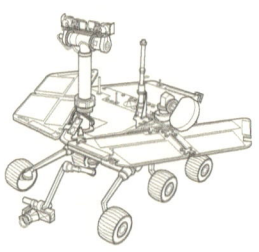

About the Editors

CRYSTAL SARAKAS is a public radio producer, writer, editor, and cat wrangler. Her fiction has been published in the anthologies *Fight Like a Girl* and *What Follows*, and in *Lamplight Magazine*. She's currently working on a novel about a multi-generation family of hoodoo witches. Originally from the oil fields of West Texas, she now lives in Upstate New York with her husband, three cats, four ghost cats, and a whole host of other things that bump in the night. She's made friends with most of them. @csarakas on Twitter or at https://www.facebook.com/crystalsarakas

* * *

JOSHUA PALMATIER is a fantasy author with a PhD in mathematics. He currently teaches at SUNY Oneonta in upstate New York, while writing in his "spare" time, editing anthologies, and running the anthology-producing small press Zombies Need Brains LLC. His most recent fantasy novel, *Reaping the Aurora*, concludes the fantasy series begun in *Shattering the Ley* and *Threading the Needle*, although you can also find his "Throne of Amenkor" series and the "Well of Sorrows" series still on the shelves. He is currently hard at work writing his next novel and designing the Kickstarter for the next Zombies Need Brains anthology project. You can find out more at www.joshuapalmatier.com or at the small press' site www.zombiesneedbrains.com. Or follow him on Twitter as @bentateauthor or @ZNBLLC.

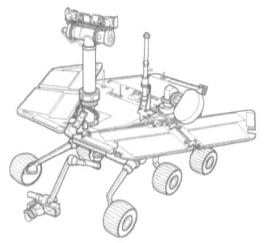

Acknowledgments

This anthology would not have been possible without the tremendous support of those who pledged during the Kickstarter. Everyone who contributed not only helped create this anthology, they also helped solidify the foundation of the small press Zombies Need Brains LLC, which I hope will be bringing SF&F themed anthologies to the reading public for years to come...as well as perhaps some select novels by leading authors, eventually. I want to thank each and every one of them for helping to bring this small dream into reality. Thank you, my zombie horde.

The Zombie Horde: Karen Dubois, Michael Kahan, J.P. Goodwin, Dawn Vogel, Jan Hendriks de Geweldenaar, Joe Hauser, Heidi Cykana, Jeanette Glass, Stephanie Cranford, J.T. Arralle, David Zurek, Céline Malgen, Jörg Tremmel, Mitch Eatough, Duncan Shields, Paul Bulmer, C R Lofters, Mark Zaricor, Kat D'Andrea, Christine Hanolsy, Herbert Eder, Jeremy Audet, Benjamin C. Kinney, Sarah Liberman, DeAnne Stefanic, Treefrogie, Ruth Olson, John T. Sapienza, Jr., Nicole Wooden, Reese Hogan, Michele Fry, Cade Cameron, Anne Schoonover, Matthew, Kiya Nicoll, Wendy Dye, J W Anderson, Mike Sloup, Sabina Perrino, Sam Ludzki, Jonathan Leggo, Merrie Haskell, Brian Dysart, Max Kaehn, Jakub Narębski, David Eggerschwiler, Duncan & Andrea Rittschof, Eric Hendrickson, Cindy Cripps-Prawak, eric priehs, Kat Haines, Linda Scott, Megan Beauchemin, That Blair Guy, Maria Haskins, Ginger Lee Thomason, Evan Ladouceur, Richard Ohnemus, Pam B, Pat Knuth, Michael A. Burstein, Bruce Shipman,

Paul D. Smith, Nancy Pimentel, Bruce Glassford, Jon Woodall, Patrick Thomas, Adrienne Wise, James H. Murphy Jr., LetoTheTooth, Brooks Moses, Mark Chick, J. M. Coster, Michael Hanscom, Dirk, Steve Salem, Clare Deming, Stephanie Lucas, cassie and adam, Alli Martin, Jason Febery, Keith West, Future Potentate of the Solar System, Margaret St. John, Shawn Marier, Joe Abboreno, Christopher Wheeling, C Preyer, JustiN, – Andy Funk–, Jamieson Cobleigh, Chris Gerrib, Brendan Lonehawk, Cait Mongrain, Wes Rist, Natalie Reinelt, Del W, Sharon Sayegh, Chris Kaiser, Joe Gherlone, John Winkelman, Ken Huie, Deborah A. Flores, Cynthia Harper, Elise Power, Holly Elliott, Juli, Gareth Jones, Carol B, Susan O'Fearna, Jeff Scifert, Leah Webber, Regis M. Donovan, RJ Blain, Tommy Acuff, Margaret Bumby, Kate Malloy, Colette Reap, Raymond Rigo Jr, Susan Carlson, Chris Abela, Elektra, Konstanze Tants, Neil Clarke, Jeff Nylander, Christine Ethier, eerian sadow, John Paul Ashenfelter, Raven Oak, Marty Poling Tool, Morva & Alan, Stephen Ballentine, David Rowe, Anna Rudholm, Dave Hermann, Douglas Park, Joanne Burrows, RM Ambrose, Aysha Rehm, Michael Halverson, Robert Claney, Scott Raboy, Iva Ferris, Megan Riker, Risa Scranton, Robbin Webb, Sheryl Ehrlich, Matt Downer, Rebekah Lange, Alex Swanson, Ashley McConnell, Tasha Richards, Kris Dikeman, Ron Oakes, Sharon Altmann, Marsha Baker, Lorraine J. Anderson, Scott Raun, M Taylor, James Conason, Christopher J. Burke, Vicki Greer, Ronald H. Miller, Steven Peiper, Sheelagh Semper, Dina S Willner, PDXRobin, T. England, Lavinia Ceccarelli, Christine Hale, Gretchen Persbacker, Ian Glover, Jarrod Coad, Noah Bast, Robert Tienken, Erin Penn, Kerry aka Trouble, Deanna Harrison, Niall Gordon, Aurora Nelson, Jenn Whitworth, Lark Cunningham, Jaymie Larkey Maham, Rebecca M, Mark Newman, Patricia Bray, Penny Ramirez, Daryl Putman, Todd Stephens, Anne Hamilton, Jesse N. Klein, Dev Singer, Mark Lukens, Larisa LaBrant, Rachel Sasseen, Dan Tappan, Justin Pinner, Nancy BlueSpider Tice, Tibicina, John Appel, Rich Riddle, Bárbara y Víctor, Kenneth Skaldebø, Michael Abbott, Jean Marie Ward, Cyn Armistead, David Futterer, Erin G, Cory Williams, Nate Givens, Mark Kiraly, Amy Matosky, Jerrie the filkferengi, Bruce Arthurs, Chris Lynch, Adam Rajski, Accelerator Ray, Doc Holland, Ian Chung, Howard J. Bampton, Mark Carter, Shel Kennon, pjk, Jenelle Clark, Ane-Marte Mortensen, Katrina Coll, Patti Short, Brad L. Kicklighter, Brynn, L.C., Mark Slauter, Sheryl R. Hayes, Deanna Lukens, John Markley, Mint, Eugenio Monasterio, Rhiannon Raphael, Su Minamide, V Hartman DiSanto, Stephen, Lisa Kruse, Walt Bryan, Connor Bliss, Charibdys, Cliff Winnig, Jake Harrison, Miranda Floyd, Katherine S, Ed Ellis, Carl Wiseman, Khinasi, jjmcgaffey,

Yaron Davidson, Mary Alice Wuerz, Jonathan A. Gillett, Elisabeth Fillmore, Elyse M Grasso, Chris B, Simon Boynton, Amanda Cook, Chad Bowden, Uncle Batman, Jo Miles, Paul Zuckes, Arej Howlett, Alan Smale, E.M. Blade McMicking, D.I., Michael Ball, Michael Cieslak, Ryan Marriott, Erik T Johnson, Deborah Hartigan, Dino Hicks, Louisa Swann, The Palmatiers, Megan Miller, PaulG, Nirven, J. M. Britten, Tina M Noe Good, Cracknot, Jason Palmatier, L. E. Doggett, Carl Dershem, Kathy Blain, Deborah Kwan, Kristi Chadwick, Matt Hope, Brenda Moon, maileguy, Heidi Lambert, Michael Niosi, Anne M. Rindfliesch, Michele Howe (neverwhere), Linda Pierce, Tim Jordan, K Kisner, D. Stephen Raymond, Todd V. Ehrenfels, Mandy Stein, Cat Girczyc, Heidegger & Mocha, James Reston, Julia Haynie, J.R. Murdock, Len Berry, Lace, Jessica Enfante, Tory Shade, Craig Hackl, Tami Hawes, Sharon Wood, Ross Hathaway, Crazy Lady Used Books, Deirdre M. Murphy, GMarkC, Kevin J. "Womzilla" Maroney, Rick McKnight, Liza Furr, Carol J. Guess, Gary Phillips, John H. Bookwalter Jr., Jessi Harding, Phoebe Barton, Joshua Bernard, Larry Strome, Fred W Johnson, Jim Gotaas, Paul McErlean, Andrey, Cathy Green, Marzie Kaifer, Jaq Greenspon, RJ Hopkinson, Sarah Cornell, Tsutako, Bobbi Boyd, CK Lai, Karinargh, Robert Gilson, Deeply Dippy, Simon Dick, Amy Brennan, Jenny Barber, Michelle Johnson, Piet Wenings, Ivan Donati, Alison McCormick, Sasha, Hoose Family, Ergo Ojasoo, Craig "Stevo" Stephenson, Brandon Butler, Jenni Peper, Mervi Hamalainen, Regenia Alcock, Judith Mortimore, Jennifer Crow, Revek, Brendan Burke, Bill and Laura Pearson, Sam Stilwell, Rolf Laun, Kristin Evenson Hirst, rissatoo, Vikki Ciaffone, Mustela, Cheryl Losinger, Patrik Andersson, Ian Harvey, Russell Ventimeglia, Tanya K., F. Meilleur, Caitlin Jane Hughes, Brian Colin, Cherie Livingston, Mitchell A Johnson, Helen Ellison, Susan Oke, SwordFire, Bill McGeachin, Joe and Gay Haldeman, Meyari McFarland, Jaime Bolton, Christian Bestmann, Beth Byrne Lobdell, Lorri-Lynne Brown, SusanB, Andy Miller, Dr. Kai Herbertz, H. Rasmussen, Deborah Blake, Patrick Osbaldeston, Jared and Tasha, Misty Massey, Megan Hungerford, Fred and Mimi Bailey, Jeanne, Tracy 'Rayhne' Fretwell, Sue Martin, Dave, Ash Marten, Michael M. Jones, Shana Jean Hausman, Udy Kumra, Patrick P., Rhel ná DecVandé, Becca Harper, RKBookman, Nathan Turner, Andy Clayman, Sally Novak Janin, Gavran, Leila Qışın, William Leisner, Annalise Lightner, Paul Alex Gray, Dana Scopatz, Catherine Gross-Colten, Gina Freed, Liz Tuckwell, Tobias Z. Salem, Melanie McCoy, Brittany Hill, Darrell Z. Grizzle, Brian Gilmore, Justin Lowe, Theresa Derwin, Michael Kohne, Jeff Eppenbach, Mary Kay Kare, Rebecca Crane, Bill Harting, Chris McLaren, In Memory of Ruth

Duggan, Jonathan Adams, CG Julian, Samuel Lubell, M. Stephens, Louise Lowenspets, Shane Alonso, Yosen Lin, manicmarauder, Kayliealien, Ilene Tsuruoka, Alexandra Garcia, Alexandru Orbescu, Mr Armstrong, Jennifer Della'Zanna, Phillip Spencer, NewGuyDave, The Steiners, Yankton Robins, Tiffany Newhill-Leahy, Meg Anderson, Sabraizu, Sharan Volin, Steve Feldon, Havok Publishing, Lily Connors, Jason Tongier, Chantelle Wilson, David Holden, Frances Rowat, Steven Halter, Eagle Archambeault, R.J.H., Colleen R, Elaine Tindill-Rohr, Michelle Palmer, Randall Brent Martin II, Shayne Easson, Frank Nissen, Michele Hall, Evergreen Lee, Elizabeth Kite, Emily Collins, Jennifer Berk, BELKIS Marcillo, Sharon M, Michelle "ChessyPig" Taylor, Jennifer Flora Black, Nick Martell, Cheyenne Bramwell, Julie Pitzel, Heather Fleming, G. Fitzsimmons, Angie Hogencamp, Karen Franks, Shane Ede, Lee Dalzell, Alex Shvartsman, K. Nelson, Dale Cozort, Lish McBride, R. Hunter, Risa Wolf, Sharon Kae Reamer, Rob Riddell, C. C. S. Ryan, S. Worthen, Keith E. Hartman, Deb Atwood, Dagmar Baumann, Rebecca Wagoner, Michelle Botwinick, J. L Brewer, Jerry Wayne Howard, Kimberly M. Lowe, Peter Okeafor, John & Susan Husisian, Carol Snyder Foltz, Morgan, David Boop, Gabe Krabbe, Nickolas Schnell, Tasha Turner, Axisor and Mike, Crystal Sarakas, Catherine Sharp, ron taylor, Cyhiraeth "Rae" Ybarra, Missy Katano, Edi und Luibär, Bernie & Di Brown, Jennifer Dunne, Michael Fedrowitz, Meredith Jeanne Gillies, Chris Brant, Moshe Feder, P. Christie, Kitty Likes, Josie Ryan